本著作受上海工程技术大学学术著作出版专项资助

汤瑶　著

Transgression, the Other and Justice:
A Study on the Narrative Art of E. L. Doctorow

越界、他者与正义：

E. L. 多克托罗叙事艺术研究

厦门大学出版社　国家一级出版社
XIAMEN UNIVERSITY PRESS　全国百佳图书出版单位

图书在版编目(CIP)数据

越界、他者与正义：E.L.多克托罗叙事艺术研究　Transgression，the Other and Justice：A Study on the Narrative Art of E. L. Doctorow：英文/汤瑶著.—厦门：厦门大学出版社，2020.7

　　ISBN 978-7-5615-4880-6

　　Ⅰ.①越…　Ⅱ.①汤…　Ⅲ.①多克托罗－小说研究－英文　Ⅳ.①I712.074

中国版本图书馆 CIP 数据核字(2020)第 122469 号

出 版 人	郑文礼
责任编辑	高奕欢
封面设计	李嘉彬
技术编辑	许克华

出版发行 厦门大学出版社

社　　址	厦门市软件园二期望海路 39 号
邮政编码	361008
总　　机	0592-2181111　0592-2181406(传真)
营销中心	0592-2184458　0592-2181365
网　　址	http://www.xmupress.com
邮　　箱	xmup@xmupress.com
印　　刷	厦门集大印刷厂

开本	720 mm×1 000 mm　1/16
印张	12
插页	2
字数	300 千字
版次	2020 年 7 月第 1 版
印次	2020 年 7 月第 1 次印刷
定价	50.00 元

本书如有印装质量问题请直接寄承印厂调换

厦门大学出版社
微信二维码

厦门大学出版社
微博二维码

前　言

E. L. 多克托罗是一位在美国当代文坛有着举足轻重地位的犹太裔美国作家。他因在作品中勇于革新，敢于突破社会准则、美学分类等各种传统界限而被誉为具有"越界精神"。很多评论家认为多克托罗属于后现代主义风格小说家，他们普遍关注到多克托罗将历史事实与文学虚构相结合、将通俗艺术形式引入文学创作的越界特征，却很少有人因此结合他的越界创作手法来研究多克托罗作品中的他者问题。

本书选取多克托罗的八部小说作为研究对象，以福柯、沃弗雷等人的越界理论、列维纳斯的他者伦理以及巴赫金的对话研究作为理论依据，通过对多克托罗作品主题以及叙事上所反映的越界性进行系统详细的研究，旨在探索多克托罗文学创作主张所体现的伦理关注，尤其是对他者和正义的关注。每一章节将分别研究多克托罗两部小说在不同方面的越界特征。

在《鱼鹰湖》《比利·巴斯格特》中，多克托罗追溯了主人公乔和比利从少年到成年时期的成长历程，强调他者在主人公寻求自我身份过程中发挥的不可替代作用。作为未来的艺术家，乔和比利成了多克托罗的代言人，他们明白了在某种程度上，写作就是建构身份，写作是基于自我和他者的不断对话，身份也是在这种不断对话中逐渐形成的，这体现了一种身份上的越界。

在《但以理书》《供水系统》中，多克托罗塑造了两位充满质疑精神的主人公叙事者但以理和麦基尔文。出于对社会伦理系统"非此即彼"模式的不满，他们创作出了另外一种叙事，打破了社会单一规范和价值观的垄断。他们的书写对"善与恶""正义与非正义""真与假"等二元对立的伦理范式的合理性提出了挑战，构成了伦理上的越界。在这两部小说中，多克托罗通过审视并质疑道德界限建立的普遍性基础，展现了道德判断的模糊性、相对性，以及它们与政治权力的关联。

在《上帝之城》《大进军》中，多克托罗将目光聚焦于社会话语的等级结构。他尤其批判了坚持自我绝对权威地位、拒绝他者声音的高位话语（宗教话语、官方历史）。在《上帝之城》中，他质疑了基督教经典《圣经》以及奥古斯丁同名作《上帝之城》坚称真理的合理性。多克托罗通过主人公佩姆和艾弗瑞特的追寻历程表明，作为宏观叙事的宗教话语根本无法解释二十世纪面临的重大问题，而且不论是在宗教或世俗领域，他们都无法维持自身的权威。《大进军》叙事则解构了官方历史的客观真实性。在这两部作品中，多克托罗实际上创作了一种碎片式、自省、具有多重叙事声音的叙事，采用边缘视角，提供了不同意见，构成了小叙事（或者称位话语），以抵制高位话语的垄断。可以说，多克托罗的叙事是一种话语上的越界。

《拉格泰姆时代》《欢迎来到艰难时世》两部小说充分体现了多克托罗在体裁和风格上的越界。在《拉格泰姆时代》中，多克托罗将拉格泰姆音乐、电影、新闻报道等流行文化元素引入小说创作，用它们来象征特定历史时期，也使这部小说的叙事结构充满了技术特征。在《欢迎来到艰难时世》中，多克托罗巧妙地融入西部体裁——一种根植于廉价小说、电影、电视剧以及商业广告等流行文化的独特美国体裁。严肃文学创作与流行文化相结合，增加了多克托罗作品的可读性，但并没有损害他的艺术成就。此外，通过在高雅与低俗之间的越界，多克托罗拷问了那些将文化分为三六九等、精英与大众的各种标准与品位，从而将公众注意力导向那些在社会话语中居于从属地位的亚文化。

总体而言，多克托罗的作品关注叙事和表征，并且强调创作过程中越界的重要性。因此，他的小说创作艺术可以被称为越界的艺术。在多克托罗笔下，越界是作为一种多变、不可控、颠覆性的力量存在的。它让作家可以用质疑的眼光来看待贯穿于社会话语和知识系统各个方面的西方形而上学中的本体论思维和独白式结构，并拷问这些系统背后权力操作的合理性。在多克托罗看来，作家在艺术创作中的越界行为源自于他对他者的关注。这里的"他者"，是指那些社会上、话语体系中或文学系统里通常被忽视、被边缘化的对象。多克托罗希望，可以通过叙事的越界力量，给这些他者带来公平与正义。

Table of Contents

Introduction / 1

    1. E. L. Doctorow's Life and Literary Career / 1

    2. Critical Responses to Doctorow / 4

    3. Theoretical Framework and Structure of the Book / 17

Chapter One   Identity and Narrative: Transgression of A Unitary Self / 24

    1. Transgression and Identity / 26

    2. The Unfixed Nature of Identity in *Billy Bathgate* and *Loon Lake* / 27

    3. The Constant Transgression of the Self to Reach the Other / 36

    4. A Narrative of Multiple Voices / 47

Chapter Two   Beyond Good and Evil: Transgression of Ethical Codes / 53

    1. Ethical Boundaries in Question / 53

    2. Justice and Truth on Trial: *The Book of Daniel* / 55

    3. Evil and Otherness in *The Waterworks* / 73

Chapter Three   From "High" to "Low": Transgression of Discursive Hierarchy / 90

    1. The Hierarchical Structure in Social Discourse / 90

    2. Failed "Sacred Text" in *City of God* / 93

    3. Recomposed History in *The March* / 108

Chapter Four   The Dialogic Voice: Transgression of Genres / 127

    1. "The Great Divide" and Postmodern Transgression / 127

    2. *Ragtime* and Popular Culture / 132

    3. Western Genre in *Welcome to Hard Times* / 152

Conclusion / 167

Works Cited / 172

Acknowledgements / 185

Introduction

1. E. L. Doctorow's Life and Literary Career

On July 21, 2015, the American writer E. L. Doctorow passed away in New York at the age of 84. In response to this news, major media like *Time*, *New York Times* and *The Atlantic* all published articles in memory of him. Bruce Weber of *New York Times Book Reviews* wrote a long essay subtitled as "Literary Time Traveler Stirred Past Into Fiction", proclaiming Doctorow's achievement as a stylist and historical revisionist, based on an elaborate introduction to his writing career and literary works. Best known for such works as *Ragtime*, *The Book of Daniel* and *Billy Bathgate,* Doctorow was, as *Times*' David Ulin points out, "perhaps the most important American novelist of his generation. More than Philip Roth or John Updike, more even than Norman Mailer, Doctorow created fiction that existed at the intersection of American myth and hypocrisy"[1]. Even Barack Obama, the former American president, acknowledged Doctorow's profound influence on his official POTUS twitter: "E. L. Doctorow was one of America's greatest novelists. His books taught me much, and he will be missed."[2]

Edgar Lawrence Doctorow, the second child of David Richard Doctorow and Rose Levine Doctorow, was born in Bronx (New York) in 1931. He belonged to the third generation of this American immigrant family of Russian Jewish origin. The old Doctorow was the owner of a small music shop and Rose Doctorow, like other women in that time, was a housewife. During the Depression, the father failed in his business and he had to work as a salesman to keep the family fed. This low-middle family milieu made young Doctorow taste the bitterness of life at an earlier age; that's maybe why most of his novels focused on characters from underprivileged social background, such as the homeless, the drunkard, orphaned youths, hapless

---

[1] From online *Los Angles Times*, titled "Remembering E.L. Doctorow, great American mythologist". http://www.latimes.com/books/jacketcopy/la-et-jc-el-doctorow-appreciation-20150721-story.html.

[2] From online *New York Times*. http://www.nytimes.com/2015/07/22/books/el-doctorow-author-of-historical-fiction-dies-at-84.html?_r=0.

immigrants, and working-class people, etc. The influences of family members on him were multifaceted. In his essay collection *Reporting the Universe*, Doctorow reminisced his family as a location of ideological tension. As he said, generations of men like his grandfather and father were liberal humanists and socialists. The women in the family, however, were pious followers of Jewish scriptures and rituals. The miraculous integration of socialism and Judaism made young Doctorow believe that the incompatible ideas could flow into one small world. It suffices to say that the ideological jumbling of his family endowed him with the spirit of freedom and creativity, which paves the way for his future career as a man of letters.

After graduating from Bronx High School of Science in 1948, Doctorow went to Kenyon College in Ohio with the expectation to study with the famous poet and essayist John Crowe Ransom. At that time of American history, it was McCarthyism that began to emerge and later permeated the American politics and society, with suspicious atomic spies arrested, writers interrogated and censored, and people living in white terror. In the chapter "Kenyon" from *Reporting the Universe*, Doctorow recalled his experiences on the campus where the atmosphere was quite idyllic. Despite the cruel external environment, the students of Kenyon College were provided with courses like "Roman and Ancient Greek history" and educated in the stronghold of the New Criticism. In relation to the silence of the academia on the social turmoil, Doctorow commented that it is the "nature of a prevailing culture not to appeal ideologically, especially to its executors" (Doctorow, 2003: 48). As a Jewish American, the sensitivity to justice and a highlight of individual's responsibility for the whole community has always been with Doctorow. The Jewish heritage led to his contemplation on E. M. Forster's well-known saying "Only connect"[1], a great inspiration for his thinking at that time. Majoring in philosophy in the undergraduate years, Doctorow developed the metaphysics of connection, by which he intended to connect everything, from the top to the bottom, from the outside to the inside, with the insight of a storyteller rather than a God-believer.

After his graduation from college, Doctorow undertook a variety of jobs. He went to the military for a few years. After that, he worked as a script reader and later as an editor. These jobs on language and words taught him how to structure a plot, and how to absorb elements of popular culture into serious literary creation to make them well received by the general market. The experiences of reading film

---

[1] "Only connect" is a sentence from E. M. Forster's *Howards Ends* (1910) and one of his lasting thematic concerns in his works. Doctorow refers to this idea of Forster in his essay collection *Reporting the Universe*.

scripts and writing comments also aroused his desire to create stories of his own. He talked to himself that all was about lies and he could lie better than these people (the playwrights). In 1969, he left the publishing industry where he already worked as a senior editor, and became a professional writer as well as a faculty member in a number of universities.

Doctorow's writing career started off in the early 1960s. *Welcome to Hard Times* (briefly as *Welcome*), his first novel in 1960, told an unconventional story of western town named "Hard Times", a dark version of the American frontier myth. In the following years, Doctorow published a series of gradually mature works. It is noteworthy that *The Book of Daniel* (1971) (briefly as *Daniel*), an effort to reexamine the Rosenberg Case that happened in McCarthy era of 1950s, was generally considered to be Doctorow's most compelling work. Four years after *Daniel*, Doctorow created *Ragtime*, an immediate and huge success, "greeted by both popular and critical acclaim" and named by the Modern Library Editorial Board one of the 100 best novels of the 20th century (Rogers, 1975: 134). *Loon Lake* (1980), *World's Fair* (1985), *Billy Bathgate* (1989), the three novels sequentially appearing in the 1980s, were all set in the depression era of the 1930s, a period which fascinated the author greatly, with its poverty, corruption and unprecedented scale of socialist movements. In 1984, Doctorow published *Lives of the Poets*, a story collection consisting of six short stories and a novella, a new attempt for the writer both in theme and genre. In this work, Doctorow addressed the fundamental issues of the nature of writing and the function of writers. *Waterworks*, a novel in 1994, unraveled a Hawthornian story of crime and evil, committed by the corporation of industrialists and a cruel scientist. Set in the postbellum New York, it exposed the bleak side of American society presumably stigmatized by the prosperity and progress at the end of the 19th century.

Entering the new century, Doctorow continued to explore new territories, and his achievements gained more widespread attention than ever from the international society. In his millennium work *City of God*, he examined many essential issues of the twentieth century, such as religion, language, ethics, narrative, etc. His intention, with deliberate use of different voices and genres, was not to generate the linear history of the whole century, but to pose question to the established faiths and institutions. In 2005, Doctorow returned to the subject of history in *The March*. Named after the famous event in American history, *The March* was Doctorow's attempt to reconstruct the famous March of the Union Army led by William T. Sherman from Atlanta to Savannah toward the end of the Civil War. The work following *The March* was *Homer & Langley*, Doctorow's adaptation of the life stories of the Collyer brothers, a sensational piece of news widely covered in the newspapers. The writer's most recent book was *Andrew's Brain*, a novel set in the 9/11 event and centered around a mentally troubled neurologist Andrew, through which Doctorow explored the world of mind, trauma, and the blurred boundary of illusion and reality in a media society.

Till his death in 2015, Doctorow had published twelve novels, three volumes of short fiction, a stage drama and three collections of essays. His literary achievements won him popular success as well as numerous academic awards, among which are National Book Critics Circle Award (1975, 1990 and 2005), National Book Award (1986), PEN/Faulkner Award (1990 and 2006), National Humanities Medal (1998), Medal for Distinguished Contribution to American Letters (2013), etc. Some of his works had been adapted for screens and turned into films and musical plays, causing great sensation among the public. Many well-known contemporary writers such as John Updike, Carol Joyce Oates, Don Dellilo admitted the enormous influence of Doctorow's works on American literature. In terms of theme, Doctorow's works touched upon the very details of American scenery and life. He inherited the great tradition of historical romance of Walter Scott and Nathaniel Hawthorne. Most of his novels were historical fiction kindled with bold fabrication, which covered a wide range of historical period from the middle 19th century to the early 21st century. Different from some of his contemporary counterparts who turned their eyes to the private inner world for inspiration, Doctorow always had a strong sense of responsibility toward writing, investing his work with concern for social problems. In terms of form, Doctorow was a bold experimenter. He was never bored of introducing new elements into his novels, from shifts in perspective and voice, to the breaking of chronology, to cinematic montage and collage, to the blurring boundary of fiction and reality. In this sense, he was simultaneously a conscientiously realist writer as well as a postmodernist stylist. It was success on both fronts that elevated Doctorow to the ranks of the most entertaining and most important writers in the American literary scenery.

2. Critical Responses to Doctorow

Generally speaking, Doctorowian criticism did not prosper until the late 1970s when poststructualism came to the public view and gained momentum. Entering the 1980s, Narratology and cultural criticism appeared in the view of Doctorowian criticism while the poststructual and deconstructive perspectives remained on the way. Since then, reviews, essays, and monographs on Doctorow's works have become increasingly various and innovative on perspective and methodology. During that period, a series of influential critics appeared with their monographs on and interviews with Doctorow, such as Harold Bloom, Paul Levin, Geofferey Galt Harpham, Carol C. Harter and James R. Thompson, and John G. Parks, to name just a few. Their works included systematic analysis of Doctorow's major works from *Welcome* to *The Waterworks*. The fact is no matter how divergent critical perspectives seemed to be, critics' treatments of Doctorow's works generally fell into two categories—the realistic and the postmodernernist. The former category tended to approach the author from his involvement with politics, history, philosophy and other aspects, and saw his works as the mimetic mode of the outside world; the latter based its analysis on the assumption that literature cannot reflect any extratextual presence, and that its existence only pointed out the fictionality of texts and our illusory dream of representation.

The first category starts with Doctorow's concern with politics. Some of the conservative critics such as Hilton Kramer, Perl Bell and Joseph Epstein considered Doctorow a representative writer of leftist ideas. They critiqued his novels as propaganda of political views, grotesque distortions of facts and truth. Attacking the initial reviewers of *Ragtime* of their blindness to the novel's ambitious political objective, Hilton Kramer, for instance, thought it "distort[ed] the actual materials of history with a fierce ideological arrogance" (Kramer 1975: 79). However, Harter and Thompson, devoting a monograph to Doctorow, acclaimed Doctorow's social commitment precious and unique, "a rare phenomenon" in the contemporary American literature. They thought that Doctorow, influenced by such writers as John Dos Passos and John Steinbeck, held "the passion of our calling" rooted in the belief that "writing matters, that there is salvation in witness and moral assignment" (Doctorow, 1985a: 23). John G. Parks shared a similar idea with Harter and Thompson, lauding Doctorow as a writer of "engagement", different from lots of contemporary writers "who have largely abandoned the social and political realm for the exploration of the self" (Parks, 1991a: 454).

Critics such as John Clayton and Paul Levin tried to connect Doctorow's concern for politics with his Jewish roots. Paul Levine, in "Politics and Imagination", analyzed Doctorow's political commitment to social justice and his radical skepticism toward all established institutions, attributing these to his family influences as well as his growing up along with the silent generation of the

1950s. Jewish radical humanism, as John Clayton elaborated, was Doctorow's most important emotional and intellectual ethos. Summarizing Doctorow's Jewish heritage, Clayton observed that "caring and doing for other people and a critical attitude to contemporary myths" were what Jewish culture insisted (Clayton, 1983, 119). The themes of suffering, social injustice and community which frequently appeared in Doctorow's works were what the Jewish writers often dealt with. Harold Bloom also thought that Doctorow was, by temperament, "closer to the central Jewish traditions than are Philip Roth or Cynthia Ozick" (Bloom, 2002: 4), and Jewish traces abounded in his works.

Many other critics noticed Doctorow's criticism on capitalist exploitation and corruption in the process of industrialization. In their essays, Marxist and Post-Marxist criticism including class conflicts, economic exploitation, and power struggle became the key words. Based on the Marxist-psychoanalytical method and a detailed examination of the economic power in Doctorow's novels, David S. Gross's perspective on the money image in several Doctorow's novels was innovative and insightful. He elucidated that modernist writers like Doctorow employed "formal strategies which seem[ed] designed to distance and protect the author from responsibility" of speaking unpleasant truth on money (Gross, 1983: 128). The result was that the "connections among money, excrement and power" were established with ambiguities and biting ironies (128). But Gross's essay, as John Williams suggested, was not so much about Doctorow's works as a use of Doctorow's works in combination with Marx and Freud to speculate on the issue of "literary modernism and American history" (Williams, 1996: 49). Despite Doctorow's deep involvement with politics in his works, some critics thought that it was improper to label Doctorow as a political novelist. To John G. Parks, such a labelling was "simplistic and misleading", for it implied that the author had "an agenda, a program, or an ideology to promulgate in fiction" (Parks 1991a: 11). Paul Levine supported his argument. According to him, Doctorow, though a relentless critic of "America's failures to fulfill its dreams and founding convictions", did not advocate new political system in place of the current one (Levin, 2002: 56). Levine thus realized that Doctorow did not belong to those political writers who wrote to promote certain ideology since he was "aware of the dangers of ideology for art" (59).

Besides politics, history was another field that had become the object of Doctorow's obsessive attention and meditation. In fact, like his political stance, Doctorow's imaginative manipulation of history gave rise to hot debates. A noticeable fact is that most of critics' research on Doctorow's treatment of history was based on a New Historicist perspective. "All of Doctorow's fiction is an engagement with crucial moment in American history" (Parks 1991b: 16), Parks suggested, but his method of using history was not the conventional one (realistic reflection). Instead, Doctorow subjected history to ambiguity and plural interpretations. Parks' study on Doctorow's plural interpretation of history was significant in that he linked narrative to social power. He pointed out that the "dialogic or polyphonic" narrative of Doctorow disrupted or even subverted "regimes of power" and restored the "neglected or forgotten or unheard voices" (19). Carol C. Harter and James R. Thompson's monograph *E. L. Doctorow* discussed a great deal on Doctorow's treatment of history. They thought, in his novels since *Ragtime*, Doctorow not only "repeatedly invoke[d] history by employing actual events but, more importantly, he fictionalize[d] a number of historical personages in unverifiable ways" (Harter & Thompson, 1990: 10). This led to their conclusion that reiterated Doctorow's famous claim that all history was composed and there was no distinction between fiction and nonfiction. Tokarczyk's analysis of Doctorow's historical consciousness cited Frederic Jameson's idea on the "crisis of historicity". Doctorow's distrust of official history and historians' role as faithful recorders of the past penetrated all his works, Tokarczyk suggested, "the uncertainty about history and interpretation is a key component of skepticism" that marked Doctorow's skeptical commitment (Tokarczyk, 2002: 9). Linking Doctorow's historical consciousness to that of John Dos Passos, Barbara Foley made a detailed comparison between their representative works *Ragtime* and *U.S.A.* He came to the important statement that both works "represent[ed] a significant departure from the form and outlook of classical historical fictions" (Foley, 1983: 168). The difference of the writers lied in that Dos Passos "subordinate[d] the fates of his invented characters to the 'plot' of history itself" and framed his narrative around facts that were held to be true and verifiable while Doctorow "treat[ed] with equal aplomb facts that are 'true' and those that are 'created', thus calling into question our concept of factuality and, indeed, of history itself" (Foley, 1983: 168).

Poststructualist approaches especially Roland Barthe's and Foucault's theories on myth were also used to analyze Doctorow's historical consciousness. In his monograph *E. L. Doctorow's Skeptical Commitment*, Tokarczyk referred to Roland Barthe's famous discussion on the relationship between myth and history to explain how Doctorow's first novel *Welcome* debunked the myth of American west. *Ragtime*, according to the analysis of David S. Gross, demystified "the nostalgic view and simple America at the turn of the century by exposing the lies that seek to conceal the realities of class and racial oppression and its support of money complex"(Gross, 1983: 133). Among numerous American myths, American Dream, a motif recurrently appearing in great literary works since Benjamin Franklin, was one of the most influential ones. Critics like John G. Parks, Arthur Saltzman, Harter and Thompson, specifically analyzed Doctorow's refutation of different aspects of American Dream in his various works. Considering *Welcome* as a rework of American west formula, Parks remarked that Doctorow's narrative actually "raise[ed] serious questions about the nature of American Dream." (Parks, 1991a: 28). Parks' comprehensive and penetrating analysis on Doctorow's skepticism of the nature of American Dream could be applied to all of Doctorow's novels. *Daniel*, according to Tokarczyk, "critique[d] American Dream of upward mobility and certainly criticize[d] the reality of American justice under the law", but more than that, it also "fault[ed] groups associated with the left" and questioned the possibility of drastic social revolution as well (Tokarczyk, 2002: 74). Arthur Saltzman thought that, in novels such as *Loon Lake*, *Billy Bathgate*, and *Waterworks*, Doctorow suggested the "relationship of criminality and American Dream" by revealing the fact that "[t]oo often it is greed and ruthlessness rather than virtues that bring success" (Saltzman, 1983: 134).

From the late 1980s to the early 1990s, Winifred Farrant Bevilacqua successively contributed three important essays discussing history and narration in Doctorow's three novels, *Welcome*, *Ragtime*, and *Daniel*. Her study covered various aspects of the New Historicist and deconstructive approaches to Doctorow's novels. In her essays, she argued that Doctorow's works subverted the assumptions about classical historical novel as outlined by Georg Lukacs as he presented history in a self-reflexive style rather than the detached omniscient style, which exposed the subjectivity of historical representation. Bevilacqua further pointed out, the three novels of Doctorow all shared a sense of the fictiveness of all discourse about reality and history; they deconstructed the stereotypical pictures of history so that readers were left to rethink why certain groups had been at the center stage and others marginalized. In this respect, Bevilacqua had something in common with Parks as both of them related Doctorow's historical consciousness and narrative to his moral concerns.

Although much Doctorowian criticism focused on his social views and treatment of history, a series of significant essays were devoted to the existentialist strain in his works. David Emblidge, in his study on Doctorow's three earlier novels, claimed that a central motif penetrating *Welcome*, *Ragtime*, and *Daniel* was "the idea of history as a repetitive process, almost a cyclical one, in which man is an unwilling, unknowing pawn, easily seduced into a belief in 'progress'" (Emblidge, 1977: 397). Harter and Thompson expressed a similar opinion in their monograph *E. L. Doctorow*: "Doctorow's vision is repeatedly of a universe where meaninglessness and absurdity are at the center of things and lead to unending and inescapable repetitions of human failure" (Harter and Thompson, 1990: 10). John McGowan made a comparative study of Hannah Arendt and Doctorow's existential thoughts (mainly based on his essays and interviews while partially based on his novel *Ragtime*) and his research provided another way to study Doctorow's writings. To McGowan, Doctorow shared much in common with Arendt's philosophy since both intellectuals agreed that freedom came from "the collective creation of a common world" where "individual actions" could "acquire meaning through their being witnessed and narrated by others" (McGowan, 2011: 168). For both, the prime political virtue was "taking responsibility for the world, acting with others to maintain it" (168). In this sense, Arendt's existential philosophy was illuminating in researching Doctorow's works.

Despite his inheritance of the realistic tradition, most of the time, Doctorow was viewed as a great postmodern stylist. In Larry McCaffery' *Postmodern Fiction*, David Gross, author of the entry on Doctorow, claimed that the novelist earned the label "postmodern stylist" chiefly by inventing a form of historical fiction that, through its pastiche and self-reflexive qualities, made readers aware of both the American past and the ideological account of it (Gross, 1986: 339). But Doctorow's reputation as a postmodern stylist, according to Tokarczyk, mainly lied in his skeptical attitude toward all kinds of grand narrative, and his determination to demystify the dominant social discourses that constructed commonly held values, norms and knowledge. In this sense, the author's practice was a version of "micropolitics" with action that was "local, situated in the community, in individual deeds and work on the self" (Tokarczyk, 2002: 23). Among all monographs on Doctorow, Christopher D. Morris' *Models of Misrepresentation: on the Fiction of E. L. Doctorow* was the most complicated and obscure one. Essentially, the whole book was a long deconstructive reading of Doctorow's fictional and non-fictional works under the philosophical framework of five writers: Friedrich Nietzsche, Martin Heidegger, Derrida, Paul De Man and J. Hillis Miller. According to Morris, the five writers had a common denominator in their thoughts: "a refusal to presuppose that texts necessarily represent a signified, extratextual presence" (Morris, 1991: 13). Doctorow's works, with their intention to demystify writing as a faithful representation of reality, shared this refusal. Most of criticism on Doctorow's works, in the eyes of Morris, was hermeneutic in regarding his works as representations of particular ideas (such as Jewish humanism, radical socialism, existentialism, or criticism of official history and capitalism). However, argued Morris, the so-called political satire was only "a seeming demystification, since the novels never rest in any 'truth' that might serve as the alternative to the political illusion they condemn" (13). In all, Morris' study was innovative in some way but it carried the skepticism of postmodernism to the extreme since it denied the ability of literary works to reflect any reality. His assumptions thus reduced literature to empty language games without any referential significance—a common sin postmodern literary works were accused of.

In the late 1980s, two important critics at that time, Frederic James and Linda Hutcheon, both started a discussion on the postmodern characteristics of Doctorow's works. In his prize-winning study, *Postmodernism, Or the Cultural Logic of Late Capitalism* (1991), James argued that Doctorow was the "epic poet of the disappearance of the American radical past" (James, 1991: 24). His impressionistic analysis of Doctorow's *Ragtime* showed that the author actually aimed to reveal the hidden power system in the history of a capitalist society. However, produced in a postmodern era, the novel undermined its attacking force for its self-reflective qualities. Linda Hutcheon, in *A Poetics of Postmodernism*, tried to defend postmodern fiction from conservative critics' general accusations. She thought their misgivings of the loss of reference were a little bit fussy. By dubbing postmodern fiction like *Ragtime* as "historiography", a term indicating both a representation of history and its self-reflexivity, Hutcheon expressed her appreciation of this new category, especially its ability to interrogate and "problemize" a totalizing system and to open for new possibilities of understanding the world. James's and Hutcheon's contradictory perspectives made clear the contemporary concern for ethics and its quandary in the postmodern context. Anyway, their comments on Doctorow, representing two related but contrasted ideas of the postmodernist school, were frequently cited as the landmarks of Doctorowian research by later critics. Tokarczky, for example, quoted James's words but considered Doctorow's skeptical commitment to history, power, social myth and non-linearity an advantage often associated with postmodernism, since it gave a writer the power to interrogate and question conventional ideas and values. But his skepticism was not that of relativism or nihilism. Disagreeing on James's idea that Doctorow's technique undercut his critique power, Tokarczyk categorized Doctorow's works into midfiction[①] which lies in the middle way between "realism and reflexivity"—the two extremes of contemporary literature (Tokarczyk, 2000: 68). Therefore, they both kept the power to put almost everything under telescope as well as to reveal some truth.

Besides his skeptical spirit, Doctorow was labelled as a postmodern stylist also because of being a bold experimentalist on narrative form and style. Most of critics have mentioned that one of the distinctive features that marked Doctorow's narratives was a blurring of boundaries between fiction and other popular artistic forms. Commenting on Doctorow's resurrection of deserted materials (genres, plots, characters, etc.), Michael Wutz described Doctorow as "a Sartor Resartus gathering, snipping, pasting and stitching worn materials into novel textures of collage and montage" (Wutz, 2003: 511). Wutz's essay, though very complicated in views, covered multiple aspects of Doctorow's works as well as literary theories. It not only used the images of garbage, rags and recycling in Doctorow's works to confirm their subversive power against the capitalist consumer culture, but also pointed out the intertextual quality of Doctorow's works. Winifred Farrant Bevilacqua analyzed Doctorow's reworking of American west genre and his creation of a self-reflexive narrator-protagonist in *Welcome*. Fowler thought that Doctorow's pedantic and ironic style of *Ragtime*, with his deliberate mockery of the dry, objective voice of official history, made the work "sardonic and urbane and directed along a privileged wavelength of attitude and allusion" (Fowler, 1992: 57). A considerable number of critical essays were devoted to the intertextual quality of Doctorow's work. Lieselotte E. Kurth-Voigt's "Kleistian Overtones in E. L. Doctorow's '*Ragtime*'", for example, made a detailed comparison of the plot, characterization, and themes between Heinrich von Kleist's novella *Michael Kohlhaas* and *Ragtime*'s Coalhouse episode. He suggested that despite the different time and settings, the Kohlhaas/ Coalhouse tragedy indicated the universal pattern of disorder individuals often encountered. Thus, Doctorow's adaptation of the Kleist story showed the recurrence of historical processes.

Narrative was another arena where Doctorow's postmodern experiments took place. Most critical approaches have mentioned the indeterminacy of the narrative discourse, the shifting voice and perspective, and the self-reflexive quality of the

---

① Midfiction is a term coined by Allan Wilde in *Middle Grounds* (1987) to refer to fiction that "situates itself between mimetic and metafictional forms of writing and uses both realist and self-reflexive modes of expression without privileging either of them." Quoted from Fran Mason's *Historical Dictionary of Postmodernist Literature and Theater*, Scarecrow Press, 2007: 300.

narrators in Doctorow's fiction. Early critical voices of *Ragtime* were focused on the anonymous and unidentifiable narrative voice. Christopher D. Morris, for instance, thought that the undecidability of the narrator was mainly caused by "the generic names" assigned to the primary families in *Ragtime*. Charles Berryman, on the other hand, identified the little Boy from the WASP family as the narrator. Berryman also linked images like the mirror and film to illustrate the relation between reality and the artistic world. But Morris pointed out some problems behind this kind of assumption. Interestingly, he proposed another bold assumption that the narrator might be a double, containing "two different entities, a specific and a separate anonymous voice" (Morris, 1991: 101). According to Barbara Cooper, each of Doctorow's protagonists represented an artist-historian figure, who often found himself trapped in the same predicament—to find the "proper alignment", which described the artist's ambition to get the "alignment of his materials, his intention, his creation, the conventions of writings, and audience expectations about the nature of the novel" (Cooper, 1980: 6). In his essay "The Stylistic Energy of E. L. Doctorow", Arthur Saltzman concluded that the experimental style of Doctorow, especially the self-reflexive qualities of his narratives actually served his thematic concern—"to demythologize America and to demystify his own craft" (Saltzman, 1983: 75). In this essay, Saltzman also explored such motifs that would be repetitively dug up by critics of later years: the narrator's radical distrust of language, and the futility of the artist to seek representation for his experiences. In the case of Cooper and Saltzman, it can be seen that different from the mimetic mode of the earlier critical essays, later studies on Doctorow's narrative turned to the poststructuralist approach. Furthermore, both Saltzman and Cooper's researches focused on the issues of literary creation in the fictional world, which made it evident that Doctorow's novels were mostly metafictions concerning writing itself.

Compared with Saltzman and Cooper, Geoffrey Galt Harpham moved a step further in the deconstructive direction. His essay "E. L. Doctorow and the Technology of Narrative" deserved a special space in the reception of Doctorow because it shifted critical emphasis to narrative itself. In this essay, Harpham, under the influence of Hayden White, claimed that "narrative, with its volatile images, is a political issue" since its "truth status always depends on the power of authorities that sanction it" (Harpham, 1985: 32). Based on the poststructualist theories, Harpham's study differed from any previous one because he put narrative prior to reality and considered that our sense of reality originated from texts, which meant "narrativity takes precedence over referentiality". His study revealed the phenomenological influence of Husserl. Another approach to the narratological study of Doctorow's works was the combination of narratology with cultural study. During the late 1970s, a great many of critics creatively integrated the theories of cultural studies especially theories of films, music, and photography into narratology, which invested Doctorowian criticism with deeper insight and broader perspectives. Anthony B. Dawson, among them, made a detailed analysis of specific filmic devices used in the narrative of *Ragtime*. Borrowing Walter Benjamin's ideas on the relationship between mechanical reproduction and art, he attempted to argue that *Ragtime* reflected a time when the mode of perception was drastically changed by mass media like films. Narrative, like other artistic forms, had become the product of industrial production without the unique aura commonly associated with traditional arts. Berndt Ostenorf, on the other hand, examined the musical works of the era's composers, and the development of ragtime music in the 1920s and 1970s. Based on the analysis of the musical history as well as the text of *Ragtime*, Ostenorf concluded that ragtime music best represented the time and the narrative, since its syncopation symbolized "the desire for progress" and "a dread of change", the typical conflicts in the era of modernization (Ostenorf, 1991: 585). If in Dawson and Ostenorf's essays, music and film as the cultural metaphor, functioned as an analogy to the narrative, Seymour and Barrett's treatment of the image of photography in *The March* was quite different. In their essay "Photography and History in E. L. Doctorow's *The March*", the two scholars examined the role of photography as objective and sacred recorder of reality in the perceptions of the characters. By repeatedly comparing photography with history, they pointed out neither of the two was transparent as medium of representation; instead, both share their "dependency upon perspective and selection" (Seymour& Barrett, 2009: 66). In this sense, *The March* showed that "objectivity is a myth", the myth employed in social discourse to secure documentary authority (66).

Since the publication of *Ragtime*, Doctorow has yielded attention not only in the United States, but also from the international society. China is one of the countries where Doctorow's works have received warm welcome and critical attention possibly because their close engagement with political issues (especially its radicalism) and social reality. Since 1986, Doctorow's works have been introduced to China and translated into Chinese. Yang Renjing, a scholar from Xiamen University, made a great contribution to the broadening reception of E. L. Doctorow in China. He translated *Billy Bathgate* in 2000 and two of Doctorow's short stories "The Leather Man" and "The Hunter" in 2001. Besides, he wrote an introductory essay, introducing the biography, major works as well as artistic features of Doctorow. He also contributed a critical essay on Doctorow's narrative strategies such as the indeterminacy of his narrative, his innovative use of collage, computer language and ironic effect in the two stories. Later in 2004, Yang published a book *On Postmodern American Fiction*, which also included an introduction to and his comments on Doctorow. His works, together with Wang Shouren's essays in *A New Literary History of United States after 1945* (2002), which recognized Doctorow's distinctive status as a writer and his important artistic characteristics, marked the earlier efforts of Chinese criticism to explore Doctorow's works.

Earlier Doctorowian criticism in China mainly undertook the political and historical perspectives, similar to the Marxist and neo-historicist approach discussed in the previous part. Yang Renjing's essay "American Postmodernist Writer E. L. Doctorow's Historical and Political Concern", for example, mainly analyzed the political background of Doctorow's novels, and his postmodern narrative strategies, calling readers' attention to the author's realistic concern. Chen Shidan's essay "*Ragtime*: A Return to Its Historical Sense" also falls into this category. Based on the textual analysis of *Ragtime*, he elaborated that Doctorow's use of history and postmodern techniques created a world where facts and fiction coexisted, but his essential intention still went to social reality. Another scholar Li Junli contributed three essays, two on the "historicity of the text" and the "textuality of history" reflected in *Ragtime*, the other one on the humanistic-realistic tendency of Doctorow. Entering the new century, the perspective and method employed to the research of Doctorow became various, among which were analyses of his Jewishness, existential thoughts, cultural elements, religion and so on. According to Li Shunchun, *City of God*, through the description of the experiences of a little boy in the Nazi-ruled Ghetto, of the Two World Wars, and of the victim's traumatic immigrant life in the United States, expressed Doctorow's meditation on Jewish identity, the meaning of Jewishness and Jewish tradition in the post-holocaust era. Employing the framework of Sartre's ideas on freedom, death and alienation, Li Junli, analyzed the protagonist Daniel's alienation as a socialist Jewish descendant in the McCarthy era of 1950s and his sense of obligation to discover the meaning of his parents' case in another Doctorow's novel *Daniel*. Critical essays including "Anti-Theodicy Narrative in Doctorow's *City of God*" by Yuan Xianlai, "Reconstitution of Belief after Post-Modernism: The Deviation and Inheriting of Aurelius Augustinus by E. L. Doctorow in *City of God*" by Pan Daozheng and Huang Xiaoli all focused on religious issues reflected in the novel, such as the predicament of traditional Christianity in the postmodern context and the difficulty of maintaining ethics in a society where faith had been desecrated.

Among the four PhD dissertations on Doctorow's works to date, two of which are carried out from cultural perspective, specifically from the view of city studies. Yuan Yuan's dissertation "Politics and Perception: A Study of Little Wanderers and the City in E. L. Doctorow's Fiction" explored how the little boy wanderers in the three novels, through their wandering experiences in the cities, perceived the urban space and how their perceptions influenced their growth and outlook on space. Xianyu Jing's doctoral dissertation "A Study of the Writing of New York City in E. L. Doctorow's Novels"(already published) was also on the topic of New York City. Different from Yuan Yuan, she mainly analyzed Doctorow's representation of the city's history, geography, politics, as well as all sorts of problems and his meditation on the solutions to these problems in eight novels. Compared with the cultural perspectives of these two dissertations, Cai Yuxia's approach was a poststructual one. In his doctoral dissertation "Demystification in E. L. Doctorow's Historical Fictions", he focused on the demythologization of history in Doctorow's four novels, *Welcome*, *Ragtime*, *Loon Lake* and *The March*. Wang Liyan's doctoral dissertation "The Trajectory of Jewish Themes in E. L. Doctorow's Fiction", as the title suggested, traced the connection between Doctorow's Jewish tradition and the development of his thematic concerns in his works.

Despite the amazing achievements on the research of Doctorow's works at home and abroad in recent years, there are still some fields to be explored and insufficiencies to be perfected such as the gender studies and ethical studies. Actually, till now few critics have paid attention to the ethical aspect of his works, except some fragmentary comments in this aspect. Besides, mass media, especially newspaper, film, and music, which have played a very important role in Doctorow's writing and therefore are closely related to his narrative energy, are barely explored in a comprehensive way, except in *Ragtime*. One or two of American scholars have noticed the feature, but in China, there are only a few essays on the films or music as separate cultural elements in *Ragtime*, still with vacancy to be filled in the exploration of the relationship between literature and media.

As a Jewish American writer, E. L. Doctorow's works showed the writer's preoccupation with ethics, especially his constant concern for the "Other". Richard Trenner, in 1983 noted that Doctorow's "most important quality" was his moral vision, his conscious and intuitive commitment to "an ideal of universal justice" (Trenner, 1983: 11). The middle-low class family background, the contact with the diversity of ethnicity in his neighborhood, and the sense of alienation and marginalization as a Jewish descendants, gave the author a kind of "hypersensitivity to otherness, by a profound vigilance to the other of language and the possibility of something different, something impossible" (Critchley, 1999: 16-7). But the ethical interpretation of his works was rare among the critical works, and till now there were few essays in this aspect and only one doctoral dissertation devoted to the narrative ethics in Doctorow's works.

Carol Iannone, in her essay "E. L. Doctorow's Jewish Radicalism", noted that the Jewish background enabled Doctorow to scrutinize American mainstream society from the angle of the other, and his works showed his commitment to politics and the ideas of justice. Michael Wutz, on the other hand, considered that Doctorow's narrative "interrogate[d] such mythic categories as good and evil, fact and fiction, as they [had] been used by the powers that [would] be in the service of ideological control" (Wutz, 2003: 521). Wutz's comment exposed Doctorow's skepticism toward traditional ethics. Catharine Walker Bergström, in her doctoral dissertation "Intuition of an Infinite Obligation: Narrative Ethics and Postmodern Gnostics in the Fiction of E. L. Doctorow", addressed the intertextual elements of Doctorow's works which opened the possibility to the face of the other and thus "provide[d] an alternative to the dominating force of scientific truth: a Gnostic intuition of the ethical role that the narrative act plays in inter-human relations" (Bergström, 2010: 33). Bergström had noticed the moral matrix of Doctorow's writing, but most of her attention was placed on Gnostics and Doctorow's romantic tradition, as she tended to interpret knowledge and truth as something intuitive and transcendental, which were beyond human capacity to understand. From the previous Doctorowian criticism in ethical perspective, it suffices to say that the research in this field is very limited while there are still questions to be raised and problems to be addressed.

My research will start from Doctorow's transgressive spirit reflected in his eight novels, specifically focusing on how this transgressive writing reflects his ethical concern for the other. As is known, traditionally, the word transgression has derogative connotations as it is always related to breaking a law or disobeying some moral codes. But nowadays, with the efforts of lots of theorists, such as Nietzsche, Foucault, Bahktin and so on, the word has been invested with ethical meanings. To them, transgression represents the rebellious spirit to walk out the confinement defined by the social norms and cultural restraints, and to cross the boundary artificially drawn due to the influence of the dialectical thoughts of the western society for over two thousand years. In an interview with Larry

McCaffery, Doctorow complained about the borders and rules set in the creation of literary works, and he declared that when writers began to write out of "a spirit of transgression" (McCaffery, 1999: 213), they could probably produce the best work. Actually, Doctorow's transgressive spirit is both reflected in his thematic concern and aesthetic technique throughout his oeuvre. This research thus focuses on the various transgressive features of Doctorow's works, including his stress on intersubjectivity as a necessary part in protagonists' pursuit of identity, his interrogation of traditional moral categories, his transgression of the demarcation of social discourses as the "high" and the "low", and his opening of narrative genre to the dialogue of different voices. By exploring the transgressive features of Doctorow's works, the book aims to dig out Doctorow's concern for the other, within the theoretical framework of Julian Wolfreys, Emmanuel Levinas, Mikhail Bahktin and some others. As is known, Doctorow's ethical conception is specifically characterized by his concern for the other, which can be understood as the existential other, the cultural other, and the other in epistemological sense. His narrative is full of transgressive quality, which constitutes a subversive power to his quest for the truthfulness, to break down the traditionally established order and mystified discourses, to deconstruct the monopoly and control of institutionalized power, and to restore the silenced voice of the other, that is, the often disempowered and marginalized group in history.

3. Theoretical Framework and Structure of the Book

This book addresses the topic of transgression reflected in E. L. Doctorow's fiction. Transgression, a word commonly known as the act to step over some boundary, to break some rules or laws, and to depart from a tradition, has become a term frequently cited in the contemporary sociology and literary practice. In this book, transgression is, first and foremost, a thematic thought that sustains Doctorow's fiction. With the drive to look beyond one's current status, including identity, time, space and established knowledge, characters in Doctorow's fiction seem to live in a state of fluidity, always ready to remake himself/herself or to move to a new territory. Their dissatisfaction with the status quo and their desire to renew themselves precipitate an inquisition on the traditional categories or boundaries which divide identity into the self and the other, behaviors into the good and the bad, social discourse into the high and the low. Furthermore, Doctorow introduces transgression as an important strategy in the literary creation. On many occasions, he emphasizes the role of transgression in a writer's career to help produce the best works. His protagonists are always self-conscious writers or historians, who seek to find a voice that transgresses the ethical and aesthetic boundaries to represent the postmodern experiences of flux, discontinuity, fragment and diaspora. Most of his works depart from some literary traditions and reflect his determination to get rid of the old codes, cliché and paradigm to come up with something new. In his eyes, the word transgression is invested with positive connotations in the postmodern context, which aims to question the totalizing system, to set free the voice of the marginalized.

Transgression, as a cultural term, was first systematically elaborated by Michel Foucault in his "Preface to Transgression", an essay to pay homage to the forefathers who have done some breakthrough researches on the development of this idea such as Marquis de Sade, Georges Bataille and Friedrich Nietzsche. Foucault's discussion of transgression starts from his analysis on sexuality, which in his opinion, opens up a fissure for the light of liberation to come in, thus providing an opportunity for our understanding of limits and taboos. According to Foucault, Sade's study on all kinds of deviant sexual behaviors makes him the frontiersman to touch the topic of transgression; his language on sexuality carries human existence to where God is absent. However, it is Nietzsche's declaration on the death of God that leads to all the profanation and reevaluation in the contemporary society. Bataille puts forward another important concept "excess" to refer to all acts that overstep the limit such as "eroticism" and "expenditure". After tracing the genealogy of these scholars' study, Foucault draws a conclusion on the idea of transgression: "Transgression is an action which involves the limit, that narrow zone of a line which it displays the flash of its passages, but perhaps also its entire trajectory, even its origin; it is likely that transgression has its entire space in the line it crosses" (Foucault, 1977: 34-35). Foucault's definition emphasizes not only the spatiality of transgressive act but also its dialectic relationship with limits, its repetitive feature and complicacy: "The play of limits and transgression seems to be regulated by a single obstinacy: transgression incessantly crosses and recrosses a line which closes up behind it..." (35).

Emmanuel Levinas's contribution to the theory of transgression mainly lies in his recognition of intersubjectivity—the subject's crossing over the boundary of the self and the other. By "putting into question of my spontaneity by the presence of the Other," (Levinas, 1969: 54) his philosophy restores the dignity of the other that has been expelled and excluded for a long time in the western society. Thus, his focus is not placed on transgression as a social behavior, but as a psychological act that constitutes the necessary step to reach the other. Like Foucault and Levinas,

M. M. Bakhtin also leads the attention of the public to the irrational and suppressed other in the traditional culture. His studies on carnivals and dialogism have enriched the culture of transgression. Following Levinas and Bakhtin, many scholars try to elucidate the relationship between transgression and the other. John Jervis, for example, thinks, "the transgressive is reflexive, questioning both its own role and that of the culture that has defined its otherness" (Jervis, 1999: 4). Similarly, Julian Wolfreys states that the maintenance of self is based on the constant approach to and exchange with the other. The point is to "get outside" myself, to "exceed my being and my world, crossing over the boundary...by proxy the events of another, of multiple others". In this sense, transgression connotes the act of going "beyond the self into any other life, losing the self in other possibilities" (Wolfreys, 2008: 15). Thanks to the efforts of these thinkers, the meaning of transgression is enriched and its scope broadened. The natural proximity of the word transgression to illegal or immoral acts endows it with a sense of revolution so that whenever linked to it, the subject (the transgressor) shows his/her strong will to break, to destroy and to subvert the decayed and irrational order.

After Foucault, with the rise of postmodern literary practice that tends to question all ideologies that once represented center, authority and the sacred, the studies on subjects like taboos, constraints, madness, desire, carnival have been on the rise. In this trend, the act of transgression is considered closely related to ethics. To Chris Jenks, transgression means a subject's escape from the center to touch the "Excluded Middle" or the grey ground, the territory that is neither "A" or "B," which is explored with great enthusiasm by poststructualists, feminists, and postcolonial theorists. A critical feature of postmodernity, says Jenks, is to transcend limits which are "physical, racial, aesthetic, sexual, national, legal and moral" since limits or taboos always generate an ungoverned desire to "go beyond the margins of acceptability or normal performance" (Jenks, 2003: 8). Using transgression as a subversive power, the postmodernists try to question the traditional categories and social hierarchies and call the attention of the public to the middle ground where the voices of the suppressed, subaltern and silenced can be heard.

Entering the second half of the twentieth century, transgression no longer merely existed as a cultural phenomenon. It was applied to the field of literature as a strategy to break the rule set by traditional literary practice, to overstep the boundary of the high culture and the low culture, and to introduce into literary creation new genres or styles. Citing Foucault's essay on authorship, Wolfreys thought that writing was actually a process of recycling. Since the establishments of ownership system and strict copyright rules made the transgressive acts in literary creation necessary, literature works had to "break, or mix or adulterate the existing genre-expectations of the time" (Wolfreys, 2008: 13). According to Frederic Jameson, postmodern artistic forms were essentially anti-elitist, more open to the spirit of diversity and tolerance, and one of its remarkable features was "the effacement of some key boundaries or separations, most notably the erosion of the older distinction between high culture and so-called mass or popular culture." (Jameson, 2002: 112). So the post-1960s literature generally witnessed more transgressions in writing techniques and styles, such as the mixture of realistic and fictive, the parody on canons, the chaotic arrangement of time and space, and the use of cinematic and musical elements, etc. These bold experiments brought new possibilities to the literature genres and styles, which were supposed to have been exhausted by former masters. On the other hand, through the acts of transgression, the postmodern narratives posed challenge to the order and hierarchy established by the division and categorization of social discourse, thus calling into question the process of their formation, coming into power, and distribution.

This book mainly employs Foucault, Jenks, and Wolfreys' theories on transgression, Levinas' philosophy of the other and Bakhtin's dialogism as its theoretical framework. It consists of four chapters, with each chapter containing the textual analyses of Doctorow's two novels. Every chapter has a special focus, and this focus is necessarily one of the reflections of Doctorow's transgressive spirit. The four aspects this book attempts to explore are respectively identity, ethics, discourse, and genre, which are connected by a common denominator—the art of writing. It is the sense of obligation the art of writing awakens that enables Doctorow to view the established systems including norms, customs, and paradigms with a skeptical spirit and motivates him to overstep the boundaries these systems have drawn and popularized. The obligation, as Levinas suggests, is a moral being's irresistible return to the other from the location of the self to respond to the other's appealing. Therefore, the transgressive energy reflected in Doctorow's fiction is a demonstration of his ethical concern for the other, the suppressed and marginalized voice in the fields of identity, ethics, discourse and aesthetics.

On many occasions, Doctorow talked of the writer's role as a "transgressor"[1]. His thought on transgression is reflected at various levels in different works. To

---

[1]   In an interview with Larry McCaffy, Doctorow says that writers should write out of a spirit of transgression. In another interview with Michael Silverblatt, Siverblatt mentions Doctorow's claim on artist as a transgressor when talking about Dr. Sartorius, a character in both *The Waterworks* and *The March*.

Doctorow, transgression is first and foremost the limitless capacity of a subject to break its own limits, specifically, to break from the fetters of the self to admit the existence of the other, which is the central concern of Chapter one. In *Loon Lake* and *Billy Bathgate*, Doctorow portrays two boy-protagonists, Billy and Joe, who in their journey of growing into adulthood inevitably encounter the other that will greatly influence their outlook on themselves as well as on the world. The protagonists constantly transgress the confinement of the self to interact and absorb the element of the other to realize their identity. Through their pursuits, Doctorow conveys the message that the formation of one's identity is a dynamic process, constantly in dialogue with external forces. In other words, the construction of an identity is based on the recognition of the alterity, the expression of uncontrollable difference. Like Levinas says, the self is always exposed to the face of the other, to whom, the former has an unavoidable obligation to respond, to speak, and to love.

Chapter two centers on the topic of ethical transgression. According to John Jervis, the postmodern expression of transgression is not only about trespassing, disobeying, or infringement but also "involves hybridization, the mixing of categories and the questioning of the boundaries that separate categories"(Jervis, 1999: 3). In both *Daniel* and *The Waterworks*, Doctorow questions the validity of traditional categorizations of ethical codes such as good and evil, justice and injustice, truth and falsity, as they have been used by institutionalized power in the service of ideological control, which reflects his skeptical perspective on ethics. The universality and foundations on which the ethical boundaries are established are also put into scrutiny. In *Daniel*, the protagonist Daniel's investigation of his parents' case does not lead to clarification but to obscurity and multiple interpretations, which reveals that in a postmodern society, the pursuit of absolute truth and justice might be a fantasy. In *The Waterworks*, McIlvaine's highly self-aware reminiscence of a past event sheds light on the grey ground of an ethical dilemma, that is, the otherness of Dr. Sartorius, whose acts cannot be easily judged by existing moral codes. In both novels, narratives' roles are examined. They are deemed as the subversive power to disrupt the hegemony of monolithic social norms or moral values.

Chapter Three deals with Doctorow's transgressing of hierarchy in social discourse. Peter Stallybrass and Allon White generally divide social discourse into high discourse and low discourse based on their position in the binary structure. The former is characterized by "their lofty style, exalted aims and sublime ends" (Stallybrass & White, 1986: 3) such as official history, law, the language of the church and so on. The latter, on the contrary, is characterized by "its popular and vulgar style, its aims to entertain the mass" which "always seek the opportunity to impose counter-view on the dominant culture" such as popular novels (western, detective genre, science fiction, pornography), folktales, songs, etc. (4). In *City of God*, Doctorow challenges the authority of the language of the church represented by the Holy Bible, thus calling into question the demarcation of social discourse into high and low. Through the skeptical pastor Pem, Doctorow tries to reveal that the religious scriptures including the Bible—the grand narrative in Leotard's term, are written by storytellers of different generations. Full of pious lies and political struggles, they are thus without much distinction from the fictional literary creations of Everett, the writer-protagonist of the novel. Everett's depictions of New York City, of modern evils and disasters, also constitute a deconstruction of another religious work, Augustus's *The City of God*. In *The March*, Doctorow presents a carnivalesque picture of American south during the Civil War, from the multiple perspectives of generals, poor white criminals, and black slaves, some real in history, some fabricated by himself. His presentation of the history of the March not only blurs the boundary between history and fiction, but also demystifies official history by pointing out its false claim to be an objective and faithful record of the past. Doctorow's perspective, in conclusion, is that of a skeptic, who always questions the categorizations and boundaries that characterize the mainstream knowledge and truth system. In these two novels, he tries to locate and break down the hierarchy existing in social discourse caused by the high/low dichotomy. Thus through the acts of deliberate crossing over the line, he actually creates the low discourse, the discourse from the perspective of the other.

Chapter Four deals with Doctorow's transgression in the aesthetic field. In the field of aesthetics, transgression happens when artistic conventions are broken, rules are disobeyed, and the previous disreputable elements are introduced into the literary system. Doctorow is always considered as a postmodern writer for his transgressing in literary genres and styles. In *Ragtime*, he introduces the elements of popular culture such as ragtime music, cinema and newspaper into the novel to epitomize a time of industrial duplication and change. The narrative of the novel is also influenced by the techniques of music, film and journalism, which makes *Ragtime* a novel of technological quality. The blending of serious literature and popular culture contributes to the readability of the novel but barely undermines its artistic achievements. In *Welcome*, Doctorow skillfully integrates into his novel the Western genre, a unique genre in American culture, which is rooted in pop forms such as penny novels, films, TV series and commercials. Despite the familiar set of characters, scenes and motifs which are typical Hollywood Western formulas, Doctorow's narrative also subverts the Western tradition with its depiction of a pessimistic picture: failed heroism, frustrated hope and the illusion of West as conquerable wilderness. In this sense, Doctorow's *Welcome* both learns from and renews the Western genre, questioning and altering the frontier myth constructed by American popular culture. As Julia Wolfreys proposes, transgression within form is usually in response to the "political, ideological, cultural and historical demands for stability and self-sameness in the constitution of identity". In this sense, Doctorow's transgression in form reflects a writer's desire to shake off the literary cliché to create something new and also his determination to break down the order and hierarchy in the political and cultural system.

Chapter One
Identity and Narrative:
Transgression of A Unitary Self

E. L. Doctorow's two novels *Billy Bathgate* and *Loon Lake* are always put in comparison by critics as they share so much in common: both of them are set in the 1930s, a period which fascinated Doctorow with its restlessness and complexities; they also depict a questing protagonist who acts as the narrator of his adolescent experience, trying to find his spiritual father as well as his position in the society. When asked why he always chooses the youngster as a hero, Doctorow says that a youngster is someone who is comparatively innocent and still with the capability of "wonder and discovery" (Sanoff, 1999: 145), so that he is still most prone to change and renewal.

In general, the two protagonists from different novels, Billy and Joe, are similar in their life track. Billy, a street boy with a crazy mother and a father who abandoned the family at an earlier time, is technically an orphan. Fascinated with the world of money and power epitomized by the gangsters, he longs to become a member of them to gain success. Finally, rummaging out the amassed wealth of the gang, Billy is able to get himself a good education, an important position, and to melt into the mainstream American society. Joe, suffocated by his callous family of working-class background, also expects to encounter some big changes in his life. In his wandering in the forest, he occasionally catches a glimpse of a private train, with its glamorous inside, and more attractively, a girl standing naked before a mirror trying her dress. He is bewitched by the scene and follows the train track to the estate of a tycoon, F. W. Bennett. After some twists and turns, he gets adopted by Bennett and becomes the legal heir of his industrial empire.

For Billy and Joe, the most important issue arising from their adventurous journey is to find who they are. In this process, they both realize that one's identity is an unfixed thing, constantly in a state of fluidity. In their pursuit of themselves, they transgress not only the limitations of their biological environment, but also the conception of self as the unitary center, which instead is continuously renewed and revised by the influences from the other. According to Geoffrey Galt Harpham, Doctorow is obsessed with the idea of "the imposition of the other on self", and his work shows that "the self is historically contingent and inconstant as the technology it appropriates" (Tokarczyk, 2002: 116). To Billy and Joe, transgression over a stagnant dichotomy of self and the other repetitively changes who they are, thus helping them construct an identity of containment and diversity.

It is not only a matter of realizing their dream of upward mobility, but it also concerns with their survival, as John G. Parks comments: "He (Joe) is the sum total of the voices he hears, denying and forsaking his own voice if, indeed, he ever knew it" (Parks, 1991a: 73). In this process, the face of the other[1], in the words of Levinas, plays an especially important role since it is the stimulus and end of their transgressive acts, just as Levinas proposes, "to go from the Same to the Other (Autre), from Self to Other" is "to bring meaning into Being" and "to give sign, to undo the structures of language" (Bergström, 2010: 82). In some sense, Joe and Billy's journeys demonstrate their continual departure from their old self to enter into the skin of the other so that they can accommodate to and survive in the adult world of unknown danger and threats.

In their pursuit of finding themselves, narrative becomes a key element. Both *Billy Bathgate* and *Loon Lake* are written by the grown-up protagonists in retrospection of their past experiences. Therefore, they suggest "the act of self-composition" (Smith, 1981: 60). According to Doctorow, *Loon Lake* shows that "we all compose ourselves from other people in our experience"(60). At the end of each novel, both protagonists find that in order to reflect their life which is "simultaneous but dissynchrous" (Doctorow, 1996: 191), they have to compose a narrative of their own, a polyphonic narrative where the voices of the self and the other intermingle and converse, with the understanding that one's identity is actually what he invents or composes for himself. In this sense, Billy and Joe become the spokesmen of Doctorow's true artist, who always transgresses the boundaries of the self to produce the best works. As a narrator and future artist, Billy and Joe succeed in creating a narrative, which is actually a resonance of their identity. The indeterminacy and competing voices inside their narrative transgress the monologic authorial perspective of the traditional realist novels to create "a heteroglossic one,

---

[1] By the face, Levinas means human face, but not necessarily thought of or experienced as a physical object. As one of the most important images in Levinas' philosophy, "the face of the other" is used to designate the expression or exposal of the other in front of the I as an undeniable reality that I must admit.

which reflects the multiple voices that shape, if not determine, human identity and constitute human selfhood". (Parks: 1991a: 73)

1. Transgression and Identity

Identity, a word from Latin language, originally means "sameness". Generally speaking, one's identity is his/her label, which marks the unique quality of a person. The unique quality of an individual keeps the same at all times and ensures its difference from that of other groups in all circumstances. So it is basically "constructed in terms of opposition" such as the oppositions of black/white, male/female, subject/object, etc. (Woodward, 1997: 2). Traditional conception of identity, as Stuart Hall suggests, always holds the conviction that there is an essential center of the self, which constitutes a person's identity. This self, continuous and unified, is endowed with the "capacities of reason, consciousness and action", which first "emerged when the subject was born, and unfolded with it, while remaining essentially the same—continuous or 'identical' with itself—throughout the individual's existence" (Hall, 1992: 598). The self, with a limit set up between it and the other, defines and reinforces its status as the center of existence, thus representing "the unreflective assumption of ontological privilege" (Holquist, 2002:19). In ontology, it becomes the collective name of anything that stands superior in the dichotomous categorizations such as God, the Soul, the Ideal, the author, and so on.

Entering the postmodern era, with the decentering tendency of deconstruction movement, the boundary between the self and the other is frequently questioned and challenged by the theorists like M. M. Bahktin, Michel Foucault, Emmanuel Levinas. As Foucault suggests, "Transgression forces the limit ... to find itself in what it excludes" (Foucault, 1977: 34). In the contemporary society, more and more people begin to focus on the realm traditional conception of self has excluded: the peripheral region where the other is placed. The postmodernists, thus, always transgress the limit established by conventional ideologies to explore this realm and try to restore the voice of the suppressed other. For Bahktin, the self should be in a dialogic relationship with the other, not only with other human beings, but also with the natural and cultural configurations we lump together as "the world". For Levinas, the self should listen to the summoning of the other, and react to the face of the other in a responsible manner. Both Bahktin and Levinas' ideas are based on the premise that the barrier between the self and the other established in the Western society for thousands of years should be broken-down. To use the words of Julia Wolfreys, the rigid line of the self and the other has to be stepped over and over to lose oneself "in other possibility" (Wolfreys, 2008: 4). The spatial movement from the center (the self) to the margin (the other) is accompanied with the shift of power.

It is against this background that a postmodern conception of identity is generated. The postmodern subject, according to Hall, "conceptualized as having no fixed, essential, or permanent identity, makes identity a 'moveable feast': formed and transformed continuously in relation to the ways we are represented or addressed in the cultural systems which surround us" (Hall, 1992: 598). In other words, the postmodern identity is a transgressive one, as it crosses over the boundary of the "completed, secure and coherent" center of self to move around in a diaspora way. Different from the traditional conception of identity that defines itself by expelling or excluding the other, the postmodern identity attaches more importance to the other—the irrational, alternate, and different voices, just as Hall proposes, "Identity is a structured representation which only achieves its positive through its narrow eye of the negative. It has to go through the eye of the needle of the other before it can construct itself" (Hall, 1992: 21). Put another way, the formation of an identity is based on the admission and absorption of the other by the self.

In this sense, the postmodern identity is historically rather than biologically defined. In fact, as Hall suggests, the subject assumes different identities in different situations: Within "us" are "contradictory identities pulling in different directions, so that our identifications are continuously being shifted about" (21). If "we" feel we have a unified identity in our whole lifetime, it is only because "we" "construct a comforting story or narrative of the self" about ourselves (21). The truth is that as the systems of meaning and representation multiply, people find them always "confronted by a bewildering, fleeting multiplicity of possible identities—any one of which they could identify with—at least temporarily" (21). In general, Hall's study conceptualizes identity as fragmented and unfixed, which for the most time exists merely in our illusion. In the subject's construction of a coherent identity, narrative plays an essential role to fabricate and edit so that the relevant are united and all the disharmonious are wiped off.

2. The Unfixed Nature of Identity in *Billy Bathgate* and *Loon Lake*

In *Welcome*, a territorial officer tells the narrator his contemplation on the volatility of the land and people: "Nothing fixed in this damned country, people blow around at the whiff of the wind" (Doctorow, 1960: 142). Indeed, the idea of transience and fluidity characterizes American national identity as a result of its immigrant culture and ethnic diversity. The 1930s (the background of *Billy Bathgate* and *Loon Lake*), with its expansion of capital, the popularization of underworld activities, and the corruption in political and economic field, provides the stage where drastic change of wealth and position seems possible. In such a time of great social restlessness and speculative profiteering, boys like Billy and Joe, both of whom are from the lowest level of the social hierarchy, can dream of upward mobility in a shortcut way. For them, an important strategy of survival is to be dexterous and adaptable enough to play all kinds of roles according to different situations. Their final success, at least in a worldly sense, is mostly based on their chameleonic quality, as Nelson H. Vienra says, "on account of their very adaptable natures—their dexterous and self-conscious role-playing", Billy and Joe's life reflect an "ethics of change" (Vienra, 1991: 365). The chameleonic feature of their personality ensures their intactness and success in a tough adult world.

2.1. "Our Temporary Identification" in *Billy Bathgate*

In *Billy Bathgate*, the poor street boy Billy lives with his crazy mother in a shabby tenement of Bronx. The family of two depends on the mother's meager income of doing laundry for a living. Like other boys on the streets, Billy feels proud of his avenue as the location of Dutch Schultz (Arthur Flegenheim)'s beer drop. He longs to become a member of his underworld, which includes bootlegging and numbers racketing, and unions. To Billy, Schultz and his gang represent the life he aspires for, the life of adventures, fast money, luxury, and excitement. It looks like a journey full of unknown factors. On why people are always interested in gangster culture and criminal activities, etc., Doctorow says:

> We're always attracted to the edges of what we are, out by the edges where it's a little raw and nervy. And gangsters bring that qualities right into the heart of the society, and we who are law-abiding have this mythic attachment to the irreverent law breakers and the audacious dissenters, asocial, nonsocial, anti-social. It reflects that atavism we all still have in us the idea of transgression, breaking the rules. (Parks, 1991a: 108)

In this sense, young Billy's interest in the racketeering group comes not only from his aspiration for money and power, but also from his will to transgress the current social order. In fact, his credo on life and morality is quite flexible. His idea of the boundary between good and evil is very obscure. Talking of Dutch Schultz's bootlegging on Bathgate Ave, he feels honored to "enjoy his confidence" and it seems he has become "part of something noble" himself (Doctorow, 1989: 24). Faced with Dutch Schultz's criminal activities like murder and bribery, he never relates them to injustice or evil, but follows instructions and engages in the tasks assigned to him in a passive way. Without valid parenthood and schooling, he tends to adopt anything practical and convenient for use. A street boy since birth, the most important quality of Billy is his dexterity, as he says,

> I was double-jointed, I could run like the wind, I had keen vision and could hear silence and could smell the truant officer before he even came around the corner. ... and what they should have called me was Phantom, after that Hearst New York American comics hero. (Doctorow, 1989: 23)

Billy's dexterity, on the other hand, is represented by his prowess as a juggler, a gift that opens the gate of opportunity to him. One day, when Billy is juggling for other boys on the street, he occasionally comes to the sight of the notorious Dutch Schultz, the great racketeer. Seeing this as a chance to catch Schulz's attention and enter his underworld, Billy juggles in a deliberately skillful way and succeeds in gaining Schultz's appreciation. Before walking away, Schultz leaves Billy ten dollars as reward and puts a prophetic hand on his shoulder as some sort of indication. In this novel, the act of juggling appears several times and becomes a metaphor for life. During his later involvement with the gangsters, Billy is able to connect juggling with reality. As he considers, America is a big juggling event, and as long as one has the superb ability of perception, understanding as well as keeping everything in balance precariously, he can make success out of nothing. After engaging in the criminal activities of the gangsters, Billy gradually realizes that like juggling, the errands he ran for the racketeering group must be unerring. Even one tiny mistake can lead to ruination and every detail of work must be completed with aplomb.

Billy's dexterity in action and mind makes him a quick learner and potential master of the principles of gangsterdom. Soon, he learns that the most critical principle of all is the readiness to change, and his ethics of change develops based on his observation of the gangsters around him. Firstly it is the big boss Schultz, the legendary racketeer who is notorious for his extreme emotions and actions of instinct. On several occasions, Schultz loses his temper, and violently kills those people who annoy him, including a former follower of his, a fire inspector, one of his business partners, and a barber. Billy is thrilled by the bloody scenes Schultz has incurred. But on the other hand, he feels attracted by his thunderous temperament, which for him represents a leader's charismatic spirit, the typical ethos of American heroes. Schultz's criminal empire undergoes ups and downs, and when Billy joins, it is the time when Schultz is charged for his tax evasion and other illegal acts. The group escapes into a small country Onondaga to wait for the appeasement of the event. Dutch Schultz comes up with a series of ideas to get rid of the accusation against him. Some of the ideas rush to his mind instinctively, which again proves that he is a man of impetuosity and improvisation. In Onondaga, he pretends to be a philanthropist who tends to the need of the poor residents in this district. He buys the hearts of prominent people like the bankers and pastors with his generosity. Using Billy his so-called protégé as the guise, he successfully secures himself the role of a patron, thus getting himself a position in the local church. Through a period of efforts, Schultz is finally declared innocent and released after the trial, for most of the jury (who has believed in his generosity and integrity) stands on his side. Awed by this man, Billy confesses, Schultz and his gang men live in a world of improvisation, "This gang, they make things up as they go along. They use what's to hand" (182). Billy's trouble is that he has to choose between his inclination toward keeping everything under control and in order just as a juggler always does, and the jungle law of disguise and constant change. As much as Billy would like things to be definite and stable, he must learn to adjust to the contingent. "And when the situation changed, would I change with it? Yes, the answer is yes"(138).

A smart apprentice to the gangsters, Billy soon not only masters the art of change, but also discovers that the consequence of one's change to adapt to the environment is the agile shifts between different roles. With more contact with and deeper understanding of Dutch Schultz, he begins to contemplate on the issues of naming and identity. Dutch Schultz, for instance, is originally named Arthur Flegenheimer. In one instant, he is the legendary hero, "a king in my eyes", who has given a kid a ten-dollar note to reward his performance. At the next moment, he changes into the crazy criminal who executes his former colleague Bo and rapes his girl in a cruel way. In Onondaga, he turns into a philanthropist, a catholic, and a kind-hearted patron of the little orphan Billy. It seems everyone in the gang puts on some camouflage and has different faces. Dutch Schultz's financial assistant Otto Berman is "in some circles Adbadabba". The heroine of the novel Drew Preston is at first Bo's girl Miss Lola. Then she changes into Schultz's mistress Miss Drew, and later Mrs. Preston according to different occasions.

From Drew Preston, Billy also finds the same quality of change and free shift in roles. The first scene of the book opens with the murdering of Bo Weinberg in a tugboat. Bo is directly taken away from a restaurant by Schultz's utility men. His fiancée Drew, at this time called Miss Lola, becomes the victim of Schultz's rage for her relationship with Bo, the betrayer in the eyes of Schultz. Drew is forced into a separate room by Schultz to suffer his rage. After a night, instead of revenging on the man who has killed her fiancé, she reaches some secret agreements with Schultz and acquiesces to be his mistress. When leaving the boat, Billy is assigned to follow Drew to her hotel to fetch her belongings. To his surprise, he finds that Drew actually lives with her husband in a grand hotel. It turns out that she comes from a very prominent family and marries a rich man. But she lives a quite independent life, separated from her husband, who is obviously gay or bisexual.

Following Schultz to the country of Onondaga, rather than behaving like a subjugated captive, Drew appears to be the upper-class lady Mrs. Preston, whose table manners show "an operation of pronounced gentility performed at ritual speed"(124). With her pantomime, "presuming to act in that way of privilege of instructing those less fortunate..."(125), she humiliates the tough gangsters including Schultz in a subtle way. To set up a positive image for himself in Onondaga, Dutch Schultz asks Drew to pretend to be the governess of Joe, his protégé in the eyes of the public. Drew agrees and more than willingly throws herself into the new role, a maternal figure full of love and responsibility. She orders proper outfit from New York for Billy and teaches him language as well as decent manner of upper class. But before the trial of Schulz, when Billy escorts her to Saratoga Springs under the order of Berman, Drew allures Billy into a dark forest and has sex with him. In this fairy-tale-like forest, Billy finds in her "a primitive voice", and her action "entirely wild" (135). It is through Drew that Billy realizes that one's identity can be so volatile, and that he actually knows little about women. As Billy concludes, she seems to quite indulge in every role she plays, "incapable of distinguishing pretense from reality" (135). In the mind of Billy, Drew is unstable, mysterious, and enchantingly "dangerous", as she "covered her tracks", "trailed no history", but "took on the coloration of the moment, slipping into the role suggested to her by her surroundings"(137). That's why Otto Berman dislikes her. As a man of reason and numbers, Otto Berman would like to keep everything under control. To him, Drew is an X, a letter symbolizing unknown factors and potential dangers.

As Arthur Flegenheimer can change into Dutch Schultz, Otto Berman is also Abbadabba and Drew turns into Miss Lola or Mrs. Preston or Joe's governess, Joe begins to realize that all names "could be like license plates you could switch on cars, not welded into their construction but only tagged on for the temporary purposes of identification" (138). Witnessing these people's free shift among their different roles, Joe comes to the awareness that "all identification is temporary because you went through a life of changing situations." Satisfied with his conclusion, he decides that he would appropriate their way of living and make it "my license-plate theory of identification"(138).

2. 2. A Self Subject to Invention in *Loon Lake*

Like *Billy Bathgate*, *Loon Lake* is also set in the Depression era and it centers around a poor homeless boy Joe in search of his identity. In their essay "*Loon Lake* and the Vision of Synchronicity: 'Exactly Like You'", Carol Harter and James R. Thompson make the observation that "[Doctorow] has always been concerned with the conditions of the self", but they conclude by claiming that Doctorow "has approached the position that there is no such thing as a unique human character, that self is both the cause and effect of processes and elements generally thought of as external to the self" (Harter & Thompson, 1990: 87). In other words, the self is not a finished statement, and it is always in the construction, subject to forces from the outside world. In *Loon Lake*, Doctorow tries to reveal that one's identity is produced and reproduced through a highly subjective narrator with the medium of language that causes its instability. Essentially, the two novels are both narrated by the participators of the main events that have happened in the story. They are the protagonists, who reminisce their adolescent experiences as a wanderer and render them into narrative. The difference lies in that *Billy Bathgate* draws upon a more realistic way of narration while the narrative of *Loon Lake* shifts between the first and third person perspective, and is full of distractions from the main narrative, such as the computer outputs, vitae, annotations and so on. Obviously, *Loon Lake* puts more emphasis on the tension between one's will to find a unified self and the discordant discourse that produces it.

Like Billy, Joe also comes from a dire family, but he does not feel any warmth from his family as Billy gets from his mentally troubled mother. To him, parents are "hateful presences", and his life only suggests to them "the terrible sequence of one mindless moment of their lust" (Doctorow, 1979: 3). Unlike Billy who finally returns to his mother, Joe denies his family and his working-class origin, seldom mentioning it in his later time. In terms of intelligence, both Billy and Joe belong to Doctorow's definition of the "criminal of perception", who possesses the prowess to perceive, penetrate and analyze, just as Joe distinguishes himself from his peers by claiming that "my brain was along in the silence of observation and perception and understanding"(4). According to Jochen Barkhausen, what makes Billy and Joe's perception criminal, is not its uncommon sharpness or subtlety, but the fact that it is not directed at the self, but at the Other (the others, the world), and that in its critical attention to the Other, it violates taboos pervasive in the fields of discourse, thought and knowledge (Barkhausen, 1988: 126). But their ambitions are the same. Joe wants to be famous just as Billy longs to be admitted into Dutch Schultz's group— a world of fast money and unconditional power. Their evolution lies in more than a change of identity from poverty and anonymity to wealth and prominence; it is also from ignorance to awareness, an awareness of what constitutes the self. However, this awareness does not originate from an individual's psychologized ego, but to a large extent comes from the influences of the other.

After running away from his birth place Paterson in a provincial town of New Jersey "where nothing important could happen where even death was unimportant"(Doctorow, 1979: 6), Joe travels to New York, then to California, and ends up in the mountain area where he encounters a carnival owned by Sim Hearn. Witnessing that Fanny the Fat Lady—a retarded woman—is gang-raped by the "rubes" to earn money for the boss Hearn, Joe is enraged. He takes revenge by eloping with Hearn's Wife, sexually abusing her, and throwing all the money made from Fanny into the air. After leaving Hearn's Wife and walking aimlessly into the deep forest, Joe catches a glimpse of a train with a brightly lit bedroom where a blond girl stands naked in front of a mirror holding a dress. In this moment of epiphany, Joe feels his heart lighted up by something glorious, so he follows the track into the Adirondacks range where the industrial tycoon F. W. Bennett is holding a party in his property near Loon Lake. Unfortunately, Joe's sneaking into the retreat is welcomed by wild dogs. Seriously injured by the dogs, Joe is temporarily kept in Bennett's property for recovery. It is during this time that he comes to know another unusual guest of Loon Lake—Warren Penfield, a poet with working-class background, who previously intends to assassinate Bennett, but instead he gives up and stays under his patronage. With the help of Penfield, Joe elopes with Clara Luckas, the girl Joe has seen in the train, the mistress of the notorious gang leader Tommy Crapo, then of Bennett, and of Penfield. On their way to California, the young couple settles down in a town and Joe works in Bennett's Autobody Factory to support his temporary family. Later, Joe is involved in the murder of Red James, a union leader he befriends with, who turns out to be the man of Tommy Crapo's espionage organization in the service of Bennett. In the emergency of his arrest, Joe comes up with a story that he is the son of Bennett who comes to the town to investigate the union activities. After the release from his detention, Joe eventually returns to Loon Lake. After the death of Bennett, he becomes his legal heir and the new master of Loon Lake.

In Joe's struggle to survive, the key element is what Penfield has taught him—to become the hero of his own narration. In the mind of the poet, one's identity is not determined by his biographical genes, nor the environment he lives in; instead, it is a matter of narrative constant in the process of reinvention and recomposition, which rests upon one's verbal talent. In fact, since a very early time, Joe has displayed the talent of linguistic creation. Like Billy who realizes that names are like license plates tapped on the car only for temporary identification, Joe also finds that one's names are subject to impromptu invention. Bedridden in Bennett's servant cabin after the dog attack, he occasionally gets access to the Loon Lake Guest Book, where all Bennett's guests invited to this property—"movie stars, orchestra leaders, authors, senators"—have left their signatures (78). With a strong desire to be a member of this prominent group, just as Billy desires to integrate into the gangs, Joe signs his name "Joe of Paterson", "a name with a false stamp of royalty and obscures the mauling under a reference to being greeted with honor" (Bevilacqua, 2012: 56), which makes Bennett notice his existence. Ushered by a maid into a grand storage room full of outfits prepared by Bennett for his guests, Joe finds satisfaction in dressing himself up as a rich boy with slacks, saddle shoes and an argyle sweater. Standing in front of the full-length mirror, Joe feels a shock of recognition:

> I was stunned by the magnificent youth that looked at me from the mirror. All the scars and deeper marks of hard life were covered in fine fashion. [...] He made a passing aristocrat. (92)

With this recognition, Joe begins to consider the possibility of a new identity for himself, "Who knew whose child I was", and he makes the bold proclamation, "I might be a Bennett son"(92). As Winifred Farrant Bevilacqua indicates, Joe's actions along the way reflect his strong intention of disguising his old identity "to cross borders and achieve desired relationships that are carried out through nominal, physical and behavioral changes" (Bevilacqua, 2011: 56). To him, nothing is predestined; labels and borders are artificially defined or drawn that can be changed with his efforts.

Like Billy, Joe's realization of his impromptu identity cannot be separated from the influences from the other. Warren Penfield, the failed residential poet who lives under the patronage of Bennett, becomes the most profound source of Joe's awareness, with the freedom he achieves in artistic creations. In his contact with Penfield, Joe is surprised and awed by the latter's verbal talents and brilliant mind, as he comments, "People from my world didn't talk with such embellishment such scrollwork. I had never before met someone who admitted to the profession of poet but believed it by the way he spoke" (Doctorow, 1979: 95). When Penfield shows him his published work, Joe feels so impressed with a sense of recognition in him that he calls Penfield a "distinguished friend" who makes him "a presence in the world" (109). Penfield also sees in Joe a shadow of himself, and feels an obligation to help and nurture him, as a father would do to his son. With the efforts of Penfield, Joe is able to escape from Bennett's realm of power and control with his beloved girl Clara. In the little town of Jacksontown where they temporarily settle, Joe is arrested and questioned by the police for his involvement in the death of Red James. Realizing himself in a position of looming imprisonment, Joe suddenly finds a voice rising from his mind, the voice belonging to a writer:

> It was an amazing discovery, the use of my ignorance, a kind of industrial manufacture of my own. And the more it went on, the more I believed it, taking this fact and that possibility and assembling them, then sending the results down the line a bit and adding another fact and dropping an idea on the whole thing and sending it on a bit for another operation, another bolt to the construction, my own factory of lies, driven by rage, Paterson Autobody doing its day's work. I was going to make it! This was survival at its secret source, and no amount of time on the around or sentimental education could have brought me to it if the suicidal boom of my stunned heart didn't threaten my extinction. (230)

Interrogated by the police, Joe makes up a story about his background, and asks the police to check the information with F. W. Bennett—the fictive father of his creation who has sent him to Jacksontown—with the private telephone number Bennett has given him. His story is convincing and coherent, and Joe attributes the art of his creation to Penfield, "the hero of his own narration with life and sun and stars and universe concentrically disposed on the locus of his tongue" (263). This is a creative act that saves him from an unjust sentence. Finally, after the disappearing of Bennett's wife Lucinda and Penfield in a flight, Joe returns to Loon Lake and really becomes Bennett's adoptive son. His fictive creation of himself turns into reality. From the beginning of the book to the close, Joe never reveals his true family name but uses the name of the street "Paterson" where he grows up as his fake surname.

Till the end of the novel, the computer data of Joe's curriculum vitae shows his name as Joe Korzeniowski, an exotic surname without any validation of its truth. As some critics suggest, the surname Korzeniowki reminds readers of Joseph Conrad, who gets the same name, a name indicating the owner's complicated origin[①].

3. The Constant Transgression of the Self to Reach the Other

3.1. The I-Thou Dichotomy

In his work *I and Thou*, Martin Buber writes that there are two basic word pairs one can speak: I-You and I-It. In the I-You (I-Thou), one stands in relation to another with one's whole being (presence). In the I-It, one experiences something or someone as an object. In his writings on the I-Thou relationship, Buber urges movement toward intersubjectivity. This intersubjectivity, a topic which many contemporary theorists find fascinating, focuses on the coexistence of the self and the other to constitute an identity. Apparently, one's self is constantly related to its inseparable connection to the other. Other, a word frequently employed in the studies of psychoanalysis, postcolonialism, feminism, etc. philosophically, refers to the opposite of the Same, the I, or the Unified. As a signifier, it always refers to the minor and inferior party in binary oppositions. The state or characteristic of the Other is "being different [from] or [alien to]" the identity of self or social identities[②].

The history of western philosophy is a process of continual expelling of the other and of continual accentuation of the subject. Therefore, a common target of postmodern theorists is to set free the other that has been imprisoned in the dungeon by the logos-centered metaphysics for thousands of years. As early as the end of 19th century, Sigmund Freud's lectures on psychoanalysis have shed light on the "dark, inaccessible part" of one's personality, which he defines as "id". To Freud, the id can be approached with analogies like "the chaos", the "cauldron full of seething excitations" or "the other", which refers to the part of psyche that is suppressed or disciplined by the "superego" represented by laws, norms, and regulations, etc. Like Freud, Michel Foucault was able to detect a new kind of disciplinary power of modern society, which aims to monitor its members in a more

---

① The background of the famous modernist novelist Joseph Conrad is very complicated. He was born Józef Teodor Konrad Korzeniowski in Berdichev (now Berdychiv), Ukraine, but was raised and educated primarily in Poland. He travelled to many places and later joined the English nationality.

② Quoted from Wikipedia. https://en.wikipedia.org/wiki/Other.

efficient way. Discursively, the system works through the various dichotomies in which social groups are categorized as normal/abnormal, sane/insane, and rational/irrational. Based on this standard, some people are labeled as the mad or deviant just because their behaviors are different from those of the majority. In other words, they represent forces of the other that the society tends to suppress or assimilate. In his elaborations on dialogue, M. M. Bakhtin analyzed the self/other relationship as the prerequisite for the development of a dialogue. To Bakhtin, self is never an isolated entity; rather, it is a relation, always in dialogue with other forces. He understands the other as the party engaged in a dialogue except the subject, the interlocutor whose participation of the dialogue makes the access to truth possible. Though the context of the other may vary, Freud, Foucault and Bakhtin's study all contribute in one way or another to the reevaluation and resurrection of the voices that are always ignored or silenced in the past.

Among all the scholars, Levinas's idea of the self and the other has the most profound influences especially in the postmodern period. In the opinion of Levinas, the philosophical tradition of the whole western society is ontological, and it is the process of obstinate effort of the self trying to perceive, conceptualize and absorb the other. Most of the time the definition of the self is accompanied by the demonization and banishment of the other, which always puts the other in a minor or peripheral place. In *Totality and Infinity*, one of Levinas's most crucial works subtitled "An Essay on Exteriority", Levinas mentions otherness as exteriority and remarks that "Moral consciousness is not an experience of values, but an access to exterior being" (Levinas, 1979: 28). Levinas calls this exterior being "the face of the other", the omnipresent presence the self encounters with, which calls for the obligation of the self to respond to.

3.2. The Transgression of the Limit of the Self

In *Billy Bathgate* and *Loon Lake*, both Billy and Joe come from a humble origin but with a strong desire to change their fate. Despite their will to gain success, they are naturally flawed in many aspects such as their lower-class family background, poor education, their manners and speech, and their limited experiences and knowledge of the world.

Before joining Schultz's gang group, Billy has some naïve recognition of himself as the king in sovereignty of his own kingdom. "[B]eing gifted with extraordinary peripheral vision", he feels that he can become somebody in America—the big juggling event in his eyes. Considering himself a good juggler,

Billy claims, "I was juggling my own self as well in a kind of matching spiritual feat, performer and performed for" (Doctorow, 1989: 25). But soon he discovers the deterministic forces that usurp the sovereignty of his kingdom. He changes his opinion: "At this moment it occurred to me that my self-satisfaction was inane. It consists in believing I was the subject of my experience" (81).

Billy has realized the limitation that his humble origin brings about by comparing himself with Drew, who is not much older than him but seems to live in an enlarged realm of choice and knowledge. For the poor kid Billy, life is left without many options, as he says "If I had lived down near Yankee Stadium I would have known where the players went in through the side door, or if I lived in Riverdale maybe the mayor would have passed by and waved from his police car on the way home from work, it was the culture of where you lived" (29). If he does not join the gangsters, he may end up like other boys on the Paterson Street, to be a peddler, a hobo, or a worker in the factory.

But to Drew, things are totally different. As Billy says, "for the same reasons of staring meditation, she might have chosen life in a convent, say or to be an actress on the stage" (153). She can choose to be an upper-class lady who enjoys horseracing, sailing and other luxury entertainments or to join the gangsters just for the excitement of adventure. Behind her, it's her prominent family as well as the huge wealth the family provides to support her willfulness. On the other hand, Billy thinks that "with the golden band on her finger", Drew lives a life beyond him in practiced knowledge insofar as he is almost a child beside her. With her wealth, Drew can have access to "all the pleasures on the planet" (153). Her experiences enable her to acquire knowledge on things that Billy may not even have a chance to hear in his whole life. Aware of this fact, Billy laments:

> So look at her now I had revelation of the great expanse of my ambitions, I felt the first acute pain of this same knowledge, which was an appreciative inkling of how much I had so far missed and my mother had missed and would forever miss... (Doctorow, 153)

Through the comparison between him and Drew, Billy learns the influence of stratification that class and power bring on the formation of individual identity. The fact is that if Billy wants to live a life different from that of the boys on the Paterson Street, and he has to transgress the deterministic force of environment, of social norms, moralities and even laws to move upwardly. In other words, he has to overcome his illusion that he is the sovereign of his own subjectivity and to open himself to the influence of the other.

Like Billy, Joe also feels the burden of his caste and he expresses his strong desire to shake free of this weight caused by his biological origin:

> Without the sling I felt the true weight of my cast. I thought of the weight as everything that had to be done before I could get out of Jacksontown. I wanted to shake this cement cast from my bones as I wanted to shake free of this weight of local life and disaster... I wanted to be back at my best, out of everyone's reach, in flight. But I had all this weight and ... there was hardly any time for which I had to do in order to lift it from me so that we could get free (134).

For once in Jacksontown, Joe feels that he can inherit the family's working-class tradition. He tries to settle down in the little town, working at an assembly line in Bennett's Autobody Factory. But then the case of Red James' murder awakens his dream of petty life: a downtrodden and anonymous guy like him is destined to be the victim of those in power as he is faced with the unjust accusation he has nothing to do with. Therefore, he chooses the way of self-invention, to create another identity for himself—to abandon his proletarian origin, and to embrace the cold and desolate industrialist F. W. Bennett.

Both Joe and Billy's experiences include their witnessing of crime and underworld activities, in which "corruption, graft and exploitation flourish, and where the values of justice and truth are indeed complex, if not downright debatable" (Vieira, 1991: 363). With no assurances in life, they have to brave a world where "appearances belie other realities and so they learn to use acute caution and their acquired disrespect for limits and boundaries, as well as their imagination, their ruses, and their skills to recover a supposedly better world for themselves"(363). For them, the limits of their despicable parents, of the place where they grow up, and of their personalities caused by their birth, must be stepped over to achieve manhood and spiritual maturity. The boundary between the self, which is supposed to be the center of subjectivity, and the other—the forces that are not self, must be broken down to open up to new possibilities.

Now, realizing the limitation of their old self, Billy and Joe employ the strategy of transgressing the boundary of the self to appropriate the other, to become the other and even to usurp the other so as to accomplish the process of transformation from boyhood to manhood.

3.3. The Influence of the Other on the Self in *Billy Bathgate*

According to Nelson H. Vieira, in *Billy Bathgate* Billy's relationship with other people like Dutch Schultz and Drew Preston—exponents of illegal and legal capitalism, "enables him to overcome his egocentrism and understand the relativity of his experience" (185). To Billy, the force of the other is, first of all, a kind of paternal influence that comes from his spiritual fathers Dutch Schultz and Otto Berman.

On many occasions, Billy has expressed his admiration for Dutch Schultz— the gangster hero—and his longing to become a man like him. Like the protagonists of many other Horatio Alger[①] stories, Billy is obsessed with the fulfillment of his American Dream, and Schultz just represents the model of the self-made man, though in a dark version, as he tells Billy: "Christ, I had to earn everything I got, nobody gave me a thing, I came out of nowhere and everything I done I done by my self" (Doctorow, 1989: 67). When Schultz gives Billy the ten dollars and holds his head for a moment, Billy is greatly inspired by his acts as some recognition of his ability, and more importantly, he understands the ritual as "a kind of investiture" bestowed from "my king"(33). With his impetuosity and brutality, Schultz becomes the charismatic father image, an idol of manliness to Billy. Billy sympathizes with him and almost completely internalizes his point of view. With his astute skill of handling with grown-ups, Billy gradually becomes a confidant follower of Schultz, and he has the chance to observe Schultz and the operation of the gang at a close distance. He notices that what maintains Schultz's leader position is his ferocious energy, as "he took things to extremes, so that what might have started out as business, like everything else up here, he would want to do the limit. He would go overboard in these feelings just as he did in his angers" (176). Besides, Schultz has the urge to appropriate, which "operated all the time and wherever he happened to be, he'd appropriated speakeasies, beer companies, union, numbers games, nightclubs, me, Miss Drew, and now he was appropriating Catholicism"(176). Billy feels himself a lucky kid to receive the intimate education from Schultz and he longs to become a man like him: "In these days I felt very close to Mr. Schultz, I was the only one cooperating in the deepest spirit with him ... I was alone with the man in his heart..." (295)

---

①   Horatio Alger (1832-1899) was a 19th-century American writer who has created many novels about impoverished boys and their rise from humble backgrounds to lives of middle-class security and comfort through hard work, determination, courage, and honesty. His writings could be defined as "rags-to-riches" narrative, which had a significant effect on America during the Gilded Age.

Otto Berman, however, stands as a "complement to Schultz", who has shaped Billy's personality in other aspects. The two fathers constitute the "two halves of a whole" which make out of Billy a complete genius-criminal (Henry, 1991: 35-6). Otto "Abadabba" Berman is Schultz's financial wizard, a man who "lived and dreamed in numbers". As a genius in mathematics, he represents the organized crime of future generations based on the real capitalist way, instead of the physical conquer in Schultz's manner. He suggests that the organization of the gang should be operated through numbers, that is, through reasonable control, manipulation and cooperation between rival gangs, like the way big capitalist enterprises operate. Thus, from Otto, Billy learns the value and necessity of business savvy. It seems that Billy takes both Schultz and Otto as his surrogate father, and after their death, he laments his loss: "Mr. Berman has failed me too, I am resentful, I feel fatherless again, a while new wave of fatherlessness, that they have gone so suddenly, as if there was no history of our life together in the gang..." (Doctorow, 1989: 303)

The maternal force of love and sex epitomized by Drew Preston becomes another affecting force of the other that contributes to the development of Billy's identity. Before Drew, Billy's knowledge of women is based on his crazy mother—a woman he reveres—and the orphaned girl Rebecca whom "he fucked two times for a dollar" (89). As Janice Stewart Heber points out, Billy's idea on gender is traditional, as he receives the stereotypical dichotomy of women as "holy mother" or "evil" whore. When he first met Drew on the tugboat in the night of Bo's death, he promises Bo that he will protect Drew for he understands her as a vulnerable existence like his mother whom he must precariously keep away from any intimation of the dangers in gangster life. But soon, he is stunned by the "x factor" that Drew demonstrates in her dealing with Schultz and other gang members. As Joseph Francese mentions, Drew is prominently characterized by her volatile energy, that is, her ability to become somebody else. In the earlier stage, Billy imagines her to be the "embodiment of the aristocracy" with her "fine features, curving neck, white shoulders and marcelled blond head" (Doctorow, 1989: 15-6), the golden girl in the Gatsby stories. But then, Billy's impression of Drew changes as she turns into a maternal image in Onondaga, who reminds Billy of his mother Lucy. He reminiscences his relationship with Drew and Schultz as this: "Miss Drew could be my mother and Mr. Schultz my father, a thought that came to me, no not even a thought worse than a thought, a feeling, when we attended mass at the St. Barnabas Catholic Church one Sunday [. . .]" (134). But until then, Billy's understanding of Drew cannot shake off the rigid dichotomy of "mother/ whore". The turning point appears when they two walk to a gorge and Billy tells Drew of her fiancé Bo's death scene. Out of grievance or guilt, Drew climbs down the bank of the gorge, and plunges into a black pool of water. This episode helps Billy come to an insightful recognition of her deeper nature: "[s]he lived an enlarged existence," not to be "contained by judgments". Billy realizes that Drew "had the character of independence, that she lived alone in some sort of mystery of her own making and that it was her integrity to be self-driven and self-communicating..."(168). At this moment, Billy feels a "new liking for her" and now Drew becomes a mysterious and beautiful woman he desires and longs to possess. In this sense, Drew turns to "an Aphrodite, a goddess of love and fertility, as well as a siren, a dangerous temptress" in Billy's fantasy as he progresses from the adolescent kid lack of knowledge to a mature man conscious of his identity (Baba, 1993: 34). After their consummate sex in the forest, Billy has a long epiphanic speech on sex:

> You can remember the fact of it, and recall the setting, and even the details, but the sex of the sex cannot be remembered, the substantive truth of it, it is by nature self-erasing, you can remember its anatomy and be left with a judgment as to the degree of your liking of it, but whatever it is as a splurge of being, as a loss, as a charge of the conviction of love stopping your heart like your execution..." (201)

The experience of sex leads Billy to the adult world of pleasure, pain and insatiable desire. As a more experienced woman, Drew teaches Billy not only the knowledge of class, of life, but also of love and sex. The combination of Schultz, Otto, Drew as well as other figures on Billy's road of quest together completes Billy's education and maturation. The same forces of the other also work out through Joe's evolution but in a more complicated way.

3.4. The Approach of the Self to the Other in *Loon Lake*

Many critics have commented on the "Father-son" relationship in *Loon Lake*. But the core of this relationship is primarily the self-other relationship, which overwhelms the whole book. To Jochen Barkhausen, Joe is the young individualist who clings to "my own kingship of consciousness" and is resolved "to take alone whatever came"(18). He not only lets his self to approach the other closely, but literally allows others to penetrate him by incorporating others (Barkhausen, 1988: 126).

In *Loon Lake*, Joe's life and the life of Warren Penfield are intertwined in an incredible way. Like Billy who has laid his fantasy of paternity on Schultz and Otto, Joe also seeks for his spiritual father from people around him especially from

Penfield and Bennett. As soon as the book begins, the readers are immediately struck by the similarities of the experiences of Penfield and Joe: both are poor sons with estranged working-class parenthood; they are attacked by Bennett's wild dogs when first stepping on the property of Loon Lake (the attack seems to symbolize the assault of working-class by the ruthless power of capitalism). In consideration of his parents, Joe thinks, "They were hateful presences in me. Like a little old couple in the woods, all alone for each other, the son only a whim of fate." (Doctorow, 1979: 1). Penfield, in comparison, is derided by his father for being chosen as the Boy of the Year, and he is admonished to give up his creative talents in writing and to follow his parents' path of mining. In the words of Michelle Tokarczyk, the two men "represent two generations of workers during the Depression" (Tokarczyk, 2002: 117), with Joe of Paterson standing for the urban Northeasterner while Warren Penfield representing the miners of the West. The dog-biting episode that so coincidentally rehappens probably indicates their common destiny: the corruption of the working class by the capitalists. Besides, both men share the birth date of August 2, with Penfield born in 1888, old enough to be the father of Joe in 1918, as does Bennett, born in 1878, implying that there are some bonds among the three.

As the successor of both, what Joe inherits from Penfield is his literary imagination, creative prowess, and romantic passion toward life. During Joe's recuperation from injuries caused by the dogs, Penfield befriends him and always reads to him the poems from his published or unpublished volumes. At that moment, Joe's initial impression of Penfield as a fat drunk who lives under the mercy of others has completely changed. He feels the resonance aroused in his heart by Penfield's lyrics:

> I heard the feeling they inspired in me, that I was living at last! That it was the way it should be, I was feeling Penfield's immense careless generosity, the boom of himself which granted me without argument everything I was struggling for, all of it assumed in the simple giving of words, so moving to this scruffy boy. (Doctorow, 1979: 97)

Penfield also expresses his sympathy with and recognition of Billy as a paternal elder. He talks to him as if to teach him the lessons he learns from life. He tells Joe, "My pain is your pain. My life is your life."(133) His words show a life philosophy of circularity: one's life is in parallel with others and the end of one's life does not mean eternal emptiness, but the shift of force from one to the body of the other. Before his disappearence in the flight with Bennett's wife Lucinda, Penfield leaves all his papers, copies of chapbooks, letters, words of meditations, journals and night thoughts to Joe, in expectation of Joe's final return to Loon Lake to take them. In his works, he says, "You are what I would want my son to be", a posture of admitting Joe as his adopted son. And he conveys his philosophy of reincarnation: "[P]erhaps we all reappear, perhaps all our lives are impositions one on another" (207). It is not until Joe's detention in Jacksontown that he realizes the influences of Penfield on him. In the time of life-or-death crisis, he finds Penfield's voice in his mind, the voice of creativity, and he fabricates the fictive story of his life as Bennett's son, which ensures his freedom.

F. W. Bennett, however, represents another side of human nature that Joe desires to possess, the absolute isolation and freedom brought about by the ownership of capital. First and foremost, he is a cold-hearted industrialist, who has accumulated multimillions of wealth through the exploitation of workers. From the biographical data inserted in the text, we can find that F. W. Bennett is responsible for the mine disaster of Ludlow in 1910. He also sends out spying organizations to secretly monitor and sabotage the activities of unions. But in the eyes of Joe, Bennett is a man of great power and freedom due to his possession of wealth; a force both attracts and dispels him. When dressed in the fancy clothes Bennett has prepared for his guests, Joe expresses his wish to become the son of Bennett. According to John G. Parks, the figure of F. W. Bennett is the encoded hero of the system that defines American culture and his power is more than material—"he is what everybody wants [to be]" (Parks, 77). He embodies the dream of self-made men, as Joe writes: "For men all over the country he was, finally, a condition of life" (Doctorow, 1979: 86). In the short period of staying at Loon Lake, Joe is fascinated by "the enormous will placed on Nature by crushing its purity and parodies the temperament of Bennett who has bought the wilderness with enormous wealth" (Ramya. B, 2013: 5). Loon Lake used to be the ancient residency of Indians, the land of sheer nature. Now it falls into the hands of Bennett, who turns it into private property, the immoral retreat to provide luxury entertainment such as hunting and bowing for his guests. In the verse written by Penfield about the natural scenery of Loon Lake, he depicts the contamination of the wilderness by human will, especially with the description of the cold lake water and the cruel scene of loon predation, which indicates the exact nature of its master:

...

Loons diving into the cold Back lake

and diving back out again in a whorl of clinging water

...

thrillingly exerting loon
taking a fish
rising to the moon streamlined
its loon eyes around and red.

Realizing Bennett's enormous will, power and influences imposed on his surrounding environment, Joe reveals his conflicted desire to become him and to escape from his control:

I had expected not to like F. W. Bennett. But he was insane. How could I resist that? There was this manic energy of his, a mad light in his eye. He was free. That was what free men were like, they shone their freedom over everyone. (122)

With the help of Penfield, Joe succeeds in eloping with Clara, Bennett's mistress at that time. He plans to live an ordinary life away from Bennett's control, after refusing the job offer of Bennett. But after the Jacksontown episode, Joe finds his dream of living as an ordinary anonymous man crushed by the capital power, which reaches almost every corner of American life. Finally, he chooses to become Bennett's son and subjugates himself to his way of living as he says to the police chief: "Tell Mr. Bennett it's his son calling. Tell him it's his son, Joe."(270) From the biography in the form of verse at the end of the novel, the readers are informed that Joe inherits Bennett's family name and his mass wealth. He follows the pattern of Bennett and becomes the self-made man through a series of upward movements: he gets educated in a college, is commissioned as the Second Lieutenant U. S. Air Corps, and is later appointed as the organization staff CIA 1947. He finally wins the title he has desired—"Master of Loon Lake". In his review "Types Defamiliarized", George Stade comments on Joe's final choice of becoming a second Bennett in this way: "In *Loon Lake*, Joe of Paterson (or Father-son) triumphs over his adoptive father by becoming him, only worse ... in America, ... the sons win; they destroy the past only to preserve the worst of it in themselves, and thereby destroy the future" (Stade, 1980: 285).

As a successor of Penfield and Bennett, Joe is affected by both in his march into manhood as he inherits from Penfield his art of story-telling and from Bennett his immense wealth, industrial empire and his life of sterility. Like Billy, there is also a female figure that has exerted great influence on Joe. Clara Lukacs, a girl also from a working-class family, serves as a foil to Joe since they both possess the ambition to acquire fame, money and a higher social position. Firstly, Clara is the golden girl standing naked in front of a mirror, who allures Joe to follow the track to Adirondacks. In other words, she awakens Joe's aspiration for something noble and glorious in life. The reason that Clara attracts Penfield and Joe is not only about her appearances, but her symbolization of desire itself. As Penfield says, "she is faithful to nothing but her own life" (Doctorow, 1979: 108). In fact, Clara never conceals her desire to live a better life. Her desire for upward mobility is fulfilled through the exchange of her youth and beauty for what she dreams of with those in power, first Tommy Crapo the notorious gangster, and then Bennett the industrial tycoon. But more importantly, she is the inspiration of literary creations, the golden muse for both Joe and Penfield.

Glimpsing Clara for the first time, Joe makes a reaction that signals his sensitivity to words and language: "Into my vacated mind flowed all the English I never knew I'd learned at Paterson Latin High School. Grammar slammed into my brain."(56) Actually before this event, Joe has described a boy watching a beautiful little girl urinating in a verse inserted after the first chapter of the book. The boy seems to have known the girl and he says, "it's you", watching the "thin stream of golden water to cascade/into the dust where instantly formed minuscule tulips/ he beheld the fruition of a small fertile universe"(15). In the middle part of the book, the urinating scene appears again but this time the boy who is enjoying his Dixie ice cream completely recognizes the little girl. The pronoun becomes you as the poet writes, "you closed your eyes and allowed the thin stream of/golden water to cascade to the tar which was instantly black and/shone clearer than a night sky"(135). Later, when Joe and Clara settle down in Jacksontown, they reveal their past to each other. To the surprise of Joe, they used to live on the same street. Till then, Joe realizes that they may have had encounters in their childhood or maybe it's only his fantasy. Anyway, the little girl's "golden water" has some symbolic meaning since it reappears. It can be the source of inspiration for Joe who has written the verses, just as the boy takes it as the "fruition of the fertile universe". Like the beautiful girl Stephen Dedalus meets by the sea[①], Clara also serves as a muse-like figure in *Loon Lake*, an epitome of beauty, youth and sexuality, who appears and disappears just to arouse the protagonist's epiphany on life and art.

---

① Stephen Dedalus is the protagonist in James Joyce's *The Portrait of the Artist as a Young Man*. He meets a girl by the sea, which awakens his inspiration of literary creation. Hence, he writes the first poem in his life. The episode also strengthens his determination to become a writer.

4. A Narrative of Multiple Voices

In *Billy Bathgate* and *Loon Lake*, both Billy and Joe play the role of the hero as well as the narrator who narrates for the most part in the first-person point of view. Their narratives are from the perspective of an adult who tries to reminisce their younger self. According to Paul Ricoeur, narrative constitutes human identity, as it is the "irreducible dimension of self-understanding" (Bergström, 2010: 83). In fact, Ricoeur's claim on the relationship between narrative and identity can be traced back to Socrates and Aristotle. According to Socrates, an "examined life" is a life recounted. Similarly, Aristotle posits the link between ethical aspects of conduct with happiness/misfortune through the "thought experiments" provided by narrative and other dramatic forms. In this sense, human experience is structured as narrative which helps introduce meaning to the chaotic reality.

Billy and Joe's narratives, rather than being monologues dominated by a single authorial voice, are characterized by the "indeterminacy in the plurality of countervailing voices"(109), which indicates the discourse of "the saying"[1], the "ethical residue of language that escapes comprehension, interrupts ontology", and "the very enactment of the movement from the same to the other" (Critchley& Bernasconi, 2004:18). In these two semi-autobiographical novels, the narrators' intention to create a coherent identity is constantly interrupted by the incoherent voices inside the narrative, which reminds the narrators of the irreducible presence of the other. Firstly, the interruption comes from the narrator himself as an unreliable or self-contradicted storyteller. In the case of *Billy Bathgate*, the readers are told that the narrator is Billy who names himself after the Bathgate Avenue. Till the end of the novel, when Billy finishes his narration, the true name of the narrator is still not revealed. The reason for this, as the narrator suggests, is that Billy has become a very prominent figure at the time of his narration and he wants to protect his disgraced past from being exposed: "Who I am in my majority and what I do, how I live must remain my secret because I have a certain renown". (Doctorow, 1989: 321)

---

[1]   In the domain of language, Levinas puts forward two contradictory concepts—the saying and the said, to represent two different discourses, the first ethical, and the latter ontological. According to Levinas, the saying, similar to the dialogic discourse of Bakhtin, is the "performative stating, proposing or expressive position of myself facing the other", indicating a process that "cannot be reduced to a propositional description" (Critchley& Bernasconi, 2004: 15). The said, by contrast, is a statement, assertion or proposition of which the truth or falsity can be ascertained. In other words, the said means closure—a state in which the meaning of linguistic contents can be identified and determined.

The readers cannot help but suspect Billy's reliability, for because of the same reason, he may have hidden some of the facts, or undercut his involvement in the crimes he has described in the process of narration. Despite Billy's claim that he appreciates the transgressive behaviors of the gangsters, and that he finds their own definition of right and wrong attractive, in Billy's narrative, he always depicts himself as a distant spectator of the criminal activities. In other words, he is never a positive participator or accomplice. So in the terms of morality, he can be exempt from the accusations from the readers as a criminal or a bad man, since all his behaviors are excused as a boy's instinct to survive under the rule of the gangster world.

Billy's unreliability as a narrator is mostly reflected in his account of Bo's murder scene in front of Drew Preston. In fact, the first part of the episode is narrated in the opening chapter of the book and then it is interrupted. When later requested by Drew to tell the death of Bo, Billy begins his narration of the other half of the event. But this time, his narration is obviously invested with sympathy and emotion, in contrast to the indifference of the first chapter. In front of Drew, Billy's narrative reveals more humanity as he describes the pains and tortures of Bo as he has experienced himself. At the same time, he justifies and minimizes his involvement in Bo's execution. When Ivy "commands" (Please notice Billy's use of words) him to support Bo's other side of body to let Bo slip into the sea, Billy describes his action as involuntary, completely under the pressure from his superior, stating that "oh this is just what I prefer not to do in my criminal training"(161). On the other hand, Billy highlights the compassionate side of his nature. When Bo whispers to him "[T]ake care of my girl don't let him do it to her get her away before he does her...", he says "I promise, I tell him in the first act of mercy in my life"(160). But as it turns out, Billy breaks the promise for he does not even try to rescue Drew from the raping of Dutch Schultz, nor has he ever thought about it, a point he chooses not to tell Drew.

Later, he reveals his deliberate ellipsis of some other important details in this narration to Drew, "I had not included everything, that for instance when Irving and the pilot were talking in the wheelhouse Bo Weinberg begged me to go below and see what was happening to her"(163). In fact, Billy has heard the fierce argument between Schultz and Drew, and even the violence done to Drew, which he has omitted again for the consideration of maintaining his moral integrity.

Approaching the end of the book, Billy declares that "these are confessions of a wild and desolate boyhood and I would have no reason to lie about any one of them" (296). But as Mathew A. Henry suggests, "if they are confessions, they admit of no fault; they are the confessions of one believing in his immaculate innocence"(Henry, 1997: 35). As the narrator who "denies any taint or corruption or complicity" in a series of criminal events (35), Billy gives reason to readers to question his authority and authenticity, thus undermining the narrative's intention to construct a unitary autobiography on Billy Bathgate.

In some places, Doctorow also creates other voices to counteract Billy's narrative, reminding readers of the fictiveness of literary creation itself. During Schultz's trial in Onondaga, Billy is sent back to New York under the instructions of Otto Berman, where he keeps himself informed of the trial by reading newspapers. In fact, Billy's act of reading newspapers to know what has happened to the gangsters happens several times. Each time, he finds that the facts depicted in the news stories are different from what he learns from those gang members. It seems that only the surface is reported and realities as supplied by Billy's account are forever missing in official history. Billy reveals his meditation on the gap between literary representation and reality: "They might have their theories but it took a while to get up an authoritative version, as with all historians going through the wreckage after the silence has set in. By contrast I immediately knew, as if I had been there" (Doctorow, 1989: 105). Here, Doctorow shows that history, as representations of language, is not as true and objective as it is commonly supposed. People may rely on documents such as newspaper, broadcasting, television for information, but as Billy realizes, the truth of an event may lie beyond our imagination, only glimpsed by very few people. History, either written by institutions or individuals, is tainted with the will of human beings, thus subject to prejudice and deliberate manipulation.

In New York, Billy reads some newspaper reports on a mysterious bloody murder that happened in a barbershop with the sensational headline, "GRISLY GANGLAND MURDER". As an intimate follower of Schultz, Billy immediately knows that it is Schultz who committed the crime in a surge of rage, based on the death scene the newspaper described. Later, when Billy meets Schultz again, Schultz talks of the murder as, "There wasn't nothing grisly about it. That was newspaper bullshit … it was beautiful and professional as could be (111)". Billy is thus able to philosophize that the news reporters are opinion-shapers, "composing for you the sights you would see and the opinions you would have ... like magicians whose tricks are words" (212). And when other gangsters hide themselves away in the crisis of the prosecution looming over Schultz, Billy returns to his neighborhood in the Bronx, dressed like a rich man. He sees that people's perception of him is altered, shaped in a large part by what has been reported in the local newspapers: "... I have realized that wherever I had been, whatever I had done, the people knew about it not in its details but in its fulfillment of their myth-knowledge of the rackets" (250-251). In Billy's skepticism on word's power to convey truth, his own narrative as a reliable and faithful account of his personal history is also called into question. The constructor of identity through narrative becomes his own deconstructor. His intention to construct a coherent and unitary identity through narrative is disrupted by the heterogeneous voices inside the narrative itself, which instead create a work of polyphony, where the authorial voice constantly converses and contests with the voices of the other.

Joe's narrative in *Loon Lake* pushes this tendency of self-deconstruction still further as its style is more experimental, with its shifts of scene, tense, along with interjections of poetry and computer biographies in the form of the resume or curriculum vitae. All these formal experiments produce the effect of cinematic montage, or what Harpham calls a "bricolage"①. As Doctorow comments, "Eventually in *Loon Lake* I realized that I was composing the book in a way that might suggest the lake itself—the way the light reflects and refracts and distorts and shimmers, and images are duplicated or broken up into many pieces" (Barkhausen, 1988: 130). The narrative of *Loon Lake*, like the Lake itself, is full of images of duplication, distortion and refractions, suggesting Doctorow's meditation on the relationship between literary forms and reality. This style is another demonstration of what Doctorow calls a "discontinuous narrative, with deferred resolutions, and in the throwing of multiple voices that turns out to be the work of one narrator."(130)

The difficulty of understanding a postmodern text like *Loon Lake* is, first of all, from its constant shift between different voices and settings. In the middle of Joe's narrative of the main plotline, the readers often find the insertion of other materials such as Penfield's poems on his earlier experiences and on his current life in Loon Lake as a residential poet. And sometimes both Joe's and Penfield's narratives are interrupted by the computer-printouts and even by the dialogue between Penfield and Lucinda. In some sense, Penfield's verse constitutes another half of Joe's life, complementing and enriching Joe's narrative, partially because the two share so much in common in their experiences. Before the airplane accident, Penfield bequeaths all his letters, journals and works to Joe. Joe inserts some of these materials into his narrative so that his limited perspective and knowledge on Penfield's life is complemented. On the other hand, Penfield symbolizes the other

---

①   In art, a bricolage is equivalent to a pastiche, which means the construction of an artistic work through putting together a diverse range of things that seem irrelevant.

part of Joe, the part with literary talents, who would like to pursue artistic freedom instead of being contented with worldly success.

According to Catherine Walker Bergstrom, *Loon Lake* displays "a multiplicity of voices in a truly human character interacting with others" (Bergstrom, 2010: 109). The intertwining of Joe's and Penfield's narratives suggests not only the synchronicity of their lives, but also intertextuality in the literature system, for as the "son" of Penfield, Joe's creative ability comes from the influence of Penfield and his outlooks are greatly shaped by Penfield. A close examination will find Joe's accounts are sometimes very close to that of Penfield's in his poems, with only a little detail changed, for example, "The Little flag in the stern flapped like a machine gun" (from Joe's narrative) (Doctorow, 1989: 50) is quite similar to "while the small flag at the stern snapped like a machine gun" (from Penfield's poem) (62). The repetition and alteration suggest literary works are never the original creation of a singular mind, but the products of multiple influences that combine the present with the past.

In *Loon Lake*, even Joe's own narrative is not coherent because the perspective frequently shifts between the first-person and the third-person. This shift first appears in the chapter where Joe decides to escape from his suffocating home:

> I decided to go to California.
> Armed only with his unpronounceable last name, he went down to the freight yards to begin his journey. He confuses this now in this mind with the West side slaughtering plant such atomized extract of organic essence, such a perfumery of disembowelment...
> I found a door that slide open, got it wide enough to slip through, climbed in, pulled the door almost shut behind me stood in the darkness breathing triumph. (Doctorow, 1989: 12)

The first-person perspective, subjective and often penetrating to the deep psychology of the narrator, simultaneously complements and contradicts the indifferent, distant and objective third-person perspective. As Jochen Barkhausen points out, "the first person narration proposes an identity of desire and subjectivity, whereas the distancing of the third person indicates the principal externality of desire's objectifications" (Barkhausen, 1988: 126). The narrative, thus, is invested with a tension between the subject, the perceiver from the inside, and the object, the perceiver from the outside, which the subject tries to objectify. The tension exists not only between human agents but also between human agents and nonhuman modes of production—computer printouts which appear like this:

> Come with me
> Compose with me
> Coming she is coming is she

In the last chapter where Joe's narrative ends with his final decision to take over the reign of Bennett, computer offers the skeletal information of Joe's later experiences of becoming a member of the elite class and a qualified inheritor of Loon Lake, thus finishing the recording of Joe's whole life:

> Herewith bio Joseph Korzeniowski.
> Born to a working-class family Paterson New Jersey
>   August 2 1918.
> Graduated Paterson Latin Grade School 1930.
>   ...

The computer writing provides another style of narrative, which is stiff and indifferent, in contrast to Joe's narrative of emotion, analysis and contemplation as well as Penfield poetry of lyrical beauty. Harter and Harpham see the image of the computer used to provide the chronologic biographical data in Joe's discontinuous narrative as a metaphor to indicate the way identity is produced and reproduced by an impersonal system that, like myth, "speaks itself" and "transcends the psychologized ego" (Harter & Harpham, 1990: 92). It is noteworthy that both *Loon Lake* and Harter and Harpham's essay were written in the days before the popularization of personal computers. So the trope of the computer programming is read by Harpham as an objective and alienating force, a "dehumanized" aspect of authorship, which co-authors the book with human agents in a mythic way.

To sum up, *Billy Bathgate* and *Loon Lake* reflect Doctorow's perception of a postmodern identity: an identity that is unfixed and subject to improvisation and invention, with a self constantly transgressed to meet the possibilities of the other. Furthermore, the polyphonic nature of Billy and Joe's narrative also suggests that a unitary identity built through narrative or other modes of representation is always an illusion, as the authorial voice in the narrative is always counteracted by the voices of the other.

Chapter Two
Beyond Good and Evil:
Transgression of Ethical Codes

1. Ethical Boundaries in Question

Ethics, a term coming from Greek, from the very start means "habit or custom", and it is later given the connotation of morality and virtue by Aristotle in his monograph *Nicomachean Ethics*. For moral philosophers like Aristotle and Epicurus, the aim of ethics is, in short, to answer the question that Socrates proposed: how should one live. The question is not a trivial one, for it actually contains a series of questions, the general concern of which is centered on human existence: who are we, how can we live a good life; how to distinguish good from bad; how can we know and gain access to truth.

For thousands of years, western ethics, including the ethical system from Aristotle to Immanual Kant, takes root in the basis of an absolute center, although the reference of the center often varies. However, this center, which means the absolute authority such as God, the Ideal, or reason, seems no longer valid in the contemporary society, in a time of uncertainty, chaos, and unruliness. The ethical standards, which categorize human behaviors into the "either-or" paradigm, are contested and challenged. The boundaries between moral judgments such as good and evil, just and unjust, true and false are problemized, blurred and transgressed in the contemporary society, thus generating a grey ground where obscurity dwells. According to Zygmund Bauman, postmodern age witnessed the decline of traditional ethics because the universality and solid foundations it's based on are lost with the dismantling of authority, as he says "the authorities we may entrust are all contested and none seems to be powerful enough to give us the degrees of reassurance we seek in the end..." (Bauman, 1993: 45) Bauman calls this situation postmodern moral crisis, and he thus declares all moral judgments are contextually, socially and culturally dependent. To Bauman, the postmodern perspective of ethics is characterized by the recognition of the ambiguity in ethical codes, of the elusive nature of its universal foundations, and of the openness to the possibility of the other.

As a skeptic, on many occasions, Doctorow stressed the dangers of absolute belief: "No system, whether it's religious or anti-religious or economic or materialistic, seems to be invulnerable to human venery and greed and insanity" (Doctorow, 2003: 59). When talking of the ethical imperatives imposed on individuals by institutions like religion or the state, he warns of their authoritarian effect as ideological control: "[I]t is inconceivable in any society where the answers are already given and the rules of life are inflexible and the authority for all thought is the ruling modality—that free expression and the multiplicity of witness can be anything but an abomination, a danger to the state or an affront to God, God or the state having done all the writing that was necessary for anyone, for anything" (56). In several of his works, he endows the characters with the inverted conception of moral judgments. For example, in *Billy Bathgate*, He has Billy internalize the gangster's twisted idea on right and wrong, thus "the criminal racketeer is the embattled hero and the reformist government is seen as the evil monster" (Wutz, 2003: 521). In others like *The Book of Daniel* and *The Waterworks*, he questions the validity of ethical categories especially the foundations they are based on and the institutions that maintain them. Doctorow's narratives, as Wutz indicates, "interrogate such mythic categories as good and evil...as they have been used by the powers that be in the service of ideological control" (521). His perspective on ethics, like Baumann's, transgresses the traditional boundaries of good versus evil, just versus unjust, noble versus abject, honest versus dishonest, and truth versus falsity, but presents a territory of obscurity where ethical judgments are relative, subject to politics and power.

But Doctorow's intention barely lies in denying or rejecting our cherished values or beliefs, as Foucault says, transgression does not negate or delete, it is simply "an affirmation of divisions" and it designates "the existence of difference" (Foucault, 1977: 34). It suffices to say that the existence of difference is what Doctorow really cares about and attempts to illuminate with his writings. In fact, as a writer with strong social responsibility, Doctorow is more interested in the law that sets up the moral divisions, since it points to the "mechanisms of power on which it rests" (340. Talking of the law that commonly draws the boundary and prohibits the transgressive acts, Wolfreys' analysis seems pertinent to be quoted here: these laws represent axioms by which an institution "asserts, defines, and qualifies its limits" (Wolferys, 2008: 4). Through the process of definition and qualification, they "take on the inevitable quality of self-evident truths" (4). The naturalization of norms and regulations as set of self-evident truths reminds us of what Foucault elaborates in *Discipline and Punish*: the disciplining of the deviants is completed by social institutions through the subtle network of power especially the power of discourse.

Therefore, Doctorow's perspective on ethics, on one hand, exposes the "essential incongruity between any power-assisted ethical code and "the infinitely complex condition of the moral self" (Baumann, 1993: 14). Furthermore, he reveals "the falsity of society's pretense to be the ultimate author and sole trustworthy guardian of morality" (14), to use the words of Baumann. Through the constant process of discipline and catharsis in the name of the collective, the other, which include all the negative party in the moral dichotomies as defined by the society, are expelled or suppressed. The significance of Doctorow's exploration of ethical predicament in the contemporary society, thus, lies mainly in his opening the gate to the admission of the other and his calling attention to the formative mechanism of the moral dichotomies.

2. Justice and Truth on Trial: *The Book of Daniel*

E. L. Doctorow's 1975 novel *The Book of Daniel* is generally an adaptation of Rosenberg Case, a famous case of great controversy in American history. The case centers on the prosecution and execution of a couple named Rosenberg who are charged of conspiracy of treason for supposedly selling secret information about atomic bomb to the Soviet government. However, Doctorow changes many details of the event, including the names of the protagonists, the family background of the couple, the gender of their kids to make it a brand new story. In this story, Daniel Isaacson, the son of the similarly prosecuted and executed couple Paul and Rochelle Isaacson, reminisces and narrates his family past, investigates the truth of his parents' case, and tries to balance his traumatized memories and restless current life. With the accumulation of investigating results, his single perspective on the event is supplemented by the information he obtains from other sources. Meanwhile, linear sequence of life episodes is disturbed by the intrusion of jumbling materials like poetry, interviews, dairies, etc. As a result, the book, originally written for his PhD dissertation, turns into a pastiche of essays, government documents, personal meditations on such issues as politics, memory, family history and national movement. The narrative of Daniel, according to Sam B. Girgus, "projects a vision of justice and truth upon American culture" at a specific historical time (Girgus, 2002: 11).

However, Doctorow's adaptation, as many critics have pointed out, shows that his concern is not the case itself—whether the Isaacson is innocent or guilty—as historians are eager to find, but the ideas that the case generated, such as the ambiguous border of ethical definitions, the conflict between individuals and the state, alienation and victimization in a political society, and finally, the artist's attempt to close the gap between artistic expressions and reality. In *The Book of Daniel*, the protagonist Daniel narrates his life stories that mainly happened in the social upheavals of counter-cultural movement and the New Leftist movement in the U. S. in the 1960s. His mind frequently shifts to the 1940s and 1950s when his parents were still alive and Old Leftism as well as McCarthyism was still popular. The story opens with Daniel's visit to his sister Susan, who was then hospitalized in an asylum. It includes four chapters respectively named "Memorial Day", "Halloween", "Starfish" and "Christmas". As the son of the notorious Isaacson family, Daniel is severely traumatized by his parents' death, his orphanage as the kid of the traitors, and Susan's suicide as a result of political disillusionment. To make his life possible, he embarks on a journey of pursuit, the pursuit of the truth of his parents' case and of the reason for his sister's suicide. During the journey, Daniel learns to be a "traitor" himself. He gives up his position as insider of the system to achieve the perception of an alien, thus able to scrutinize social values and moral judgments in a transgressive way. In an interview, Doctorow talks about the sense of absurdity as an existential influence on him and his opinion on ethics as a human invention:

> I grew up on Sartre and Camus and others like their predecessor Husserl. I trust the existentialist vision. Like much metaphysics it is really a form of poetry, but I trust it insofar as it forgoes dogma and accepts the creativity of man as a kind of glorious noise in the midst of silence. I think that is what an existentialist means by absurdity. So then ethics is only a human invention.... The sense of absurdity is very pragmatic, skeptical of absolutes, of easy answers and political messiahs. (Friedl & Schulz ,1999: 183)

In *The Book of Daniel*, he endows Daniel with the sense of absurdity, with the ability to suspect all absolute beliefs and easy answers. During the investigation of his parents' case, Daniel ends up discovering that the truth known to the public is only one of the versions about the past—the historical product of co-work from multiple forces. He also understands that the justice he tries to seek for his parents is elusive and indeterminable. Thus, the boundaries between just and unjust, true and false is not absolute, but politically and socially constructed. Daniel has to receive this moral obscurity as a ritual of growing into manhood and of becoming a writer. During the process, Daniel also realizes the immense power of narrative in creating transgressions of the established knowledge. Daniel's moral consciousness belongs to what Doctorow advocates as an artist's trangressive spirit, that is, to perceive norms and values with suspicious eyes and always to "sin" against something to reach other possibilities of knowing.

2. 1. The Perspective of A Traitor

In *The Book of Daniel*, one of the central concerns that bother the Isaacson kids and the readers as well is whether Paul and Julia Isaacson have committed treason for which they are prosecuted and electrocuted. According to the elaboration of Daniel, treason is one of the most serious crimes committed against one's country or organization. A traitor thus is considered to be extremely immoral, often executed with harsh punishment. Daniel especially investigates that for the English monarchic government, a particular form of execution is designed for the transgressors:

> [They are] hanged and cut down before he was dead. Then he was emasculated, disemboweled, and his entrails were set on fire in front of his eyes. If the executioner was merciful the heart was then removed from the body, but in any case, the final act of the ritual was then performed, a hacking of the body into four parts, the quarters then being thrown to the dogs (Doctorow, 2006b: 91)

This description, through the association of transgression with punishment, indicates the horrible consequence a transgressor may face if they ignore laws and social regulations. Among all transgressive acts, treason is the most serious and its consequence correspondingly the most severe. In another chapter, Daniel starts a long discussion on the topic "traitor". He thinks that apart from the lists of traitors known to the public, America forgets to mention one of its archetype traitors—the master subversive Poe, "who wore a hole into the parchment and let the darkness pour through" (218). To Daniel, Edgar Allan Poe is treacherous mainly in two aspects. Firstly, his life and writings touch the taboos and prohibitive contents of the society, transgressing the commonly received values and shocking the cognition of the public, as Daniel describes in a poetic way,

> This is how he did it: First he spilled a few drops of whiskey just below the Preamble. To this he added the blood of his thirteen-year-old cousin Virginia, whom he had

married and who hemorrhaged from the throat. He stirred these fluids in a small, elliptically stressed circle with the extracted tooth of the dead Ligeia. Then added some raven droppings. " (218)

More importantly, Poe, like a magician who performs dark magic, conjures up "dark hellish gases like soot, like smog, like the poisonous effulgence of combustion engines over Thrift and Virtue and Reason and Natural Law and the Rights of Man" (218). His writings, therefore, poison American myths on democracy, rational order, and dominant virtues by penetrating into the deepest of human nature and social discourse, thus reaching the peripheral terrain inhabited by the subconscious, desire and chaos. Daniel hence comes to the conclusion that "It's Poe who ruined us, that scream from the smiling face of America"(218). He desires the transgressive energy of Poe and wants to emulate him to pierce the smiling face of America. In this sense, a traitor like Poe, according to Herwig Friedl, "uncover[s] the machinations of power hidden behind the magnificent fictionalizations of legal documents, behind assumptions of the possibility of an enlightened existence in a rational world" (Fridl, 1988: 28).

Doctorow, in his essay collection *Reporting the Universe*, explains that he gets his first name Edgar because his father loves the works of Edgar Allan Poe. It is until very later that he became aware of his father's serious intention behind the naming, as he begins to recognize Poe as a heterogeneous phenomenon in American letters, "a poet of lost loves" and the "psychologist of the perverse."(Doctorow, 2003: 10) Daniel, like Doctorow himself, expresses his appreciation for this literary giant. In fact, he becomes a follower of Poe, another traitor "whose point of view and ideas of reality always will be difficult and multidimentional" (Girgus, 2002: 12). He becomes what he is due to the Jewish-Communist background of his family and his experiences as an alien in the American society.

In the novel, the name Daniel is often related to the biblical figure Daniel, a Jewish prophet in Old Covenant who survived on his gifts of analyzing and interpreting dreams for the king in a foreign land after his exile. Yu Jianhua, when talking of Jewishness—the motifs that typically characterize the works of American Jewish writers, states that "a sense of loneliness and psychological alienation" shadows the characters in their works (Yu, 1990: 22). The Jewish people, though dispersed over the world, always try to keep their own culture and customs intact and not to be assimilated into the mainstream society of their immigration. Therefore, they are always excluded by the local civilization and haunted by the sense of alienation. As Yu says, the Jewish are "eternal strangers."(22) Daniel, like his Jewish forefathers, is also a stranger who lives in a foreign land and he is doomed to be estranged from his surroundings. He realizes this situation by describing it in a passage: "it is a bad time for Daniel and his co-religionists for they are second-class citizens, in a distinctly hostile environment" (Doctorow, 2006b: 34). The alienation of the Isaacsons is firstly reflected in Daniel's mad grandmother, who murmurs and curses in Yiddish in a self-absorbed way. Daniel traces the reason for her alienation to the suffering in her past experiences:

> Grandma goes mad when she can no longer consider the torment of her life. My mother's catalogue of the old lady's misfortunes—the abandoned parents whose brown picture she still keeps in her drawer, the death of her first-born in the street, the death of her two sisters in the big fire, the death of her second-born from the flu, the death of her husband, my grandfather who would have loved me if he'd lived... (85)

But as Daniel says, alienation is a family heritage, which passes through blood and only death can end the process. Though there is no clear indication of his mother's mental state, Daniel has shown his aunt to be an eccentric and paranoid. His sister Susan also inherits her grandmother's madness: she suffers from mental deterioration and commits suicide in her twenties. On the other hand, the family's alienation is caused by their choice of political stance, which is radical socialism. The post-WWI America, as Daniel suggests, witnesses the rise of frenzy fear of the Red over the country, which is called the "Red Scare." In this atmosphere, workers' strikes are attacked and assembly besieged by police. Any terrorist activities, no matter who should be responsible for, are attributed to the communist groups. Laws are passed to prohibit seditious speech and to sentence the convicts of espionage and sedition. The press "exacerbated the public feeling" by focusing on all kinds of suspicious events and propagating the governmental ideology of "finding out enemies."(56) The nationwide anti-communism movement gradually goes to extremes following the enactment of President Truman's Executive Order 9835:

> There were speeches against "foreign ideologies" and much talk about "100 percent Americanism." The teaching of evolution in the schoolbooks of Tennessee was outlawed. Elsewhere textbooks were repudiated that were not sufficiently patriotic. New immigration laws made racial distinctions and set stringent quotas. Jews were charged with international conspiracy and Catholics with trying to bring the Pope to America. (30)

In this social milieu, the lives of socialists were made tough. Daniel's father Paul Isaacson, however, is a faithful leftist who believes that communism and revolution can change the status of poor people like them. But at the same time he is an idealist who believes in the American system, full of hope on national ideals such as democracy, freedom and justice. The communist belief causes his arrest, imprisonment and indictment. The illusion on the American law and judiciary system lasts until the last moment of his life. In fact, it is the law that Paul thinks will do him justice but it actually leads to his tragic death. The family's connection with communism determines their marginal position in the American society and their vulnerability to victimhood.

As Daniel recalls, the family has only a few friends, who, like his father the repairman, are working-class people holding similar socialist beliefs. They would gather together in the shabby apartment of Daniel's family in Bronx to talk in big words of American politics, Marx and Lenin, union and so on. Their self-assurance makes young Daniel mistakenly think that they are a group of important people in the world. It is only until Daniel grows up that he understands that they actually live in the periphery of society, with their voice unheard and demands ignored. Their race and political belief determine their position in social hierarchy and the concomitant sense of alienation Daniel will never get rid of, as if it is a stigma left on his family. In a burst of outrage, Daniel claims that no matter what he does, the government will not give a shit since he is "deprived the right to be dangerous" (89). He is invisible in the eyes of the authority, as they have held every detail about him and his family criminality, so Daniel says, "There is nothing I can do, mild or extreme, that they cannot have planned for" (89). A prisoner in the cell of a panopticon[①], Daniel senses the surveillance and the disciplinary power from the politicized society at all times.

Like his ancestor Daniel who survives as an outsider with the ability of analysis and interpretation, Daniel also becomes a traitor with "the perception of a criminal" (41), in order to deal with the alienation penetrating Isaacson family. In fact, only with the subversive spirit of a traitor, with the perception to see beyond the system, and the ability to analyze independently despite of the prevailing national ideology,

---

[①]   A panopticon is a type of institutional building designed by Jeremy Bentham in the late 18th century. This building is designed to make the inmates imprisoned in the cells of the circular structure observed by the single watchman in the central tower without knowing if they are watched or not. The panopticon later becomes a metaphor employed by Michel Foucault in his *Discipline and Punish* to refer to the inclination of modern disciplinary society to observe and normalize its citizens.

can Daniel survive and progress in such an antagonistic social milieu. His position as a traitor does not come from nowhere, as he is trained as a kid by his father to be "a little criminal of perception."(41) Daniel recalls his father's training on him against the prevailing social ideologies by teaching him to read commercials,

> He wanted me to grow up right. He wrestled society for my soul. He worked on me to counteract the bad influences of my culture. That was our relationship— his teaching me how to be a psychic alien. That was part of the training. He had to exorcise the influences, the bad spirits. He'd find me reading the back of the cereal box at breakfast, and break the ad down and show what it appealed to, how it was intended to make me believe something that wasn't—that eating cereal would not make me an athlete."(42)

It is obvious that what Paul teaches Daniel is the perspective of an outsider, who tries to get rid of the influences of American mainstream culture by perceiving and analyzing in a critical way. "This analytical mode of thinking remains with Daniel in his adulthood", as Marandi Seyyed Mohanmad and Zohreh Ramin state, "and becomes the grounds by which he tries to find the truth of his parents' case. (Mohanmad & Ramin: 2013: 2944). Meanwhile, the perspective of a criminal makes Daniel a thinker instead of an activist, a skeptic instead of a believer. His moral vision, thus, is sharply contrasted with that of his sister Susan, although Daniel thinks that she is the only one in the world that connects with him. He says, "Susan and I, we were the only ones left" (Doctorow, 2006b: 79). Different from Daniel's critical perception and analysis, Susan is an absolute believer who believes in the innocence of their parents and the ideals they hold. A faithful follower of the radical career of her parents, Susan participates in the New Leftist movement with great enthusiasm in honor of their martyrdom. Daniel uses a long paragraph to analyze Susan's rigidity in insisting on her ideals:

> In Susan resides the fateful family gift for having definite feelings. Always taking stands, even as a kid. A moralist, a judge. This is right, that is wrong, this is good, that is bad.... (11)

To Daniel, Susan's problem comes from the fact that she takes stands and makes moral judgments based on her stands. Daniel disagrees on the absolutist stance she and his parents hold. He ridicules that Susan has become "a dupe of the international moralist propagandist apparatus" and has been made into a "moral speed freak"(11). Daniel and Susan's difference is mainly reflected in their attitudes toward the Paul

Rochelle Isaacson Foundation for Revolution, the trust fund set up in the name of Isaacson children, "a proper assumption of their legacy" (223). Though Susan tries hard to persuade Daniel to participate in the administration of the foundation, Daniel refuses and suspects that it is an advertising of the Communist Party for selling their ideas by making use of the Isaacsons' death. In some sense, Daniel is also the traitor of the Isaacson family, because he follows neither the Old Leftist ideas of his parents nor the New Leftist ideas of his sister. He has the inclination to analyze the deep motivation behind every event and make broad connections before his action. As Susan accuses, he is a modern cynic with the "cynicism bag" that conveniently saves him from doing anything.

But Daniel is not a Hamlet-like thinker troubled in the "to be or not to be" dilemma. He is not a dwarf in action. To experience the radical career of his sister, he even attends the anti-Vietnam-War parade in front of the Pentagon and gets beaten by the police. His spiritual crisis is caused by his skeptical perception and analysis of all beliefs, whether it be political tenets, religious dogma, or social norms. As a follower of Poe, he uses the alienated consciousness of the artist to "instigate a revolution in the values and thought of his times", always prone to penetrate into the deepest nature of things.

Under his "insistent gaze and tortured backward glance", to use the words of Herwig Friedl, "the pretensions to power not only of the establishment, the government and the FBI are exposed". (Friedl, 1988: 28). In contrast to Daniel, Susan fails due to her inability to make deep analysis, as Doctorow says, "She had to come to a very strict, defensive judgment and eventually it broke her" (Doctorow, 2006b, 198). Unlike Daniel who always has doubts on their parents' beliefs and acts, Susan prefers to believe, worship and idealize them as martyrs who are murdered by the counter-revolutionary forces. This failure of analysis leads to her mental chaos and final suicide, since she cannot deal with the contradictions of the past and the disillusionment of political ideals in her present life. She retreats to her own world, as Daniel describes, like a starfish reduced to the center, finally reaching to the point of limit.

Therefore, to Daniel, the traitor's position becomes the key element of his survival. With the perception of an outsider, he is able to question and explore different aspects of epistemological system of the American society, including political belief, law, moral codes and other social discourses, thus tearing off the ideological pretensions of institutions that guard and maintain these discourses. His perception makes him a traitor or a criminal, who transgresses the norms, values, and boundaries regulated by the society to seek his own truth about the past.

2. 2. Truth and Justice on Trial

Usually, a trial is a procedure attended by a group of relevant people to settle some disputes or resolve a conflict with authority invoked as the agent to reach a verdict. But some trials in history such as the Rosenberg case based on which the *The Book of Daniel* is inspired, instead of appeasing disputes and conflicts, bring more controversies than consensus among the public. The existence of these trials forces people to rethink some fundamental values of the culture that produce them. E. L. Doctorow talks of the controversial trials in his essay "False Document" in this way:

> Yet the most important trials in our history, those which reverberate in our lives and have most meaning for our future, are those in which the judgment is called into question: Scopes, Sacco and Vanzetti, the Rosenbergs. Facts are buried, exhumed, deposed, contradicted, recanted. There is a decision by the jury and, when the historical and prejudicial context of the decision is examined, a subsequent judgment by history. And the trial shimmers forever with just that perplexing ambiguity characteristic of a true novel. (Doctorow, 1983: 23)

In *The Book of Daniel*, one central issue that concerns Daniel's life and narrative is the truth of Rosenberg case, the result of which will determine American judiciary system as just or unjust, and the judgment of his parents as innocent or guilty. But as Doctorow suggests, facts can be "exhumed, deposed, contradicted, recanted", historical judgments of truth and justice thus become obscure and unreliable. Daniel's pursuit actually puts the concepts of truth and justice on trial, exposing the instability of the contemporary value system, especially that of ethical judgments, which are subject to the power of ideologies.

For French sociologist Louis Althusser, the word ideology refers to "a system (with its own logic and rigor) of representations (images, myths, ideas of concepts, depending on the case) endowed with a historical existence and role within a given society" (Althusser, 1969: 231). That is to say, in a society, one is inescapably influenced by certain dominant knowledge and values that will define his/her position within the social order. According to Sacvan Bercovitch, ideology establishes "the ground and texture of consensus...the system of ideas interwoven into the cultural symbology through which 'America' continues to provide the terms of identity and cohesion in the United States" (Bercovitch, 1993: 255). Through the mandatory force of national institutions and the power of ubiquitous social discourses, the dissents are disciplined, the nation's dominant logic is iterated and consequentially its ideological cohesion is assured.

Daniel's study of American politics in the 1950s describes a time when the national ideology of patriotism is at its peak among the public. In his essay "True History of the Cold War: A Raga", Daniel offers a picture of the rise of domestic anti-communism, using a revisionist perspective. His perspective reveals the real intention of the government to issue the cold war against Russia, pointing out that government always digs out new enemies to agitate the emotional fever of its citizens and stimulate national solidarity. The strategy is always useful, because by focusing on making a common enemy, public attention on domestic crisis will be shifted to international conflicts. Daniel hence comes to the conclusion that "EVERY MAN IS THE ENEMY OF HIS OWN COUNTRY" and "All government stands ready to commit their citizens to death in the interest of their goverment" (Doctorow, 2006b: 90). In this sense, the Isaacsons are nothing but the victims of politics, the "unfortunate but logical outcome of American foreign policy after the Second World War" (Bevilacqua, 1990: 99). Even if they are innocent, they have to be chosen out as the scapegoat to be the common enemy of the country.

Daniel's investigation on the truth of the case also includes interviews with people who are directly or indirectly implicated in the event. Jack P. Fein, the reporter who does the reassessment piece in the *Times* on the tenth anniversary of the Isaacson execution, provides extra information on the case when receiving Daniel's interview. He defines the trial as "piss-poor" and thinks that Dr. Mindish's testimony—the only thing that the government has to accuse the Isaacson of— is invalid and deficient to testify their crime. Fein also suggests that the government has used the power of media to exaggerate the danger of the crime to national security. Personally, he meets some guys from the Justice Department dropping hints about evidence they have but will never release because of the concern for security. One of his friends in the Justice Department tells him "if the report has evidence like they claim they would have released it"(Doctorow, 2006b: 258). Fein thus tells Daniel the inevitability of Isaacson's victimization, "between the FBI and the CP your folks never had a chance" (258). Daniel's study on cold-war politics, along with Fein's words, shows that the Isaacsons' case is far from a legal procedure that can be judged with words like just or unjust. Instead, it is severely framed by cold-war politics and public opinion. Now that the Isaacsons are only minor communist party members and the FBI cannot find out significant evidence against them, their arrest suggests that "callous political pressures may have produced a tragic miscarriage of justice". (Harter & Thompson, 1990: 195). In other words, in the special time of nationwide anti-communism and prejudice against Jews, the case's transparency and objectivity are impaired, as Daniel suggests. Thus the moral judgment of the Isaacsons is made problemized.

Robert Levin, Daniel's foster father who has partially participated in the defense of the case, provides his interpretation of the case from the perspective of a lawyer. He thinks that several elements have influenced the fairness of the case, one of which is the media manipulation of public opinion long before the trial of the Isaacsons. Concerned with the trial, he thinks that the Judge in the case "would today be ruled prejudicial" (273). Similar to Fein, he questions the validity of Mindish's testimony as he thinks that "it seemed enough to show that Mindish might conceivably feel threatened by deportation, and therefore testify to anything the government wanted him to say"(273). Levin's opinion on the case is that the top concern of the government is not to convict the Isaacsons and manifest justice, but to make the Isaacsons name other traitors, so that the whole event can continually ferment. Levin's words, from another angle, point out the limitation of the law at the time of Isaacsons' prosecution, thus supplementing the opinions of Daniel and Fein. Together, they provide other possibilities of truth about the past, which is divergent from the identification of the Isaacsons as conspirators and traitors in the "authoritative" version constructed by the FBI.

Thus, Daniel's analysis of his parents' case with information from different sources reveals that truth, rather than objective and authoritative as it's supposed to be, is politically, socially and culturally constructed. Justice, the judgment of which based on truth, has been depraved of its foundations and also becomes a shattered existence. They turn to myth, a symbolic system that is closely bundled with politics and national ideology. Since the founding of the nation, the American culture has produced a set of myths, such as the myth of "city upon the hill", the myth of self-made men, and the myth of the West, all suggesting the model role of America to the other parts of the world—American exceptionalism. Daniel's quest, however, puts the American ideal of truth and justice on trial, demystifying American judiciary system as well as its social values. As Arthur Saltzman points out, if there is a lesson Daniel manages to dredge up from his investigation, that is, " 'justice' is a myth perpetrated by an ambiguous yet formidable THEM, a ruling elite, whose power pervades not only government and law enforcement, but also advertising, restaurant chains, vending machines, Hollywood—all the attributes to unreality that anesthetize us to the ignominious facts of our heritage" (Saltzman, 1983: 85). In the novel, Daniel reveals his illusion on justice:

> Banks and churches and courtrooms all depend on the appurtenances of theater. On illusion. Banks, the illusion of stability and honorable dealings to hide the rot and corruption of capitalist exploitation churches the illusions of sacred sanctuary for purposes of pacifying social discontent. Courtrooms of course designed to promote illusion of solemn justice. (Doctorow, 2006b: 167)

Even entertainment culture like Disneyland, disguised as neutral and unharmful, plays a role in promoting the national ideology. Through "a radical process of reduction"(350), Disneyland turns into a symbolic manipulation by impressing and educating the mass as a substitute for experience. As Daniel claims, people come to the park only to get a short-hand of fast culture, "a sentimental resonance compression of something that is itself already a lie" (350). However, its glamorization and trivialization of "historical reality of mercantilism and exploitation into cartoon shadows for mass consumption" are often unnoticed (Saltzman, 1983: 86). Daniel is almost lost in the network of power constituted by the interweaving of different institutions of the American society, the political, the cultural and so on. Far from reaching a final clarification from his investigation, Daniel finds that these interpretations around the trial and execution of his parents bring more obscurity and uncertainty than before, which makes him realize the elusive nature of all sorts of ideas,

> Of one thing we are sure. Everything is elusive. God is elusive. Revolutionary morality is elusive. Justice is elusive. Human character. (Doctorow, 2006b: 52)

However, at this time, Daniel still has not given up his search for truth, which is so important to him. With the imagination of a writer, he tries to restore the whole espionage event based on his childhood memories about his parents. In his narrative, Daniel's father Paul appears as a naïve communist full of idealist hope, different from the calculated and unscrupulous spy image depicted by the public. As a radical of 1950s, Paul fully realizes the exploitation and suppression in the American society but is still optimistic about the U.S. system to restore its founding ethos. Daniel remembers one particular episode of his father's naivety: One day when the family and other friends went to a Paul Robeson Concert, a mob besieged the bus they were taking. When all the men on the bus were scared and silenced, only Paul stepped out of his seat to stop the attack of the raging crowd, calling that the violence should not be permitted. Recalling the event, Daniel can't help exclaiming: "Why did he expect so much of a system he knew by definition could never satisfy his standards of justice? A system he was committed to opposing because he had a better one in mind" (49). After his arrest under the name of suspected treason, Paul would not implicate his friend although his confession might possibly get him released. Even before his electrocution, Paul still believes in America's judiciary system which will finally give him a just judgment as he believes in the existence of truth and justice as the natural order of the world: "I have it on good authority—public sentiment will gather for us. You cannot put innocent people to death in this country. It can't be done. The truth will reclaim us. You'll see." (304) In contrast to Paul the naïve idealist, Daniel's mother Rochelle is a realist who can always brave the cruel reality of life. When talking with their lawyer Ascher in the prison, she is clearly aware of her doom and the disaster falling on the family, "Before our trial even started we were found guilty by the paid hirelings of the kept press. There was no possibility for a fair trail. On that ground alone."(304). Like Daniel, she is able to penetrate the surface of democracy and justice claimed by the state to see the nature of the trial.

Although Daniel intends to restore the truth of the trial with his childhood impressions, he admits, "Probably none of this is true. There is a lot more I can't remember"(305). He places the last hope on Dr. Mindish, the dentist friend of his family and also the witness who testifies against his parents. After some years of imprisonment, Dr. Mindish disappears from the sight of public. Through an investigation spanning over a long time, Daniel succeeds in locating his new settlement. He flies to California where Mindish and his daughter now reside in the hope of talking to him to clear his epistemological mess. But their meeting at Disneyland is disappointing since now Mindish is a senile man, he cannot provide any significant information about the past. Once again, the truth Daniel is seeking eludes him and instead of "moving from a confusion of clues to meaningful order and reaching a plausible verdict", he "proceeds from mystery, to possibility, to doubt" (Bevilacqua, 1990: 99), and in the end, to uncertainty.

Finally, Daniel receives this uncertainty as a necessary part of knowledge and life, as Bevilacqua says, he has to acquiesce "contradictions, paradoxes and unanswered questions of history" to cope with the reality which itself is chaotic and disorderly (99). Applying this uncertainty to writing, he offers three endings for the novel, indicating his expectation of multiple interpretations from readers.

2. 3. Ethics and the Power of Narrative

Doctorow's works, from *Welcome to Hard Times* to *City of God*, always center around one persistent motif, that is, the writer's role in the world (Most of his protagonists are narrators/writers baffled by the relationship of reality and representation). *The Book of Daniel* is exactly the case as Daniel the narrator struggles desperately to find a proper voice to project his own vision on truth and justice. In one interview, Doctorow claims that a writer has to possess the subversive spirit to break away from the bondages social system has placed on him. "In the largest, most philosophical sense, "Doctorow remarks, "the writer has to be subversive, of course. If he exists simply to endorse the complacent vision or the lies of the society then there's no reason for him to exist" (Levin, 1983: 193). In this sense, Daniel belongs to the category of Doctorow's subversive writer, as he finds the great power of narrative and appropriates the power as a weapon of subversion to resist the ideological power imposed on him. His narrative, a fragmentary and speculative one, crosses the complacent realm of the norms, values and truth defined by the prevailing ideologies, thus offering a different voice on the truth of the Isaacson case.

In *The Book of Daniel*, Daniel finds that his pursuit of truth and justice is unavoidably related to the power pervading all walks of the society, such as political power, media power, and the power of images, of words. "The idea of truth belongs to the rhetoric of power"—this is what Daniel realizes after his investigation of the case (Doctorow, 2006b: 211). The dispute about whether his parents have betrayed against their country is not only a matter of veracity or falsity, but "simultaneously the contest about the right of some to speak with the authority which some others should obey" (211). In this sense, the controversy around the ethical judgments of truth or falsity, justice or injustice, innocence or guilt is political in essence: the outcome tells about "the establishment or reasserting the relationship of superiority and inferiority, of domination and submission, between holders of belief". (Bauman, 1997: 112).

Daniel's realization of power as omnipresent is reflected in the recurrent metaphor of electricity in the novel, in the words of T. V. Reed, "Ubiquitous electrical metaphors come to embody the simultaneously destructive and productive nature of power" (Reed, 1992: 289). It is electricity that lights the library of Columbia University where Daniel writes his doctorial dissertation, and stimulates the operation of the whole Disneyworld where he meets his father's dentist friend

Dr. Mindish. When Daniel first walks into his father's repair shop, he is stunned by the scenery of images and voices presented by television, which is also electricity-powered. But for Daniel, the electrical power is not only productive as the source of energy, but also frequently connected with suppression, torturing and death, just like fire. In his mind, electricity derives from the natural elements of fire and he claims, "technology is the making of metaphors from the natural world. Flight is the metaphor of air, wheels are the metaphor of water, food is the metaphor of earth. The metaphor of fire is electricity". (Doctorow, 2006b: 241)

Actually, Daniel's life is closely intertwined with the metaphor of fire/electricity. His ancestor the Biblical Daniel faces the punishment of three Israelite fellows by the king Nebuchadnezzar. If he cannot interpret the king's dream to the king's satisfaction, the punishment—a fiery furnace with burning fire engulfing everything, will fall on his fellow men. Daniel Isaacson, when reading this passage, reveals his identification with his biblical namesake: "God sees that they survive the fire, but the strain on Daniel has to have been considerable." (11) He thinks his family members have followed the same fate of the ancient Israeli exiles, as they suffer from the same torturing symbolized by the fire/electricity execution. His parents, Paul and Rochelle, for example, are electrocuted with the brutal power of electricity. When visiting his sister Susan in the asylum, he finds that electricity is also used for the shock therapy applied on Susan's nerve system, which constitutes for Daniel an inhuman and unforgettable picture:

> A strong electric current is applied by means of electrodes fastened to the scalp earlobes shoulders nipples bellybutton genitals asshole knees toes and soles of the feet, to the nervous system of the patient. The patient does a rigid dance. The current is stopped and the patient relaxes. The current is applied again and the patient dances again. (206)

It is from the image of fire/electricity that Daniel realizes the immensity of electrical power, which forms circuit connecting all objects wherever it goes. In one passage, he portrays the characteristics of electricity in a quasi-poetic language, using the measure of electrical resistance "ohm":

> what is it that you can't see but you can feel
> what is it that you can't taste and can't smell
>   And can't touch but can feel
> ohm ohm ohm ohm ohm...
> what makes you smell when you touch it, blacken

when you feel it, die when you taste it.

ohm

what is it that lightens the life of man and
    comforts

his winters and sings that

he is the master of the universe; until he sits in it.

ohm (226)

This passage depicts electricity as an element invisible but omnipresent, invading human consciousness and taking effect in a subtle way. As a special epitome of power, it "provides an illusion of mastery to those who appear to possess it" and then "suddenly unmasks itself as destroyer" or killer (Harpham, 1985: 86). Based on this metaphor, Daniel learns to make broad connections, that is, the interpretative ability to grasp the ideological essence behind the knowledge system and social values. This practice of interpretation is, for Daniel, a token of his radicalism, as Jieun Kwon states, "The radical discovers connections between available data and the root responsibility. Finally he connects everything" (Kwon, 2014: 140). With this ability Daniel begins to discover the connection among events that look random on the surface: his parents died not only because of the conspiracy of government agency like FBI, of the testimony of some treacherous friends, but also of the co-work of multiple forces including the foreign policy at that time, the propaganda of media, and even their own complicity—Paul's naiveté in believing the system and Rochelle's rigidity and self-sacrifice. Daniel also learns the relativity of social categorizations such as truth and falsity, justice and injustice: the idea of justice or truth in itself is an idea "which in effect has been invented and put to work in different types of societies as an instrument of a certain political and economic power or as a weapon against that power"(Foucault, 1984: 6). Yet, the truth and justice Daniel has been seeking is obscure and inapproachable not just due to the manipulation and control of macro-power[1]. They are caused by the power of images and words—the micro-power, which influences human consciousness in a more subtle way like electricity does.

The great power of images is revealed in the remarks of Daniel's friend

---

[1] Traditionally, power is understood as issued from the above to the bottom, which aims to dominate, exploit, suppress, such as the political power. To Foucault, power works through the network of social relations. It is through this network, the society completes its discipline and standardization of the citizens without being noticed. In the opinion of Foucault, the political power belongs to the macro-power while the disciplinary power of the social institutions such as schools, hospitals, and the press is micro-power.

Artie Sternlicht, a representative of the New Leftist in the 1960s. Unlike the old communists such as Paul Isaacson, Artie never expects mild revolution inside the American system can bring about any substantial change to the society. He despises the naïve optimism of the old generation. With his apartment walls full of collages of posters, Sternlicht tells Daniel that he will wield the weapon of media like television to "Overthrow the United States" with images for them are inevitably ideological (140). However, Daniel shows his worry about images as he thinks that they are the building blocks of narrative and they have an uncertain relationship to the narrative that binds them. Narrative, with its constituents of words, images and metaphors, can exert a tremendous power on people's perception. One can accept the truth a document has claimed, or he can be susceptible to the influences of a document's infringement of truth just because he believes a document is the faithful record of reality. In the contemporary society, some forms of narrative (such as document, history, scientific report) are presumed to be more reliable than others (fiction). As a result, they are invested with more power to justify, to convince or to dissuade.

Daniel's meditation on the power of narrative is also what Doctorow elaborates in his essays. As Geofferey Galt Harpham points out, one of Doctorow's lasting concerns is "narrative itself and its relation to power, imagination, and belief" (Harpham, 1985: 89). To Michelle Foucault, power is not a thing, but a relationship between two parties, so "every time one side does something, the other one responds by deploying a conduct, a behavior that counter-invests it, tries to escape it, diverts it, turns the attack against itself, etc." (Foucault, 1996: 144). This pervasive power network Daniel discovers actually includes the power of narrative, which can be used as the instrument for ideological control and also as a way of resistance to counteract the control. Narrative, with its volatile images, is "a political issue—perhaps the quintessentially political issue, since its truth status always depends on the power of the authorities that sanction it" (Harpham, 1985: 84). The state apparatus including the FBI and the media have worked together to compose a narrative about the Isaacsons, "gradually perfect[ing] the scenario" with eight, then nine, and finally ten overt acts (84). Daniel, in order to contest the national account of Isaacsons case, has to become the authority of an alternative account and release his own voice. He has to employ the imaginative faculty of a writer to step outside the system of knowledge and truth framed by political and cultural institutions of the antagonistic society, thus providing other interpretations of truth. As Doctorow says, the writer should discover "the secret the politician is born knowing that good and evil are construed, that there is no outrage, no monstrousness that cannot be made reasonable and logical and virtuous, and no shining act that cannot be turned to disgrace—with language" (Lorsch, 1983: 393). Daniel's task as a writer, then, is to reveal how good and evil are construed, how the immoral are made moral with the power of language by providing interpretations different from the official version about the past. Finally, he has to find a voice of his own, like the Biblical Daniel, as an interpreter and analyst.

It turns out that Daniel's version of the Isaacson's story is highly subjective, full of individualistic color. In Daniel's narrative, the Isaacson couple is far from being the demonized espionages who have sold the atomic secret to the Soviet Union. Instead, they are ordinary people who struggle to make a living in their shabby environment. Paul Isaacson, a naïve communist, enjoys talking with his friends who share the same socialist belief with him. Even after his arrest, he believes in the justice of law, still with the hope that he and his wife will soon be declared innocent. In contrast to the child-like Paul, Rochelle Isaacson is a strong and independent woman. She loves her husband and kids, devoting herself wholeheartedly to the family despite of their poverty and low social position. Until the death sentence, the couple refuse to confess or involve other friends in their case, with Rochelle acting in an almost defiant way toward the upcoming death. She thinks that the outcome of their prosecution is pre-determined. In a letter to the family lawyer, she writes on her confession: "Everyone is waiting for us to confess.... Suppose I confess that I love my husband, and confess as to how I fell for him on our first date—a Loyalist rally on Convent Avenue!"(Doctorow, 2006b: 208). Her letter, which reveals the "domestic ordinariness and devotion" of a wife and a mother, actually undercuts the effort of the government to "portray the accused couple as monstrous and alien" (Detweiler, 1996: 72). Isaacsons' refusal to confess and their rejection to name others, according to Robert Detweiler, "provide the character[s] a degree of integrity based on a willingness to sacrifice themselves"(73), which contradicts the image of traitors.

In the process of creation, Daniel encounters the biggest obstacle—sequence, which he claims as "most monstrous". He thinks the sequence cannot render the discontinuous and non-causal life experiences. Enlightened by the image of switch thrown into a circuit to block the electricity, Daniel invents his own narrative—a narrative of short-circuit. His narrative, different from the chronological account of the FBI and mainstream media, appears to be fragmentary, random and sometimes unreliable. The time sequence is broken down. Narrative voice is shifted between the first and third-person perspective, revealing the discrepancy of the subject's inner world and external reality. Irrelevant images and scenes are bonded together to create the psychological effect of a traumatized narrator. Apart from Daniel's memories of the whole events, which cross the boundary between the past and the present, there are numerous references interrupting the main plot, including Daniel's essays, his interviews, dairies, poetry, and even letters from the participators of the case. In this sense, Daniel's narrative forms a counter-narrative, in response to the documentary records of the Isaacson case by the governmental institutions. The key organizing principle of his narrative is electricity, the power that flows everywhere and can be cut off with a switch, both productive and resistant. In a word, electricity "serves as a principle of desire as well as the force that transforms experience into artifact" in Daniel's personal narrative (Harpham, 1983: 88).

The multiple perspectives, the collaged genre, as well as the obscurities and uncertainties, make Daniel's narrative a polyphonic one, which questions the ethical categories such as truth and falsity, justice and injustice. It also challenges institutions that define and maintain such categories especially the government agents like FBI, law, and media. In this sense, Daniel is a transgressor, who moves beyond the social norms and values with the subversive power of words and images. His narrative, "disruptive or even subversive of regimes of power, and restorative of neglected or forgotten or unheard voices in the culture" (Parks, 1991b: 455), becomes the weapon of an individual to resist the mighty national ideology that constantly infringes the private realm.

3. Evil and Otherness in *The Waterworks*

In *The Waterworks*, Doctorow continues his exploration of ethical predicament that troubles individual human existence. But this time he sets the story on the stage of the end of 19th century New York City when modernization was just initiated and social ideologies faced drastic changes. Briefly, the novel tells a Hawthornian story of evil and corruption, with the main plot of a mad scientist, the exhumation of a grave, and the living dead. It is narrated by McIlvaine, the chief editor of a NYC newspaper *Telegram*, an "old lapsed Scotch Presbyterian", who recalls the whole events in a retrospective tone. Finding his best freelance writer Martin Pemberton missing, after Martin's weird claim of having seen his dead father reappear in a horse-ridden omnibus, McIlvaine embarks on the journey of pursuing the hidden truth behind the occult incident. In order to locate the young man, McIlvaine visits many people related to him, including Martin's friend, the minister of his family, his fiancée and stepmother, but nobody seems to know what happens to him. With the help of the municipal police Edmund Donne, McIlvaine and a few others are able to discover the underground world of corruption led by Boss Tweed. In the process, a secret crime is revealed: several wealthy and powerful men, including Martin's father Augustus Pemberton, after the clinical diagnosis of their fatal disease, secretly transfer their wealth to fund the scientific research conducted by Dr. Sartorius to prolong their lives. The lab for Sartorius experiment is set inside a construction of the waterworks, patronized by Tweed himself. In the lab, the old wealthy men are kept animate by being injected with blood and tissues drawn from the street orphans. With the efforts of Donne, his policemen and McIlvaine, Martin is saved from the dungeon where Sartorius right-hand assistant Eustace Edmund has imprisoned him. Dr. Sartorius, making no effort to resist, is sent to the asylum and later killed by the psychics there. As the novel approaches its end, Boss Tweed's criminal organization is sued and dismantled, with Tweed himself in exile.

In the novel, Doctorow firstly shows his concern for the motif of evil, like Hawthorne, Poe and Melville do in their works. Hawthorne and Poe's influences are visible throughout the novel while Melville's is "less a matter of literary traces than that of a great shadow cast on Doctorow's moral imagination", "urging him to see darkly and negatively all the way to the end of sanity and morality..." (Solotaroff, 2000: 137). Through the portrayal of evildoers like Augustus Pemberton, Simmons, Boss Tweed and Dr. Sartorius, Doctorow suggests the permeation of evil in every corner of the society despite social progress. He also indicates the elusiveness of evil due to the monolithic social discourse. Some of evil behaviors, like that of Augustus Pemberton, Simmons, Boss Tweed, can be safely categorized according to the moral norms of society. However, some of them, like that of Dr. Sartorius's, challenge human knowledge on evil and transgress moral standards commonly known to the public.

Dr. Sartorius, the doctor who collaborates with the wealthy to conduct scientific experiment, resembles Faustus and Prometheus in his extreme pursuit of knowledge. In fact, as Adam Kelly explains, Dr. Sartorius is the otherized figure in this contest of goodness versus evil, for his undue pursuit of knowledge, though "without breaking clearly any of the hallowed moral laws that society lays down for itself", "interrogates and exceeds conventional social boundaries", thus is intolerable to the institutions of his time (Kelly: 2006: 49). In the novel, Dr. Sartorius's moral ambiguity is reflected in McIlvaine's narrative, which, full of ellipsis and self-awareness, not only shows the narrator's dilemma of representing this figure, but also gives rises to the readers' uncertainty of judging him. Through the case of Dr. Sartorius, Doctorow intends to examine how society, as the "ultimate author and sole trustworthy guardian of morality"[1], refuses to change itself by absorbing or suppressing the forces that transgress its rules and norms in the name of community and how narrative plays the essential role in breaking down this stasis.

3. 1. The evil that is unsettled

3. 1. 1. The city of evil

In the interview with Michelle Tokarczyk, Doctorow admitted the influence of Hawthorne and Poe when he wrote *The Waterworks*. Indeed, the focus on the theme of evil and the plot of uncanny scientific experiment remind one of Hawthorne's dark tales like "Rappaccini's Daughter" and "Birthmark". On the other hand, Poe's influence is reflected in the gothic elements such as the exhumation of grave in the dim light, the mad scientist, the old man in the suspense of life and death and the lovely fragile women. Speaking of important ideas that inspire him to create the book, Doctorow says that what concerns him most is villainy and its elusiveness, as his narrator McIlvaine claims "It is the nature of villainy to absent itself, even as it stands before you. You reach for it and close on nothing....This is the story of invisible men, dead men or men indeterminably alive...of men hidden, barricaded, in their own created realm behind the thick walls of brownstones of New York .... You have seen them, except in the shadows, or heard them speak, except in the voices of others." (Doctorow, 1994: 214)

Doctorow describes villainy as pervasive in the New York City after the Civil War. He notes, evil is the soul of the city, represented by the old man Augustus Pemberton, his factotum Eustace Simmons, Boss Tweed, and Dr. Sartorius. In the opening pages of *The Waterworks*, the narrator reveals that the soul of the city is his subject of study. New York City, as McIlvaine complains, under the control of gangsters and unscrupulous politicians, becomes the place" raucous in its dissembling, a city falling into ruin, a society in name only?"(10). As David Louis Edelman suggests, NYC in McIlvaine's description is the center where "dark matters" dwell. It belongs to the powerful men who regulate themselves beyond any moral concerns. On top of the hierarchy, Gangster Boss Tweed's power is everywhere to be discerned. As Doctorow remarks in his essay "The Nineteenth Century New York", Tweed Creates "a model for systematic corruption that is the envy of politicians today" (Doctorow, 1993b: 143): he has his own judges in the court, his own mayor in City Hall and even his own governor. Under his power, politicians become tools of corruption for Tweed's underground organization. They

---

[1]   Bauman's words. It has been quoted in the previous part in chapter two.

collaborate with gangsters and criminals for the sake of profits. Municipal police sell services like the "practice of nightstick in the skull" and police job positions are also on sale according to the ranking (Doctorow, 1993: 34). Industrialists are ruthless and shameless in their way of making money. People from lower class live a calamitous life. Everyone doing business in the city has to "pay a fee up front and then forever kick back a percentage of his salary" (34) to Boss Tweed; anyone who dares to resist his dominance is either bribed or silenced with violence. Children, known as street rats, wonder in the city even without a name, which McIlvaine bemoans as the failure of our civilization. These orphans may beg, do menial work, or run the errands of the underworld. They are starved, exploited, prostituted and abused, and as they sometimes turn up "in hospital wards and church hospices so stunned by the abuses to which they'd been subjected"(65). Even church, in servitude to money, becomes the patronage for rich people to whitewash their ignominious past.

Recalling the chaos and corruption of New York City in the late 19th century, McIlvaine warns the readers that the progress of civilization may only be an illusion, since evil is perpetuated even when the society moves into modern times. On many occasions, he interrupts his narration to underscore the fact that it is modern time with its almost miraculous development of technology. Martin's friend Harry Wheelwright, when telling McIlvaine and Donne that he and Martin exhumed Augustus's grave only to find his body replaced by the corpse of a shrunken child, exclaims, "Good God! These are modern times! Our city is lit in gaslight, we have transcontinental railroads, I can send a message by cable under the ocean..."(105). Both McIlvaine and Wheelwright express their disbelief in the unspeakable evil revealed to them when they think civilization has made such achievements.

Among crimes participated or patronized by Tweed's Ring, the one narrated in the book is the most uncanny and hideous one. For fear of the panic and chaos it may arouse among the public, McIlvaine confesses, he chooses to keep silent and is never able to publish the story. Actually, he is so shocked and awed by the sins our civilization has committed that he finds it difficult to put the whole event into words. Some of the evil in the city, according to McIlvaine, can be safely defined and categorized despite their elusiveness. Tweed and his organization, for example, are evildoers in the most obvious sense. Tweed, the gangster leader who successfully whitewashes his criminal pasts and turns to a senator, is the God of this city in his supreme power. He maintains his dominance by bribing, threatening, plundering and murdering. With the secret wish to live and dominate eternally, Tweed permits and patronizes the operation of municipal orphanage of Little Wanderers and Sartorius's lab inside the municipal waterworks.

August Pemberton, the father who disinherits his son Martin Pemberton, is a representative figure of the ruthless industrialists. A poor immigrant in his early time, Pemberton makes a fortune by providing "shoddy" war supplies to the Union Army and by engaging in slave trade. His experiences, in the words of the narrator, are enough to "shame and mortify their line for generations to come" (5). In private, he is a selfish father and husband. At fourteen, Martin, his son with first wife, is sent to the boarding house for his opposition against his new marriage. Later, Martin writes a thesis on his father's ungraceful profiteering experiences and sends a copy to the old man. Pemberton, irritated, drives his son out of his mansion, severing their relationship and disinheriting Martin as his legal heir. Knowing he is irrecoverably ill, Pemberton fakes his death and transfers his financial assets to fund Dr. Sartorius's experiment to prolong his life, leaving his second wife Sarah and their son Noah in penury. Like the vampire, he, together with the other old businessmen, depends on the life of the orphans, sucking their blood and bone marrows to keep their already dead body alive.

If Tweed and old Pemberton belong to the powerful class that constitute a miniaturized "universe of moneyed entities who manipulate the affairs of their 'lesser' brethren without qualms, motivated solely by the basest instincts of self-preservation" (Edelman, 1994: 57), then Eustace Simmons, "a cadaverous man" (Doctorow, 1994: 181), represents social scoundrels from the lower class. He would betray, bully, exploit others only for the sake of money. Simmons, the former deputy chief clerk in the office of Port Wardens, is lured away by Augustus Pemberton's offer as an assistant in slave trade. He also plays an important role in Pemberton's conspiracy to transfer the latter's wealth. After Pemberton' s death, he begins to work for Sartorius, helping him deal with worldly issues so that the doctor can focus on his research. It is he who kidnaps and buys children to keep them in the orphanage of Little Wanderers as the subject of experiment. Under his governance, Martin is incarcerated in the dungeon and almost starved to death. Finally, Simmons is killed for the thing he loves most: on his way of fleeing the police's arrest, he is accidentally smashed on the head by the case where he keeps the rest of Pemberton's wealth.

Individual villainy taints the city, but the evil of the city is more than that. What is more horrible is the social discourse that tries to cover and distort the facts on villainy. Boss Tweed's dominance maintains for dozens of years, and the voices that try to resist him are suppressed by violence or eradicated by bribery. Pemberton's ignominious past, through his donation to the Church, is buried. He is appraised by Minister Grimshaw as a decent citizen before the exposal of his scandal. With its glamorous appearance, New York's scar is hidden down below. Like McIlvaine claims, the city moves forward its modernization at the cost of the downtrodden who are victimized by those in power.

3. 1. 2. Evil Beyond Human Understanding

So far, reviews and critics have been almost unanimous in their attribution of villainy and immorality to Dr. Sartorius. A rare exception is Luc Sante, who remarks that the scientist is "not the real bad guy here" but "the man of future" (Sante, 1994: 12), and that "like many of his fictional predecessors, he has been assigned Faustian and Promethean attributes by an uncomprehending society"(10). Adam Kelly also argues for Dr. Sartorius's position as a social outsider and his unfair treatment by the community, which is unable to tolerate different voices. Both critics seem to agree that Dr. Sartorius's evil is controversial since it cannot be judged and pinned down by the moral standards of his time. The uncomprehending society, represented by characters who fail to define and represent Dr. Sartorius, reflects the limitation of knowledge at a specific historical time and the prejudice this limitation brings about.

Early in their investigation, McIlvaine and Donne have spotted a street scum named Knucks, from whom they learn about the sensational news that someone is purchasing homeless children for suspicious intention. Linking the news with his later discovery of Sartorius's conspiracy, McIlvaine writes:

> I myself was thinking that what I had heard was in the continuum of original sin... not pleasant to contemplate but not disconnected from anything else either. I was anxious for us to get back to the matter at hand. Then Donne asked me the question that flashed across my brain and spanned the poles of our dark universe: "Who do you suppose would want to buy them, Mr. McIlvaine, when they are in the streets for the talking?" I know you will think this is overwrought fabulation of an old man, but the means of human knowledge are far from understood, and I am telling you here, it was this question that afforded me my first glimpse of Dr. Sartorius... or sense of the presence in our city of Dr. Sartorius...though it may have been nothing more than a moment's belated awareness of the shadow cast by his name as it was uttered by Sarah Pemberton (Doctorow, 1994: 94).

In this passage, McIlvaine puts in parallel two kinds of evil: the one he's familiar with, represented by Boss Tweed, Pemberton, Simmons and so on, and the other one, represented by Dr. Sartorius, which human knowledge "far from understood". The former are wrongdoings in the normal sense that can be judged by the laws of the human society. They are the "continuum of original sin ... not pleasant to contemplate but not disconnected from anything else either" (94). However, Dr. Sartorius's mind and behavior, according to McIlvaine, cast a shadow on human awareness. He belongs to the dark universe beyond our understanding. In contrast to the evil within traditional moral categories, his evil is disconnected from anything, and lies beyond the narrator's "comfortable perceptions of sin and villainy" (Kelley, 2006: 56).

McIlvaine's narration, like all detective stories do, portrays the process of discovering the truth, the truth on Martin's missing, and also the truth on human nature. The former ends with a result to clarify the whole event while the latter proves to be a failure. The characters in his narration, unexceptionally, express their bewilderment on defining Sartorius and his behavior, which leads McIlvaine to the conclusion that truth is so deeply hidden behind the intricate phenomenon that it is almost inaccessible.

In Conrad's *Heart of Darkness*, Kurts's image is revealed gradually through Marlow's impression based on what he hears and learns from his journey along the Congo River. Similarly, Dr. Sartorius's image is not unveiled until the telling of his life stories, experiences, and personalities by his former colleague Dr. Mott, Martin, and finally himself during McIlvaine's interview with him. Like Kurts' shadow that hangs over Marlow's entire narrative, Sartorius's shadow also hangs over *The Waterworks*. His presence penetrates every word of the account but is unable to be located until McIlvaine's last meeting with him.

In their interview with Sartorius's former colleague Dr. Mott, McIlvaine and Donne are informed of Sartorius's excellent skill as a surgeon, his ability to make innovations in medical field, and his unsociable nature, which makes him almost an enemy-like existence in his circle. In fact, Dr. Mott, as a distinguished physician and an upright citizen, objectively evaluates Sartorius's achievements as a field surgeon in the Civil War, whose medical innovations successfully mitigated soldiers' pain and saved thousands of lives. But to him, Sartorius's arrogance and "intolerance for opposing points of view" is not Christian at all (Doctorow, 1994: 126). He comments on him as "unfeeling", "quite unpopular with his brother physicians", and thinks his estrangement from the medical association is caused by himself, instead of "we", the "we" who "would never put social quarantine on a man so brilliant"(126). Dr. Dott's clear distinction of "we" and "him" suggests Sartorius's marginal position in the medical field. He is an outcast, an ungraceful being that Dr. Dott would rather not refer to.

Following the clues on the kidnapped children, McIlvaine and Donne find out the orphanage of Little Wanderers where the children used for experiment are kept and Martin is confined. Rescued from the dungeon, Martin becomes a bag of bones without any consciousness. After his convalescence from a long spiritual crisis, Martin is encouraged to tell his nightmarish experiences in the Sartorius's lab of the waterworks. His frame narrative contributes to the largest part of readers' information on Sartorius.

Undoubtedly, Dr. Sartorius's image in Martin's mind is complicated and contradicted, as he admits, "The doctor himself I find difficult to represent to you"(183). On one hand, Martin is repulsed by the doctor's cold and selfish nature that reminds him of his father Pemberton. Talking of Sartorious's role in the conspiracy of old rich men, Martin says "[t]hough he scrupulously fulfilled his part of the contract, he was entirely without care or concern for his patients except as they were the objects of his thought"(200). Falling into their hands, Martin is at first friendly treated. He is even allowed to watch Sartorius's experiment and read in his library, because the latter intends to use him as a subject for his cerebral experiment. Once Martin disobeys his will, the doctor immediately loses interest in him, leaving him to the disposal of Simmons.

But on the other hand, Martin is attracted by Sartorius's obsession with knowledge and can't help following his steps in scientific research. As McIlvaine says, "Martin seemed to have been seduced by the doctor's intellect to the point of working for him"(193). Especially after he has read Sartorius's books and learns his academic ambitions, Martin comes to understand "the pure scientific temperament as it shone from this man"(199). Even when Sartorius's vicious plan is exposed, he defends for the doctor's behavior and explains to his listeners, "Normality obstructed the scientific vision"(199). The truth is that the cynical Martin, who dares to break from the fetters of his family and critique the most famous writers in his column, looks like a child casting his look of admiration to an idol in front of the doctor. He is overwhelmed by the doctor's persistence in his belief—science, which to him is no less sacred than the Christian belief of Rev. Grimshaw.

According to Martin, Dr. Sartorius is essentially different from the criminal type like Simmons. He should not be labeled as immoralist, since he behaves like an ancient aristocrat, who "never attempted to justify himself" or to lie or to indicate in any way he feels "culpable"(179). He cares about nothing worldly like fame and wealth, so his such lack of "self-consciousness" that he does not even take the trouble to record his experiments (198). Feeling himself "a foreigner", "estranged, a born alien, dissynchronous with my times", Martin finds resonance in the doctor's incompatibility with his environment. In this sense, Martin is sympathetic with the doctor. Even after so many sufferings in the dungeon, he does not blame him or express hatred in his narration, which is full of "peaceful resolution"(179). Actually, the doctor's influence is so overwhelming that people around him, including Simmons and Wrangel, all work voluntarily in his need as if they have been assigned by God to complete his requirements.

After hearing Martin's narration, McIlvaine comments that everything around Martin seems to be willed by Sartorius: "He took the shape of everything— the painted iron bed, the wooden chairs, the white plaster walls and the chair rail..."(176). Even McIlvaine himself, when knowing that Sartorius will not get a public trial but instead will be sent to the mental asylum, he feels pitiful for the man. In his mind, he seems to agree with Martin and refuses to define Sartorius as an unforgivable criminal. Rather, he considers him as a man of future his contemporary society cannot understand. Sartorius's evil, if that can be called evil, unsettles the moral categories of good and evil in the latter half of 19th century American society. His deeds, as Rev. Grimshaw exclaims, are "cataclysmic", a hammer blow to the society which is "not prepared" for the shock (141).

3. 2. The Otherization of Dr. Sartorius

Adam Kelly, in his essay "Society, Justice and the Other: E. L. Doctorow's *Waterworks*", uses the term "other" to refer to the "role that Sartorius plays for the discourses and codes of institutional New York" (Kelly, 2006: 58). He emphatically analyzes how the society's intention to bring justice in the name of community causes Sartorius's silence in the social discourse. In *The Waterworks*, Dr. Sartorius is essentially a transgressor of social norms and ethics. A figure like "H. G. Wells' Dr. Moreau and Robert Louis Stevenson's Dr. Jekyll", Sartorius "shuns the ordinary rules of human behavior that most people depend on"(Edelman, 1994: 57). His fanatic pursuit of scientific knowledge, while ignoring the Christian ethics of American society in the 1980s, makes him an outsider who "go[es] beyond the margins of acceptability or normal performance" (Jenks, 2003: 3). As a result, he is punished with the label "madman" and confined to an asylum. In fact, as Doctorow remarks, compared with the other evildoers, Dr. Sartorius is an ethical outcast, for he has "his own standards, not society's" (Tokarczyk, 1995: 36). To some extent, Sartorius's case causes cognitive chaos among the community and brings danger to the order of the society. That's the reason why he is linked with insanity—the alien force that must be expelled or silenced.

In his essay "commencement", Doctorow refers to Sherwood Anderson's theory of grotesque: if a person "took one of the truths to himself, called it his truth, and tried to live his life by it, he became a grotesque and the truth he embraced became a falsehood" (Anderson, 1976: 25). According to Doctorow, it is no big deal that one holds some truth, but if the truth is clutched too tightly, the person turns into a grotesque (Doctorow, 1993b: 85). So it can be inferred that the cause of the grotesque is one's excessive embrace of some truth, which is just the case of Sartorius. New York City at the end of 19th century was at the crossing road when the old value system was breaking down and the new one had not yet come to shape. Christianity remained the overriding influences on social ideology, in rivalry with the power of natural science and technology, which was just in the rise. Sartorius's problem, first of all, comes from his holding of one kind of truth—knowledge. The extreme pursuit of knowledge leads to his contempt for other forms of knowledge: religion, social regulations and norms, to name just a few. Sartorius, when asked about his religion by Martin, regards Christianity as "no more than a poetic conceit" which he doesn't even "bother to criticize", to "mock" or to "disavow" (Doctorow, 1994: 185). MacIlvaine realizes his loose connection with society, and his ignorance of social norms: "Society, as I've said, made no impression on him. He did not see himself in any relation to it. Certainly not to its laws." (213)

Martins' narrative shows that Dr. Sartorius is a master in several languages, a keen reader of different disciplines and a frenzy pursuer of scientific knowledge. He uses everything at hand in order to discover the terminal truth, which according to him is "so deep inside, so interior" that it operates "in total blindness, in the total disregard of recognizable world that would give us comfort..." (242). The truth, in the mind of Sartorius, is provided by the diction of science, through which, "we can find the language, the formulae, or perhaps the numeration ... to match God."(243). The conservatory Sartorius has designed inside the waterworks, with its greenish light from the roof, its Romanian bathing pool, and music of a concert band, effects "a forbearing harmony and peacefulness". This place insinuates "another universe, a Creation, like ... an obverse Eden"(188). The old men living inside the conservatory, is a league of immortals, maintained animate only by Sartorius's medical procedures. In this sense, Sartorius is empowered with God's capability to access the secret of eternity and to create an Eden with the magic of his knowledge, which is forbidden by God in the Genesis. Contemplating on Sartorius's occult attraction to people surround him, McIlvaine also links him with God:

> Sartorius mentioned his requirements and left it up to the others to fulfill them ... on the model, I suppose, of God giving free will to the human race. It was a measure of the degree of loyalty this doctor inspired that everyone in his employ was free to create what was needed to serve him. The driver of the omnibus and all-around handy-man of the place ... or the cooks, the nurses ... the member of the board ... and his hospital—if you want to call it that—administrator, Eustace Simmons, formerly in the employ of Martin's father as slave-trade expediter ... all of them lived and worked with the relish of free people. (123)

Like God, Sartorius arouses awe and voluntary obedience among his followers. His power is blasphemous, which infringes the Christian ethics on humility, piety and subjugation to God's authority. His scientific obsession, in the eyes of McIlvaine, is enthusiastic but dangerous since McIlvaine is a man of reason, who tries to narrate in a realistic and objective way. Put it in another way, Sartorius's bigotry on knowledge suggests excess[1], the abundant energy that a society-looking toward reason and order cannot tolerate. According to George Bataille, excess or the surplus must be "unloaded, expended, wasted, consumed, defecated, squandered, discharged in what can only be a profane manner" so that the ecological equilibrium of a society can be maintained (Jenks, 2003: 107). On a large scale, excess is reflected in such catastrophic events like war, earthquake, and holocaust. On a small scale, it is released through individual behavior like eroticism, blasphemy, or the offense against norms and values. Sartorius's excess is consumed with his transgression of social norms of his time. That's the fundamental cause of his otherization by the society. As soon as his conspiracy is revealed, the municipal office immediately sets up a Commissio[2] to examine if their decision of committing him to an insane asylum is appropriate or not. After a hasty discussion, the decision is consented even though Dr. Sumner Hamilton, the leading psychiatrist of the city and the head of the Commissio, thinks that Sartorius is only "a man ahead of his time." (251) But he has to be categorized into the mad because "he kept going ... through, beyond ... sanity, whatever that is. Or morality, whatever that is."(251)

With the efforts of the municipal office, the police, and the Commissio, Sartorius's fate is determined. He is never publicly tried or committed. No written record is left for the Commissio's deliberations. The report of the whole nonofficial judgment is sealed by court order and to the day of McIlvaine's narration has

---

[1]   Dr. Sumner Hamilton, Sartorius's medical colleague, calls his behavior "insanely excessive".

[2]   The Latin word for commission

never been released. He is imprisoned in the asylum until the day of his tragic death. There is no chance that he will speak out his story. In this way, Sartorius is otherized and silenced. His otherization is completed through the power network of several institutions including the municipal office, the police, the courthouse, and the asylum, which constitute the social disciplinary system. This system, as Foucault expounds, operates with the method of division, which divides citizens into normal and abnormal, moral and amoral, mad and sane, etc. The disciplinary system also offers the logic of normalization, in the process of which individuals are "distributed around a norm—a norm which both organizes and is the result of this controlled distribution" (Foucault, 1984: 18). In Sartorius's community, Dr. Dott and Dr. Sumner Hamilton represent the norm of medical practice. Sartorius, however, because of his excessive behavior, is deemed as the other—the different voice that needs to be punished and suppressed. Rather than get a public trial, he is secretly judged and confined to the asylum, because if there is a trial, "his ideas will be heard" (Doctorow, 1994: 233). Since "the city has suffered several shocks to its spirit" (233), it cannot suffer another one caused by Sartorius' ideas, in the words of Dr. Hamilton. The asylum actually represents the disciplinary power of society to "reduce differences, repress vice, [and] eliminate irregularities" (Foucault, 1984: 149). As Foucault analyzes, "denounc[ing] everything that opposes the essential virtues of society...", the asylum "sets itself the task of the homogeneous rule of morality, its rigorous extension to all those who tend to escape from it"(149).

On the other hand, Sartorius's otherization also shows the unwillingness of society to accept new ideas. McIlvaine, feeling outrageous that Sartorius cannot get a public trial, comments on the tendency of the society to keep intact with its institutional thoughts:

> But let me tell you about institutional thought. Whatever the institution ... and however worthy or substantive ... its mind is not an entirely human mind ... though it is made up of human minds. If it were really human it would be capable of surprises ... if it were really human it would be motivated by all sorts of noble or ignoble ideas. But the institutional mind has only one mental operation: It abhors truth. (Doctorow, 1994: 228)

McIlvaine's conception of institution, as Adam Kelly points out, portrays "a self-consistent, persistent and predictable sameness" (Kelly, 2006: 58). A society with this sameness is destined to fail to brave the challenge posed by Sartorius's case. In fact, the 19th century New York, in McIlvaine's description at the end of the novel, seems "frozen in time" with everything "still, unmoving, stricken, as if the entire city of New York would be forever encased and frozen, aglitter and God-stunned" (Doctorow, 1994: 253). McIlvaine's narrative ends with the wedding of two couples, a banal ending, like most stories do and readers commonly expect. Ice becomes the final metaphor of this city. All of these symbolize the inability of the society to meet surprises and to open to the changes brought about by new ideas and thoughts. In the name of the interest of majority, society punishes and segregates those transgressors of social norms, who are otherized and silenced. In this way, uniformity and order are ensured for the convenience of surveillance and dominance of the ruling class.

3. 3. Narration as an ethical event

Narrative practice and ethics are inseparable. According to Andrew Gibson, the narration of a story functions as a particular kind of ethical concern as it usually involves "a mode of activity in which a subject takes another, others and the world as the object or objects of knowledge and claims possession of them"(Gibson, 1999: 26). Gibson further espouses, as a mode of knowledge, narratives are related to "questions of what is 'known' in a given narrative, who by about whom or what, form what perspective, articulated in what terms, qualified in what manner", thus they have an ethical bearing (54). With reference to Levinas, he thinks postmodern narrative provides "a diffuse and heterogeneous narrated space" where Levinas's "encounter with the alterity" happens (49). As befits the label of postmodernist novelist, E. L. Doctorow often produces such "diffuse and heterogeneous" narrative spaces in his fictions. They highlight "the voices of the marginal or 'eccentric' strata who previously had an unheard presence in the society and create[s] a sort of dialogism or heteroglossia in that all the voices from different groups of people are heard and there is no longer the dominance of the monolithic, monologic voice". (Amani & Ramin, 2014: 69). His *The Waterworks*, employing frame structure and a highly self-reflexive voice, creates a narrative of "movement" in which traditional moral categories are "opened up to the alterity they appeared to exclude" in which morality has no "distinct, determinate or final form" (Gibson, 1999: 50). In this way, the readers are led to suspend their judgments and read the texts as injecting what

Dollimore calls the "transgressive reinscription"[①] into mainstream culture. (50)

Ethics, according to Gibson, appears in a relation between two planes of a narrative, the plane where representation takes place, which can be understood as the authors, narrators, readers, etc. and the plane of the represented like the characters. Normally, the authors or narrators have a firm grasp of the objects they intend to represent. In the case of *The Waterworks*, McIlvaine occupies the first plane but he always shows his inability to represent the object, which seems to have eluded from his mastery. Like most of Doctorow's narrators who are troubled by the dilemma of representation, McIlvaine, the narrator of *The Waterworks*, tells the story in a hesitant, elliptical and self-doubting way. He constantly complains his loss of memory, his inability to render chaotic events into sequence, and the limitation of human cognition as a whole to understand things beyond their realm of knowledge. The book's mode of narrative, as Brien Diemert comments, reveals "its deep suspicion about earthly authority" (Diemert, 2003: 354), which mirrors the skeptical spirit postmodernists often celebrate. Marshall Bruce Gentry also argues that McIlvaine's monologue presents itself as "unauthoritative" and Doctorow actually creates him to project a narrator who "expresses all of Doctorow's darkest suspicions and Poesque pessimism, and then to exorcise some personal demons by subtly revealing that narrator's limitations, inaccuracies and evil traits" (Gentry, 2002: 66).

As McIlvaine claims, "it is important for you to know who is telling the story"(11), the readers should bear in mind McIlvaine's occupation and personality, which inevitably influence his way of narration. As the former chief editor of the newspaper *Telegram*, McIlvaine considers himself a realist who obtains the sense of stability from the newsprint world. To him, the newsprint world is where chaos is slugged into sentences and "arranged in columns on a page of newsprint" (Doctorow, 1994: 14). McIlvaine thinks that without daily paper, "there is no order in the universe, no discernible meaning"(14). Depending on the objectivity of newspapers for the sense of security, McIlvaine finds himself somehow drawn into his freelance Martin's occult event. Through his narration of Sartorius's case, McIlvaine realizes that "the story was not ... reportorially possible ... that there are limits to the use of words in a newspaper (208)".

McIlvaine's sense of unrepresentability is firstly shown in his failed

---

① In his essay "Subjectivity, Sexuality, and Transgression: The Jacobean Connection", Jonathan Dollimore argues for a valorization of "transgressive reinscription," in which transgression takes the form of inverting or reversing ideological categories. Jonathan Dollimore. "Subjectivity, Sexuality, and Transgression: The Jacobean Connection,'' *Renaissance Drama* 17 (1986), 53-69.

interpretation of Martin's words. One day, Martin enters McIlvaine's office in despondency and declares that his father is alive. Like Martin's fiancée and Reverend Grimshaw, McIlvaine is unable to understand Martin's statement literally. On the contrary, he interprets what he says "as metaphor, a poetic way of characterizing the wretched city that neither of us loved, but neither of us could leave"(8). In fact, as early as the opening line of the first chapter, McIlvaine has described this faltering of textual realism: "People wouldn't take what Martin Pemberton said as literal truth, he was much too melodramatic or too tormented to speak plainly"(1). As the mystery is unfolded, Martin's father, who is supposed to be lying in his grave, really appears in the omnibus with other old men. Biologically, he is alive, depending on the injection of blood and tissues from the orphans. McIlvaine and other's failure to abstract meaning from Martin suggests that they live in a world of reality—a world of common sense and banality. This world of reality welcomes no surprises and is to be shocked by the otherness of Sartorius's story. In the frame narrative of Martin, he expresses similar opinion, "The doctor himself I find difficult to represent to you. He doesn't expend his energy on the formation of a ... social self" (201).

The narrator's insistence on the limits of representation undercuts his mastery over the story, reducing his reliability and authority. In fact, even McIlvaine's own account shows his suspicion toward the reliability of the story. He tells the readers that he is now an old man and as his memory collapses, he is not sure whether the names, places, dates and other details in his story are accurate. On many occasions, he expresses his anxiety that the readers may not believe in what he narrates. Digressed from the main storyline, he reveals to the readers, "You will just have to trust that this, like everything I tell you, has a bearing on the story (6)". Finding that the Sartorius's story is horrible and incredible to such extent that he cannot find exact words to pin it down, he says, "If you're not convinced, let's just say that I didn't think the story was reportable, accurately, until it was all in"(207).

All these self-reflexive qualities of the narrative suggest that the relation between the narrator and the narrated is not that of subject and object since the narrated has fled the control of the narrator. The truth is that Sartorius's deeds have posed a challenge to the moral cognition of the narrator, rendering his realist thinking useless. The ethical power of a story comes from the narrator's certainty on moral knowledge and the clarity of moral categories. In a realist novel, the readers are led to take a stance; they are either persuaded to feel sympathetic or resentful for some characters. However, in a postmodern novel, the narrative gives a sense of uncertainty, which shatters the moral ground of readers. In a state of continuous confusion and shock, MacIlvaine feels temporarily relieved when Donne's intuition leads him to some important discoveries of the case:

> Donne's researchers had provided an answer of a kind... that where, before, all had been chaos and bewilderment and hurt, now it was clear that something understandable ... an act ... had been committed ... a deliberate act or series of acts ... by which we could recompose the world, comfortably, in categories of good and evil. (141)

The disturbed sense of moral categories becomes the essential reason for MacIlvaine's failure of composition. Although MacIlvaine tries to put the story in the realist newsprint world where reality will be objectively transformed into words, Sartorius's story denies such transformation. MacIlvaine complains the disturbance of reality on linear thinking, "I have occasionally to tell you things not in the order in which I learned them." (30) As he realizes that Sartorius's case makes chronology impossible, he gives up chronology and changes the order of the events he writes down:

> I withhold here the circumstances of our first sight of Sartorius. I want to keep to the chronology of things but at the same time to make their pattern sensible, which means disrupting the chronology. After all, there is a difference between living in some kind of day-to-day craw through chaos, where there is no hierarchy to your thoughts, but a raucous equality of them, and knowing in advance the whole conclusive order ... makes narration ... suspect. (123)

The introduction of Martin Pemberton as a second narrator also weakens the power of MacIlvaine's narrative. What MacIlvaine intends to write down is a story that happens in New York, a story of evil and horror. However, the core figure of his narrative—Sartorius resists his interpretation and representation. In his account, Martin reveals his complicated emotion toward Sartorius. Rather than recognizing him as a demon-like doctor, Martin's account reflects Sartorius's personal charm and expresses his admiration for him. MacIlvaine admits that Martin's account greatly influences his judgment of Sartorius and he even feels sympathy for him because the doctor cannot get a fair trial. Contrary to the official record that narrates Sartorius's case in a newsprint way, McIlvaine's narrative provides an anti-totalizing space where the voice of the other is filtered in. When Reverend Grimshaw urges for a public trial, Donne explains the reason why everything around Dr. Sartorius should be kept secretly:

If you have a trial, he will have to be heard. Any lawyer would see that the only hope of a defense would be in taking his testimony. He could argue in his perversity that our interruption of his work cost the lives of his patients. And our proofs, you know... are largely circumstantial. At the least his ideas will be heard ... his ... genius will be on the view. I can't think that would be of any benefit to a Christian society... (238)

His account constitutes the "gaps and fissures"(Gibson's words) where the present is crossed and the otherness comes in. Donne thinks that if there is a trial, Dr. Sartorius's voice will be heard and the public may have a chance to learn another version of the truth on the case. The fact is whoever has the right to say masters the power to disseminate truth, as Martin's friend Harry Wheelwright says, "When I write my memoirs I will be the subject of the narrative.... My own fate will be another story ... not this one."(109) In this sense, narrative plays a crucial role in deciding the moral quality of a character. McIlvaine's narrative, in contrast to the official record where Sartorius's name is hardly recognized or distorted by the institutions, offers what Andrew Gibson calls the "redemptive perspective" that estranges and displaces the world (Gibson, 1999: 116). It is ethical in core as through indeterminacies and the dismantled authorial authority, the discursive totality constructed by a monolithic and static society is broken down and the face of the other is admitted and properly responded to.

Chapter Three
From "High" to "Low" : Transgression of Discursive Hierarchy

1. The Hierarchical Structure in Social Discourse

Social discourse is quite hierarchical. Adjectives such as "lofty", "noble", "sublime", "obscene", "debased" are employed to describe the two extremities of the high/low opposition in discursive practice, which is "a fundamental basis to mechanisms of ordering and sense-making in European culture" (Stallybrass & White, 1986: 3). Peter Stallybrass and Allon White, in their collaborative work *The Politics and Poetics of Transgression* (1986), generally divide social discourse into high discourse and low discourse based on their status in the hierarchy. According to them, the high discourse, exemplified by political statecraft, law, church language, and official history, are characterized by "their lofty style, exalted aims and sublime ends" (3). The low discourse, with "its popular and vulgar style, its aims to entertain the mass", and its root in the sub-culture, which "always seek the opportunity to impose counter-view on the dominant culture" (4), includes such genres as popular novels, folktales, songs, etc. Employing the Marxist analytical method, the two scholars think that the formation of this high/low structure is normally associated with "the socio-economic group existing at the center of cultural power"(4). The categories on top of the hierarchy always attempt to reject and eliminate the bottom for the sake of dominance, only to discover, not only are they to some extent dependent on the low-other part of the culture, but also they "include that low symbolically, as a primary eroticized constituent of its own fantasy life"(6). The result is "a mobile, conflictual fusion of power" in the construction of subjectivity in the society, with social others as both a necessity and the objects of opposition and exclusion (6).

Doctorow is quite conscious of the hierarchical structure of social discourses. On many occasions, he warns that the public should keep on guard against the discourses on top of the hierarchy that attempt to convey absolute ideas and claim universal truths. According to Doctorow, these high discourses need to be constantly discredited since no system, whether "it's religious or anti-religious or economic or materialistic, seems to be invulnerable to human venery and greed and insanity" (Levine, 1983: 65). Of all the high discourses commonly referred to, the language of church and the History in upper case[①] are fields that Doctorow concerns most. They are what Doctorow considers myth in American culture, or in Jean-François Lyotard's terms, metanarratives— "apparatuses of legitimation" (Lyotard, 1984: xxiv) used to "validate knowledge and universal values, but have become untenable in the cultural heterogeneity" of contemporary society (Bowen, 2010: 17). The myths, according to Doctorow, if not "examined and questioned and dealt with constantly", will "harden and become dangerous" (Marranca, 1999: 211). Eventually they will turn to a structured belief, make people insane and lead to a monolithic and despotic society.

In his novel *City of God*, Doctorow calls the validity of religious classics into the question such as the Bible and Augustine's work *The City of God*. Through the spiritual pursuit of Pem and Everett, Doctorow shows the failed mechanism of religious classics as metanarrative to explain crucial issues concerning the twentieth century and to maintain its authority in both theological and secular sense. *The March*, on the other hand, questions the validity of official history as a faithful representation of the past, through a reconstruction of General Sherman's famous march in the Civil War. In contrast to History in upper case, it is history in plural forms, written from multiple perspectives, including those marginalized in official history. By exposing the discrepancy between historical records and fictional creation, Doctorow's *The March* reflects the false claim of official history on absolute objectivity and faithfulness. The common features of such high discourses (the language of church, History), Doctorow elucidates, are their insistence on absolute authority and rejection of the voices of the other. They are Levinas's "the said", the statement, assertion or proposition of which truth or falsity can be ascertained and meaning can be pinned down.

In *Reporting the Universe*, Doctorow questions the language of church based on Hebrew scripture "sacred texts". The only and absolute author of the sacred texts is God, whose authority is uncontested. Doctorow further points out, if a portion of a sacred text is "illogical, opaque, self-contradictory, bipolar, enigmatic", "God

---

① According to the New Historicists, History in upper case refers to the conception of history as a continuous and coherent unity. In fact, they think history is individualistic and subjective. It is made up of histories, the plural voices from different perspectives.

in the biblical sources. Generations of men in the service of God have interpreted, edited and amended it and so it can work as a relative unity. *The City of God,* St. Augustine's apology for Christian doctrine written from A.D. 413–426, can be seen as his commentary on and interpretation of the Bible. As Doctorow writes, the Bible becomes what we read today due to " 'this scissors-and-paste job' of Bible interpreters" (Doctorow, 2000: 114). They know when to "erase the inconsistencies and neaten things up" so that the process of interpretation becomes the struggle "to apprehend and accept the awesome completeness and creative totality of the Unnameable" (114). The key words here are "completeness" and totality", which suggest that like other texts of grandiose style, the sacred text of God is Levinas's "the said", the discourse of "unification and totality", which always seek to "encompass and articulate the whole"(Gibson, 1999: 60).

One of the most distinct characteristics of the language of totality is its exclusion of the voice of the other. As Doctorow notes, in the Bible, God is the only writer and narrator, who "made a text from nothing" (Doctorow, 2000: 209). He is the One, the logos, "the supreme transcendent reality or hypostasis" (Gibson, 1999, 85). As Levinas points out, the One is the unity with whose bonds "this world of plurality and variety is contained"(85). Thus, his voice throughout the Biblical texts is monolithic, a "rhetoric" in the terms of Levinas, which closes off all the possibility of dialogue with the other in his/her irreducible difference. By rhetoric, Levinas means the discourse of ontology in contrast to the discourse of ethics. The former represents authoritarian violence, which refuses to listen, rejecting "exchange, assimilation, hybridization, self-reflexivity"(62) while the latter welcomes conversation and maintains the reciprocal relation with the other.

The history of Christianity is the continual debasement and rejection of the other (the non-Christians) to define itself. In the Bible, the Israelites who turn their face from God to worship other idols always got stern punishment from God. Historically, the pagans or heresies were prosecuted and exiled by Christians in a crude way (just think the treatment the European Jewish have received for as long as thousands of years). Just as one of the Jews in this novel says, "...we had lived among them, the Christians, for generations upon generations, only to see ourselves bent and twisted to the shape of their hatred. We had been turned into Jews so that they could be Christians"(60).

Augstine's *The City of God*, as Yuan Xianlai says, "reflects the grand narrative of Latin Church at its extreme level" (Yuan, 2014: 17). It is written as a "vindication of Christianity against the attacks of the heathen in view of the sacking of the city of Rome by the barbarians" at a time when the old Græco-Roman civilization was on the decline, an a new Christian civilization was beginning to rise on its ruins (Philip Schaff, 1890: 3). Augustine's purpose of writing the book, as Philip Schaff elucidates, is "to expound the Christian faith, and justify it to enlightened men: to distinguish it from, and show its superiority to, all those forms of truth"(3). In this voluminous work, Augustine puts forward some well-known propositions of theodicy, one of which is that God is perfect and thus his creation is perfect. The perfect God creates a world of evil because he gives human beings free will to choose either to embrace or eschew from evil. Most importantly, Augustine develops the system of theological law based on the studies of his predecessors like Aquinas and Cicero. In this system, the law of God is deemed as supreme and eternal. By eternal, Augustine means that the justice that God's law embodies will never change. As for the issue of how justice can be done in such a world of evil, Augustine's answer is, God's justice will be revealed in the time of Apocalypse. In this sense, both the Bible and *The City of God* try to defend God's supreme power and His eternal dominance in the theological world. The discourses in these two narratives, with God at the center of the power, tend to establish a universal order and hierarchy among its believers.

As Nietzsche claims, every proclamation of truth is the expression of a will to power. Meaning, thus, becomes "a contested event and the struggles over meaning" and "the material conditions of textual production are read as inherently political partisan and personal" (Bowen, 2010: 25). Critiqued for the ideological color in his works, Doctorow says it is to echo Nietzsche that narratives are inevitably political. In his novel *City of God*, sacred texts are shown to be highly subjective. With the endless efforts of their storytellers, they are often employed as a tool of political control.

In Everett's story "Heist" in *City of God*, Bible's account as a reliable and objective history of God and his son Jesus is in many ways interrogated. As Pemberton claims in his sermon, all these sacred texts are the results of the communal efforts of inventing, selecting, tailoring, deleting by its adherents after several generations: "The biblical stories... But they didn't write themselves. We have to acknowledge the storyteller's work" (Doctorow, 2000: 13). The process of editing the Bible is also the process of defining, justifying, and fighting for power. Pemberton recalls his conversation with a widow friend Samantha who has been reading Pagels[①] on early Christianity. She tells the rector that all is politics, and the story about God is "all made up" and "an invention"(13). Troubled by his own doubt about Christian narratives, Pemberton cannot find a proper answer to refute her. While his visiting one of his terminal patients, Pemberton's service is rejected as the patient calls his gospels pure bullshit. All these events, together with Pem's study on the power struggles of earlier gospelers and the twentieth-century history, lead to Pem's skeptical introspection on the faith he used to be so firm with. Pem's spiritual crisis, reflected in his outrageous sermons, incurs anxiety from the bishop of his parish, who sends an examiner to inspect whether Pem is still appropriate to remain in his position. As usual, Pem tells the examiner his meditation on the relation between Biblical stories and political struggle after reading Pagels' book:

> So there was a power struggle ... it is also true that the struggle for Jesus was a struggle for power, ... and that the struggle to define Jesus and canonize his words, or interpretations of his words by others, was pure politics, ... with the desire to perpetuate the authority of Jesus...(70)

Pem's ideas find resonance in Doctorow's essay "The Politics of God". Tracing the history of disputes between earlier gospelers of different branches, Doctorow comes to the conclusion that Jesus was politicized from the beginning since he was created out of conflict. It has been a politicized Jesus ever since if one looks at the long history of European Christianity, "with its crusades, its inquisitions, its demonization of Jews, its contests and /or alliances with kings and emperors, and with the rise of Reformation, its active participation in all its forms in the wars among states and the rule of populations" (Doctorow, 2003: 91). Not only the Bible is full of pious lies and political struggles, St. Augustine's *The City of God* is also like this, or even worse. Pem's repugnance on this book originates from Augustine's narration that babies are born damned to hell unless some water is sprinkled on them, which is in discord with Pem's humanistic spirit. Pem thinks, compared with storytellers, editors' job is more dangerous, which is the case of St. Augustine:

> Migod, there is no one more dangerous than the storyteller. No, I'll amend that, than the storyteller's editor. Augustine, who edits Genesis 2–4 into original sin.

---

①   As a young researcher at Barnard College, Elaine Pagels changed forever the historical landscape of the Christian religion by exploring the myth of the early Christian Church as a unified movement. Her findings were published in 1979 in the best selling book *The Gnostic Gospels*, which won her the National Book Critics Circle Award and the National Book Award.

> What a nifty little act of deconstruction—passing it on to the children, like HIV. As the doctrine of universal damnation, the Fall becomes an instrument of social control. (Doctorow, 2000: 65)

Pem's discrediting of Christian discourse culminates when he addresses to God that He is not the embodiment of justice as claimed in the Biblical stories. In fact, in the past centuries, men used God at will for "their most hideous purposes" (266) while God the supreme author, does not seem to give any response. In an outrage when talking of the sins and crimes committed in the name of God, he makes a metaphor: "You are bought and embraced like the lowest, most pathetic streetwalker" (266). It is this inner disbelief in the grand narratives of Christian classics that leads to Pem's pursuit of a sound metaphysics, which can compromise his religious beliefs and humanistic stance.

2. 2. The failed mechanism of God's narrative

As is stated, religious classics like the Bible and St. Augustine's *The City of God* are written supposedly to defend the power of God, to maintain His dominance among the followers and to establish the order and hierarchy of the Christian realm. The general proposition of these works is that God is perfect and justice will finally be done in his presence. God, as Abraham consoles himself in Genesis, the "judge of all the earth", would assuredly "do right"[①] (Gen. 18:25). But in Doctorow's novel, God's presence and justice are constantly questioned and challenged especially against the background of a postmodern society. The postmodern condition, described by Lyotard, is "in credulity toward master- or meta-narratives" (Lyotard, 1984: xxv). As a postmodern novelist, Doctorow is acclaimed as a writer of skeptical commitment to all kinds of social ideologies. One of his central thematic concerns in *City of God*, as the narrator in the novel asks, is that "Where is God". As Stanley Trachtenberg notes, thematically, the novel explores "the difficulties each of the clergical figures has trying to reconcile the traditions of their faith with the apparent lack of a moral equation in human destiny" (Trachtenberg, 2000: 1).

In his religious work *The City of God*, Augustine distinguishes two kinds of realm in the world, the city of God and the earthly city. The city of God, as its name

---

① In Genesis 18: 25, Abraham poses the rhetorical question to God: "Far be it from You to do such a thing, to slay the righteous with the wicked, so that the righteous and the wicked are treated alike. Far be it from You! Shall not the Judge of all the earth deal justly?" By posing a rhetorical question that is asked to emphasize rather than to expect an answer, Abraham puts much trust in God's ability to distinguish between right and wrong.

suggests, is built by God, and inhabited by those people with wisdom who hold the "love for God, even to the contempt of self" (Augustine, 1890: 455). For the earthly city, it is vice versa. In the opinion of Augustine, the city of God is a utopian realm. He demonstrates "the superior morality, the true doctrine, the heavenly origin" of the city and ensures its final success (Schaff, 1890: 8), contrary to the fallen state of the earthly city. On many occasions, Doctorow claims that New York City, the place where he grew up, is the subject matter of his study, one of his everlasting interests. In *City of God*, Doctorow ironically cites Augustine's book name as an implication of the New York City. In fact, the association of NYC with the city of God starts with Boss Tweed in Doctorow's earlier book *The Waterworks*. The notorious gangster used to collaborate with a scientist who conducts medical experiment to try to discover the secrets of eternal life. After the exposal of his criminal activities, Tweed escapes to an island of South America and falls into madness, claiming that he has discovered the secrets of eternality and turns NYC to a city of God.

Part of the irony here lies in that the NYC of Everett's depiction ostensibly resembles Augustine's city of God as both "call[s] out citizens from all nations and so collects a society of aliens, speaking all languages" (Augustine, 1890: 17). The most prosperous metropolis in America, NYC attracts numerous immigrants from all over the world to pursue their dreams. It is a place where diverse cultures collide and integrate. To recover his lost crucifix, Pem wanders aimlessly along the New York streets, which offers him a superb opportunity to observe and to know the city. His wandering also guides the readers to experience the great achievements of civilization, such as skyscrapers, cruisers, waterworks, metro system, etc. Interspersed in the narrative of "Heist" is the narrator's elucidation on modern scientific theories on the creation of the universe. Albert Einstein's voice is introduced to speak out his life stories, his theory on relativity and his meditation on religion. The avatar of Ludwig Wittgenstein also makes a statement which can be understood as the footnote of the book: "Even if all the possible scientific questions are answered, our problem is still not touched at all" (Doctorow, 2000: 87). Just as Wittgenstein claims, the technological development of modern society does not resolve all problems, nor can it make a city immortal.

New York, as Pem demonstrates, is far from a blissful city of God; instead, it is filled with evil, corruption, immorality and faithlessness, a pathetic picture of the earthly city, "the vessels of wrath" (Augustine, 1890: 462). Walking on the street of Manhattan, Pemberton sees a chaotic and bustling scene of modern metropolis life:

Fire sirens. Police-car hoots.... Hissing bus doors, sidewalk pileups for the stars at their screenings. All the restaurant booked. Babies tumbling out of the maternity wards. Building facades falling into the streets. Busting water mains. Cop crime. (Doctorow, 2000: 10)

More than that, New York is a space of polarities, with the good and the evil, the richest and the poorest, the grandiose and the ugly existing simultaneously. Social discontent spreads due to the widening gap of wealth distribution. The rich does not need to work to maintain his wealth while the poor works day and night only to scratch a living. In this city, racial discrimination and conflicts run wild: "Every day a cop shoots a black kid, chokeholds a perp..."(10) It is the capital of immigration, swarmed with "the migrant wretched of the world". It is the paradise of crime, with rate of burglary, robbery, murder, rape much higher than that in other parts of the country. In a conversation with a tourist, Pemberton is surprised to know that his lost camera can be bought back on the second-hand market of Manhattan. In the indoor crime-site of his church where the altar brass cross is missing, Pemberton finds that this place, supposed to be sacred and glorious, is full of rotten smells: "[H]ashish in that pantry. Male body odor. But also the pungent sanguinary scent of female pheromone."(18) His church St. Timothy, due to the slumping fiscal budgets and diminishing parish, becomes dilapidated, indicating the loss of faith of New Yorkers. It is later remodeled as St. Timothy Theatre after Pemberton is defrocked. But the story on New York is more than that. Everett's film script tells a tragic story of an actress whose nose is eaten by a psyche, which indirectly reveals the loneliness and alienation of metropolis life. As Julia Eichelberger notes, the novel's depiction of New York City of the late 1990s can invite such a reading: "a post-industrial urban chaos where the ruthless and the desperate prey upon the weak, while the affluent withdraw into well-furnished isolation" (Eichelberger, 2004: 84). It is against this background that Pemberton embarks on his pursuit of the lost cross.

Thomas Pemberton, the rector of an Episcopal church called St. Timothy, feels himself deeply trouble with the doctrines, beliefs and visions inscribed in Biblical scriptures. To his horror, he realizes that the twentieth century history is so full of evils, crimes and disasters that the sacred law of God cannot reveal its justice. Among all the atrocities in history, he finds that the Holocaust disturbs him most. In one of his sermons, Pem asks his parishioners to imagine as a Christian how to respond to a disaster as inhuman as genocide. His anxiety intensifies after the brass crucifix of his church is stolen, which he interprets as a sign for God's absence and his own loss of belief. The whole story of "Heist", in essence, is Pem's pursuit of "a believable God", just as Pem claims, we need something to assure us of "the holy truth of our story", something "as earthshaking in its way as Auschwitz and Dachao"(49). He reproaches God's absence in face of the uncountable injustice and human sufferings, meanwhile longing for His revelation: "If I can't find God in my church, my ritual, the sacred texts that my logical and scientific mind rejects, then where else?"(53) After waiting in vain for God's revelation, he confesses that he can no longer perceive his presence and he complains in misery: "...God, as usual has ignored my communications (no offence, lord), I do feel somewhat isolated"(41). In this spiritual crisis, Pem pleads with God to speak to him or send him an email to prove his presence. Shortly afterwards, it turns out that the missing crucifix appears on the roof of the synagogue of the EJ, presided by the Jewish couple Joshua and Sarah. No one knows how the event happens, by accident or vile manipulation. The convict of the theft has never been found. Pem is invited into the rabbis' house for the restoration of the crucifix. The heist connects Pem and Sarah as well as two different religions. With this accident, Pem feels his "houses of worship desecrated, the entire Judeo-Christian Heritage trashed" (30).

Besides Pem's story in "Heist", Everett outlines his family history in the form of verse in the part of "Author's bio", including his father and brother's war experiences. Indirectly, "Author's bio" supplements Pem's reference to the twentieth century history of disaster since it includes the description of two world wars. Everett writes that his father Ben, a member of U. S. navy in WWI, was impressed by the European beaches which were "adrift with sanded bones" of earlier times (135). His brother Ronald, during his enlistment in American air force in WWII, accidentally landed on a beach after his bomber was shot down in a flying mission. To his surprise, Ronald found that the beach used to be the ancient war fields "reopened by an errant shell of this war":

> It was the improvised graveyard of ancient bones
> and skulls
> still helmeted in the stylish French couture,
> and phallic German,
> the skeletal warriors of his father Ben's generation (182)

From the war experiences of his family members, Everett comes to the awareness that civilization moves in circular pattern instead of progressing forward linearly. Hatred is passed over from one generation to another, and bodies are buried over bodies without any weight. Human history, full of blood and violence, is the stage where nightmarish scenes reappear and it can be chastened in no way. Based on the information he hears from Sarah on her father's childhood experiences in Kovno ghetto, Everett creates the Holocaust story, which fills the gap of Pemberton's questioning of Christianity for its permission of such disaster. Joshua (Sarah's father), the protagonist of the Holocaust story, gradually loses everything in the German invasion, including his parents, friends, home, foster father, etc. Working as a little messenger for the secret committee of the ghetto, he witnesses the cruel treatment his people have received during the rule of the German army. Almost killed in the atrocities of the Nazis, Joshua narrowly escapes to America to start a new life. Although during the later dozens of years, he receives education, gets married and works like a normal man, his life has been never the same, with huge trauma inside. As Sarah recalls, his father never talks of Jewish faith and the family rejects anything connected with religious rituals such as Passover.

Pem, in the speech delivered when he and Sarah get married, bemoans the souls tortured in wars, in genocides, and the masses of dead in the past century, including Sarah's father and her husband. The father dies in a stroke, after a lifetime's sufferings caused by his earlier experiences in the ghetto. The husband is accidentally killed in his journey of recovering the secret documents (the evidence against Nazi's crime) delivered out of the ghetto by his father-in-law half centuries ago. Outrageously, Pem points out that although it is proclaimed that God's justice will be eventually revealed, the most notorious convicts in the Holocaust have escaped the earthly law. Schmitz, the German commander of Kovno ghetto in the Holocaust story, forfeits a new identity after the war and begins his life as an American citizen. He dies naturally in his sleep, never put in trial in the court and his crime is never publicized before his death. It is a disgrace, Pem says, since those dead "are not resurrectable, they cannot and will not resurrect even in the imagination of your Christian faithful" (266). With "the genocidal cruelties shuddering across the world", he interrogates, "how a supposedly omnipresent God such as Yourself would allow these human catastrophes to occur." (266) Pem thinks that due to the catastrophic history of the past century, people can no longer find comfort in God in the biblical narratives. In other words, God as the absolute writer and narrator is no longer able to convince people of his presence and authority. His law of justice cannot be maintained after the crime and atrocities committed on such a large scale in the past dozens of years. Even the illusion of Apocalypse is not sufficient to justify God's law and appease the wrath of those who used to hold faith on him. The traditional God, with His words of "totality", is brought into disrepute and degradation for throwing its believers into "the despair of cursing Your name and impugning Your existence"(266). Like other concepts that will evolve, the Old One (Einstein's reference to God) also needs to be abandoned and remade into a new one.

2. 3. The Petty Narrative of Multiple Commoners

If Augustine's work is for the vindication of Christian doctrines, Doctorow's central preoccupation in his novel is "the question of authorship and dialogue", question that is at the core of his ethical concern (Ludwig, 2010: 82). In a broadcast interview with Scott Simon, Doctorow was asked about his ideas on religion and fundamentalism, "themes that are at the heart of the conflict in the Middle East and, by consequence, the terrorism here in the United States"[1]. Doctorow's response to the question is pertinent, a reiteration of his opinion in *Reporting the Universe*. Citing Ralph Waldo Emerson's line "Anything which can be thought can be written. The writer is the faculty of reporting" (Doctorow, 2003: 2), he claims that to prevent some universal truth (in that context he means religious fundamentalism) from dominating social discourse, the writer should be able to report anything in the cosmos. By report, Doctorow remarks, Emerson does not mean the term in journalism but refers to being witness. According to Emerson, the universe is the possibility of being reported and writer is the faculty of reporting. In Emerson's mind, there is no definite answer and the story is not completed, as long as human imagination is not exhausted. Therefore, whatever institutions give definite answers—"Church, government, society, family"—they are "up for examination"(2). In such a society as described by Emerson, Doctorow claims, "The right of authorship has slowly through history devolved from gods and heroes and prophets and priests and kings to all of us, to the commoners"[2]. Talking of a democratic milieu in which authorship is a free choice, Doctorow further points out: "A true democracy endows itself with a multiplicity of voices and assures the creation of a self-revising consensual reality that inches forward over the generations to a dream of truth." (Doctorow, 2003: 3)

City of God, Doctorow's "most disjointed, variegated, playful novel"(Oates,

---

[1]   It is from the introductory words by the host Scott Simon when he was having an interview with E. L. Doctorow. The script of the interview was later published in *Weekend Edition* Saturday 15 on Sept. 2001.

[2]   Quoted from the interview with Scott Simon.

2000), is such a narrative with "a multiplicity of voices", in contrast to the monolithic voice of the sacred texts. Francisco Collado Rodriguez thinks that this is a novel which best embodies Doctorow's transgressive spirit for the blurring of boundaries that exists at many levels: "the crossing of narrative levels or metalepsis (Genette, 1980); the crossing of ontological levels (mostly regarding the role of cinema and the figure of a writer who writes an embedded biography)...the crossing of traditional gender roles; the postmodern blurring of genre barriers (parody of the detective novel); the mixture of Christian and Jewish religions; and, finally, the dissolution of borders between religion and contemporary scientific theories" (Rodriguez, 2002: 62). In fact, Rodriguez should have added one more on his list: the crossing of hierarchy in social discourse. Compared with the high discourse of the sacred texts, which claim absolute authority and attempt to convey universal truths, Doctorow's narrative, with its multiplicity of voices from commoners, comply with Peter Stallybrass and Allon White's definition of low discourse. According to the two scholars, low discourse contains the vulgar, popular and dialogic voices from the bottom of society, which are diverse and full of vigor. Different from the "global and totalizing" narrative schema of high discourse, "which orders and explains knowledge and experience" (Stephens, 1998: 5), they are more individualistic and de-generalizing, focusing on local conditions. The low discourse, such as the folk humor, curses, mockery in Rabelais's works, is "opposed to all that is finished and polished, to all pomposity, to every ready-made solution in the sphere of thought and world outlook" (Bakhtin, 1968: 3). The dispute between the high and the low inevitably involves the political struggle. The shift from high to low is often accompanied by the transfer of power from the super to the sub- in the cultural network.

The novel *City of God* is centrifugal in both its structure and subject matter, with its multiple narrative levels, polyphonic narrative voices, a hybridity of genres and self-reflexive quality. As Melvin Bukiet notes, "the apparent formlessness of the book paradoxically reveals its structure" (Bukiet, 2000: 2). The miscellaneous records of stories, birds observations, family histories, scientific theories constitute a narrative without a center or authority, in accordance with its thematic concern—the incredulity toward totality. Like a film, it involves "frequent interruptions, flashbacks and flashforwards, quick cuts, dissolves" (Oates, 2000). What penetrates the novel is the "Heist" story, with Pemberton as its protagonist. Pemberton's friend Everett turns out to be the writer of the "Heist" story, who is also responsible for the Author's bio, a long verse about his family history. The lost crucifix leads to the union of

Pemberton and Sarah at the end of the novel, after Sarah's husband has been killed. On hearing Sarah's conversation on his father, Everett creates a touching story on the holocaust experience of a little boy, with Sarah's father as its prototype. Interspersed in these main story lines, are Einstein and Wittgenstein's narration of their life stories as well as the crucial scientific/philosophical problems, both of which represent the most important turning point in history. There are some other anonymous voices (maybe Everett himself ?), discussing his/her meditation on Big Bang theory and other scientific theories. The existential songs of a band called the Midrash Jazz Quartet are recorded and interpreted in different ways. On many occasions, Everett breaks off his narration to describe his design of a film script. All these segments seem random on the surface but are interrelated in a cryptic way, contributing to the central theme of "a quest for an authentic spirituality" (Elie, 2000: 22).

First of all, Einstein and Wittgenstein act as the spokesman for the past century with their scientific/metaphysical discoveries. Einstein is mostly famous for his unprecedented notions such as relativity theory, and the immeasurability of electrons, which is later formulated by Heisenberg as the principle of uncertainty. The notion of uncertainty shocked the cognition of modern men who had expected the power of science to help them figure out all ultimate truths about life. Wittgenstein's subversive opinion on language, on the other hand, crashed all modernist beliefs in the magic power of language to know the world. As Wittgenstein claims in the novel, truths that can be spoken from the truths exist only in silence and "the truth of silence when spoken out, are no longer true"(Doctorow, 2000: 86). Wittgenstein's claim, like those of poststructuralists, questions the power of language to represent reality, pushing the modernist dream of pursuing truth through the medium of language even further. His ideas on language will later find resonance in Lacan and Derrida's views on the same topic: "language traps us in a prison-house where ultimate clear meanings can never be found as more signifiers can always be added on to the message commenting on the previous ones and so demanding a continual shift of meaning" (Rodriguez, 2002: 63). The elucidation on the scientific theories/ philosophical issues by two of the most crucial figures in the twentieth-century history, not only provides the background for the unfolding of other story lines, but also relates the scientific to the metaphysical—the two interdepending and conflicting forces of modern world.

The Heist story, with Pemberton as its protagonist, tells the rector's investigation of the lost crucifix in his church. It is disguised in the form of a detective story—a strategy Doctorow has employed in his previous novel *The Waterworks*. Pemberton, the skeptical rector, describes his searching journey as the job of a divinity detective. As a rector, he never conceals his predilection for detective novels, from which he can find comfort and the sense of security. The world of detectives, according to Pem, is "circumscribed and dependable" on its final unraveling of mystery and revelation of truth (Doctorow, 2000: 8), which can never be fulfilled in his world. Coincidentally, he finds out that Joshua Gruen, rabbi of the Evolutionary Judaism (EJ) synagogue, also shares this interest in detective stories. As Ludwig notes, Pem's quest in the story, along with Joshua and Sarah's, is a quest for meaning rather than for clear-cut answers of a case as normal detectives do. The quest is doomed to failure given Wittgenstein's statement on language and truth. However, Pem's spiritual quest for a believable God does not end up with complete despair. He finds hope in the EJ, the belief of Joshua and Sarah. According to Sarah, God is not to be found in the Bible, through the mediation of language. The old God in biblical classics needs to be reinterpreted and recast, according to the Jewish tradition of Midrash[1]

The Midrash tradition gives the inspiration that there exists not only one authoritative meaning which we must find (like detectives...like Pem, who attempts to fill in the gaps of a story) but many possible meanings the interpretive process of which we must participate in. In Midrash, readers look in-between words (the gaps of a text), as well as in space between God and man so as to keep the rabbinic belief that meaning comes to be in dialogue between man and God. One of the most important points that Sarah makes at her Friday night seminars is that the story of God is never finished. "The Jewish tradition of commentaries on commentaries is", says she, "the group voice trying to enunciate over time what it means to be a civilized human being... but the key to all of this is over time" (128). Since time is not finite, the everlasting need to improve upon and revise the story of God is for Sarah a "never-ending work-in-progress" (Bergstrom, 2010: 157). Continuous efforts to renew interpretations of this story should, in its inherent multiplicity, be an underlying theme of our stories. Therefore, for the followers of EJ, faith originates not from the God who is "sacramentalized, prayed to, pleaded with, portrayed, textualized, or given voice, choir, or temple walls", but from the God who is "imperceptible, ineffable, except... for our evolved moral sense of ourselves" (Doctorow, 2000: 256). Finally, under Sarah's influences, Pem chooses to convert to EJ and honor God not by "mechanical adherence to each and every regulation but by

---

[1]   Midrash is a practice in Jewish religion. The word literarily means the interpretation of scriptures.

going to the heart of them all, the ethics..." (250).

The trope of Midrash also makes the popular songs that appear in the novel seem relevant. These songs are interpretative commentaries on popular lyrics narrated by an anonymous voice. They are called Standards and played by a band named The Midrash Jazz Quarter, whose name also suggests the important role of Midrash. The songs appear here and there to suspend the narrative of stories, creating the fragmentary effect. For instance, a song named "Dancing in the Dark" is interpreted in three different versions, which shows the great power of interpretation to proliferate meaning. Besides this, there are notes of some unknown ornithologist (or Everett himself), recording his/her observation on the realm of birds. On many occasions, Everett the writer is shown to go out for a drink and have a conversation with the Pemberton, the figure in his fiction. He talks of the role of a writer and the creative process, which makes readers realize the fictive quality of literary writings. When the news of the lost cross is published in the newspaper, Pem complains to his friend Everett about the inaccuracy of the report. Everett responds by telling him his opinion on writing:

> "Well, Father, when you compose something, that's what you do, you make the composition. Bend time, change things, put things in, leave things out. You're not sworn to include everything. Or to make something happen the way it did. Facts can be inhibiting. Actuality is beside the point. Irrelevant" (48)

Everett's words reflect the metafictional element of postmodern narrative. The metafictional, by exposing the fictiveness of literary creations, points out the unrepresentability of reality and truth as they use language as medium, thus undermining the authority of writer as the ultimate arbitrator and instructor. As Foucault notes in "What is an author", in contemporary society, literature is made of a language game in which writing becomes "a question of creating a space into which the writing subject constantly disappears" (Foucault, 1984: 118). With the removal of the author, the meaning of a narrative is allowed to proliferate without constraint, and will eventually rest upon the different interpretations of the readers.

Doctorow's *City of God* is such a creative space where the writing subject constantly disappears. As Ludwig notes, Doctorow "creates a discourse in which he, the author, is in every passage, but is not the ontological subject of the text" (Ludwig, 2010: 80). Instead, the voices of the writing object seem to be writing the text. In fact, Doctorow himself expressed similar opinions on this matter: a novel is written "at the expense of the novelist's being" and that an author's identity is "dissolved" into the writing of the books. In the end, the writer becomes "mysterious to himself" (Bergstrom, 2010: 129). The presence of an author character (Everett) who co-exists with his writing object reminds us that the text is a fictive product created by the author. However, the author is but one of the many voices that appear in the novel, which produce a number of perspectives. Many a voices endows the novel with a multiplicity of witnesses, which makes it a polyphonic novel in Bakhtin's definition:

> A plurality of independent and unmerged voices and consciousness, a genuine polyphony of fully valid voices... What unfolds in his works is not a multitude of characters and fates in a single objective world, illuminated not by a single authorial consciousness, rather a plurality of consciousness with equal rights and each with its own world, combined but are not merged in the unity of the events. (Bakhtin, 1984: 6-7)

As a polyphonic novel, Doctorow's *City of God* surrenders the egoism of the sacred text. Its polyphonic structure fully matches Doctorow's thematic concern in the novel: the interrogation of the grand stories created by sacred texts and the pursuit of multiple interpretations in a diversified society. The focus on the individualistic and subjective experiences instead of on the universal conditions makes it a petty narrative with multiple perspectives, perspectives from commoners including the scientists, a writer, a clerical staff, a Holocaust survivor, an ornithologist, and some anonymous narrators. Its meaning is produced not by the author nor the narrator, but based on the conversations between its fragmented but interrelated texts, between serious genres and popular genres, between the texts and the readers. The ongoing conversation in the novel reflects an ethics of co-dependence—"a disposition to reach out to the "other" as a necessary part of self-affirmation. In this sense, *City of God* is a novel of "the saying", the "performative stating, proposing or expressive position of myself facing the other", which indicates a process that "cannot be reduced to a propositional description" (Critchley& Bernasconi, 2004: 15).

3. Recomposed History in *The March*

In his 1977 essay "False Document," Doctorow addresses the issue of history, a subject matter he constantly deals with in his novels. According to Doctorow, earlier novelists such as Cervantes and Defoe cunningly pretend that their fiction are based on real events so that the writer can achieve some sort of authority with their art of verisimilitude. Doctorow calls their work "document" because of their claim on the faithful representation of reality, but they are "false" for the pretension cannot change the fictive nature of their novels. The examples of Cervantes and Defoe serve to illustrate Doctorow's viewpoint that the historians are usually writers and there is no clear borderline between history and literature works. Citing Nietzsche, Doctorow states that, since facts—the necessary constitutes of history, cannot exist without prior introduction to meaning, they are inevitably influenced by "an organized consciousness", "instrumental" or "moral" (Doctorow, 1983: 23). As far as human history is concerned, facts are constantly "buried, exhumed, deposed, contradicted, recanted (23)". Specifically in American history, some people, such as the blacks, the Indians, and Chinese were written out of historical textbooks by historians of the country. Doctorow thus comes to the realization: "There is no history except as it is composed"(24).

Generally, Doctorow's analysis reveals two kinds of history, the one that is written by historians premised on the absolute authority of the writer, and on the objectivity of its content. It is the History in upper case—text of documents dominated by the authorial voice from the higher rank of society. In ancient China, only those officials assigned by the emperors or kings have the right to compile history. Even nowadays, history is written by the intellectuals who work in some specific institutions (universities or research centers, for example) for a unified national identity, in one way or another. The language of History, according to Doctorow, belongs to the language of regime as it depicts "a verifiable world". The other one is "histories", an alternative version of the History, completed by novelists such as Servantes and Defoe. They create the kind of "histories" out of imagination that exposes itself as fictive. The "histories" is in plural form because often multiple interpretations are given and meaning is produced in dispute instead of a certain one. The language of "histories" belongs to what Doctorow defines as the language of freedom because it inheres in "a private or ideal world that cannot be easily corroborated and verified" (17-18). Literarily, our society bestows the language of regime with more power as it is supposed to be more closely connected to truth. Doctorow thus claims: "the regime language" derives its strength from "what we are supposed to be" and "the language of freedom" consists of the power in what "we threaten to be"(18).

Doctorow's view of history to some extent fits Peter Stallybrass and Allon White's hierarchical conception of social discourse. According to the two scholars, high/low opposition exists in the field of history and some histories are deemed with more value and authority because their authors are located in the central position of power network. For Stallybrass and White, "[h]istory seen from above and history seen from below are irreducibly different and they consequently impose radically different perspectives on the question of hierarchy" (Stallybrass & White, 1986: 4). So the dispute between history seen from above and history seen from below is actually the fight for power or voices to represent different social groups. But the view on the past inevitably influences the present, as Croce claims in *History as the Story of Liberty*: "However remote in time events may seem to be, every historical judgment refers to present needs and situations"[1]. To prevent one dominant voice of history from submerging the other, Doctorow suggests, history has to "be written and rewritten from one generation to another", and the "act of composition can never end" (Doctorow, 1983: 24).

The March is actually Doctorow's recompositon of history from the various perspectives of the peripherals, a reflection of his idea on the language of freedom. In an interview with Charlie Rose in 2006, Doctorow reveals that his inspiration of the book comes from his reading of "a topical history of Sherman's campaign through Georgia and the Carolinas by a historian named Joseph Glatthaar"[2] some twenty year ago. He also draws upon some ideas from his occasional sight of a photograph of "Sherman and his generals sitting in front of a tent in the field"[3] and a picture of a Civil War photographer sitting in his wagon. Loosely following General W. T. Sherman's infamous scorched-land march from Georgia to North Carolina, and then to South Carolina, Doctorow's novel offers multiple perspectives of this historical event participated by people of different races, genders and social positions. Some of the characters are real and recorded by official history, while others are fictive, purely a product of imagination by Doctorow. Unlike official history that often centers on one or two important figures in a certain period of history, Doctorow's narrative moves like a painting continuously unfolding itself in front of the readers, characters appear and disappear while new faces are introduced into the canvas.

Among the major characters are confederate soldiers Will Kirkland and Arly Wilcox, Pearl, the milk-skinned daughter of a salve and slaveholder, Colonel Wrede Sartorius, an excellent military surgeon, Emily Thompson and Mattie Jameson, the white southern women who lost their home in the war, and General Sherman himself, a military strategist and a man full of humanity. There are also minor figures

---

① Quoted from Doctorow's "False Document" on page 24.

② "A Discussion with Author E. . Doctorow," interview by Charlie Rose, The Charlie Rose Show, January 2, 2006, from online sources, page unknown.

③ Ibid.

such as Sherman's adjutants Morris and Teack, the Civil War photographer Josiah Culp and his assistant Calvin Harper, General Grant and President Lincoln, who only appear at the end of the novel. The characters from different walks of society, with their multiple perspectives, offer a new interpretation of the March, a heterogeneous one with voices supplementing or contradicting each other. Noticeably, Doctorow creates the perspective not only of those generals, soldiers, but also of people from the bottom of the society whose life are inevitably involved in such a disaster. Marginal groups such as the deserters, poor whites, homeless women, the blacks are all given equal right to tell their stories. According to Eric Seymour and Laura Barrett, Doctorow's *The March*, by "giving voice to the marginalized and the repressed", "fashions alternate possibilities in order to reclaim historical agency for the individual" (Seymour & Barrett: 2009: 60).

Another feature of the novel is the blending of facts and fiction, which is not new in Doctorow's work. As earlier as 1975, he already employed this strategy in *Ragtime*—his most influential work so far. To Doctorow, there is no distinction between fiction and nonfiction; there is only narrative. History shares with fiction "a mode of mediating the world for the purpose of introducing meaning, and this is the cultural authority from which they both derive that illuminates those facts so that they can be perceived" (Doctorow, 1983: 24). So in *The March*, the readers are stunned to find General Sherman involved in an assassination plotted by a fictive confederate soldier Arly, who tries to shoot the general when the latter is posing for his photographing. Sherman's meeting with Lincoln in a small cabin—a famous event in history, is witnessed by an imaginary figure Dr. Sartorius, with his long monologue on the President. To Doctorow, his literary creation of history claims no less truth than official history, or even more. As Barbara Foley points out when he compares Doctorow with Dos Passos in their use of historical materials: "Doctorow treats with equal aplomb facts that are 'true' and those that are 'created', thus calling into question our concept of factuality and, indeed, of history itself." (Foley, 1983: 175) By commingling facts and fiction, *The March* questions the presentation of historical events to be transparent in official discourse. The history presented by Doctorow in *The March*, belongs to the history in plural form and in lower case. It is history seen from below, with multiple points of view from the least empowered group, thus is able to bear witness to the irrecoverable past and to inch forward to the dream of truth.

3.1. The Illusion of Objectivity

In 1864 when the Civil War had almost approached to its end, General Sherman marched a troop of 60,000 Union Soldiers through Georgia, South Carolina to North Carolina, joined by freed ex-slaves and white refugees who sought the protection of the army. This magnificent episode in American history left behind abundant information to its posterities—"letters, journals, memoirs, pension records, oral histories—which [enables them to] attempt, in some way, to interpret their [the recorder's] individual and collective experience" of the war (Hales, 2009: 146). Even General Sherman himself wrote a memoir, recollecting and commenting on this military operation. But it seemed that this memoir had aroused great controversy among the veterans who had been following him all along the way. Obviously, they had a different version of the events narrated by the general. Sherman therefore said, maybe the only satisfactory answer of this history lied in the materials locked in the cabinet of War Department in Washington, D. C. In defense of his own account of the Civil War, he wrote the following passage:

> In this free country every man is at perfect liberty to publish his own thoughts and impressions, and any witness who may differ from me should publish his own version of facts in the truthful narration of which he is interested. I am publishing my own memoirs, not theirs and we all know that no three host witnesses of a simple brawl can agree on all the details. How much more likely will be the difference in a great battle covering a vast space of broken ground, when each division, brigade, regiment, and even company naturally and honestly believes that it was the focus of the whole affair! (Sherman, 2000: 5)

For Sherman, history is dependent on the impressions and experiences of individuals. There is seldom unanimous opinion on what happens in the past since the participators may stand from different angles to view and present the event. Sherman's opinion on history coincidentally accords with that of Doctorow. The democratic view he invests in writing history is remindful of Doctorow's claim on the multiplicity of witnesses in *Reporting the Universe*. But his hope of finding the authorial and faithful record of the past in official history (the archive of the state) may prove to be an illusion. As Doctorow claims, meaning must be introduced before the representation of facts. During the process, the realm of facts is inevitably intruded by organized consciousness, political or moral. In the novel, Doctorow's individualistic account of the March exposes the ideological intrusion into facts in official record. By revealing the discrepancy between historical account and reality, his narrative deconstructs the authority of official history as the only reliable source of understanding the past.

The novel begins with the scene of the imminent invasion of the marching corps into the city Fieldstone in Georgia, where the owner of a plantation John Jameson, his wife Mattie Jameson and the whole family are struck by panic and planning to escape. Through the complaint of Mattie's aunt Letitia Pettibone, General Sherman's image comes to the view of the readers and he will reappear only pages later. According to the Southern Lady Letitia who once invited Sherman into her house and was impressed by his civilized manner, the famous general is drastically different internally and externally: Despite of his genteel appearance, he is a demon-like existence, "a savage with not a drop of mercy in his cold heart" (4), for he allows his men to loot, burn and kill wherever his army marches.

After the Jameson family's fleeing, Pearl, the fifteenth-year-old illegitimate daughter of master John Jameson and his slave Nancy, is left in the deserted plantation by herself. She comes across the Union officer Clark and his foraging group, who ride out to rummage the plantation for supplies they need. Colonel Clark comes from a prominent family in Boston. As a young man enlisted in the midst of the battle, he is unfortunately sent to the foraging column, a service ungraceful in his opinion. Different from his junior officers who are "scarcely literate", Clark is a cultured man prone to serious contemplation. Viewing his men slaughtering, looting, burning, laughing, and leaping around as if they were holding a party, Clark feels horrified and troubled by the scene, knowing that he had better not look at their savagery acts.

In fact, on November 9th of 1884, the historical Sherman issued a Special Field Order No. 120, outlining the foraging policy his army would adopt through the southern land: "the army will forage liberally on the country during the march" under the strict provision that "[s]oldiers must not enter the dwellings of the inhabitants, or commit any trespass" (Sherman, 2000: 652). Sherman, in his memoirs, proudly claimed that all the details of the order had been faithfully carried out by the soldiers, declaring that '[the] general orders made for this march appear to me … so clear, so emphatic, and well-digested, that no account of that historic event is perfect without them … I insist that these orders were obeyed as any similar orders ever were."(647) But in the novel, the anarchic acts of soldiers are everywhere to be seen, which turn the south into a land of rubbles and ashes. Even a civilized officer like Clark knows that he can do nothing to stop his man and what he has witnessed is only "an example of orders issued unspoken from the rank and file."(Doctorow, 2005:

11) When writing a letter home, he feels he cannot give a coherent explanation of what really happened in the war so that he has to keep reticent on sensitive matters. Through his experiences in the army, Clark realizes the discrepancy between official record of the war and the real situation: even the generals issue orders "for the sake of record only" while the army has its "strange currents of willfulness and self-expression" that flow out of military discipline (11). With an indiscernible desire for the beautiful Pearl, Clark disguises her as a drummer boy in his column to keep her under his protection. But soon, Clark is captured and crudely killed by the southern guerrillas in an operation, leaving Pearl roaming on the road again. Accidentally, the disguised Pearl encounters Sherman's army.

The image of Sherman in *The March* is far from the war hero or demon general oversimplified by historical textbooks. Instead, he is represented as a multifaceted and contradicted figure. The multifaceted character of Sherman is filtered through different perspectives on him by various figures in one way or another related to him, his adjutants, doctor Sartorius, the freed salves, the mix-colored girl Pearl, etc. Sherman firstly appears in the eyes of Pearl as a casually outfitted man sitting on a disproportionately little horse, "with his tunic covered with dust and half unbuttoned"(74), not at all like an officer in either deportment or dress. Mistaking Pearl as a white drummer boy, Sherman treats her with patience and tolerance, like a real father will do to his son (In fact he has just lost his son Willie). Faced with the terrified Pearl, Sherman comforts her gently, admitting that "Sometimes I want to cry, too"(75). But to Major Morrison, a West Pointer on the General's staff, Sherman's sloppy uniform and behavior of sharing hardships with soldiers do not match his position. He feels demeaned by Sherman's appearance and manners although he does his job as a signal officer impeccably and never shows any expression of disrespect. As a "good student of human nature"(77), Morrison also finds that the true General is not the man who cares little about honor as he demonstrates to the public. After the fall of Atlanta, the General pretends not to take seriously the mails that come in, "the plaudits, the expressions of gratitude akin to worship"(77). But in private, Morrison observes the "joy of triumphal vindication in his soul and his obvious feeling of superiority to all those, including the President, who had sent their congratulations", which is in stark contrast to the "calm rectitude" and modesty displayed in his correspondence (77). Like tiny fragments in a painting of collage, the various viewpoints provided by these spectators juxtapose the image of a famous general of flesh and blood.

In chapter XV, the perspective is shifted to General Sherman himself, whose inner monologue reflects that the true motivation behind the Civil War may not be as justifiable as that proclaimed in official discourse. It is known that the Civil War was fought between the northern Union and southern Confederacy because the southern states attempted to found an independent country to keep its slavery system intact. Although President Lincoln stated in his famous Gettysburg speech that the war was waged for their forefather's ideal—liberty and equality[①], Sherman's monologue shows him not as a hero devoting himself to the great cause but a racist who fights the war for political reason. One of Sherman's infantry, chased by the confederate army, destroys the pontoon bridge they have built after the last soldier crossed the river, leaving thousands of ex-slave followers to the prey of revengeful slave masters and guerrillas. To Sherman, the strategy is not blamable as the life of his soldiers are more precious than that of the blacks. Critiqued by Secretary of War Edwin Stanton for his cruel treatment of ex-slaves, Sherman feels outraged:

> I must abase myself to the slaves. Damn this Stanton—I am sworn to destroy the treasonous insurrection and preserve the Union. That is all. And that is everything. (120)

For Sherman, the war is waged to preserve the Union from separation. As he thinks in the novel: "I am no abolitionist" (120). In fact, historical record indicates that his wife's family possessed large amounts of slaves and she brought some to her new home as part of dowry when marrying Sherman. In a letter to a friend, Sherman confessed that Mrs. Sherman couldn't run the family normally without the assistantce of the slaves. In this sense, Sherman is far from the hero who "dedicated [himself] to the great task" as claimed by President Lincoln (Lincoln, 2000: 337). In the novel, it is in order to "shut up Edwin Stanton" and "disengage the niggers" who have become the burden of the army (Doctorow, 2005: 120), that Sherman gives Field Order Number 15: The Sea Island from Charleston south, and all the abandoned plantation along the rivers for thirty miles inland in South Carolina, and part of Georgia and Florida, are reserved for black resettlement. In other words, the order is given not for the interests of the blacks but due to political and military consideration. An irony of this part is when Stanton secretly interviews a black elder in Sherman's army, asking of his opinion on this racist general, the black man shows

---

① Abraham Lincoln's Gettysburg speech starts with: "Fourscore and seven years ago, our forefathers brought forth upon this continent a new nation, conceived in liberty, and dedicated to the proposition that all men are created equal." Lincoln, Abraham. *The Life and Writings of Abraham Lincoln*. Eds. Philip Van Doren Stern. New York: The Modern Library: 2000. p.336.

high regard for the general, a fact Sherman only knows later.

Marching into Columbia, the capital city of confederate south, Sherman feels that his order can hardly constrain the soldiers, who after a long time of toiling and fighting, turn to remorseless fun-makers, rapist, looters, and arsonists. Under their anarchist destruction, Columbia loses everything and becomes a city on fire. Stunned by the magnitude of fire in Columbia, Sherman walks onto the street, only to discover the scenery of the earthly hell:

> His troops were everywhere drunk. Some stood in front of burning houses cheering, others lurched along, arms linked, looking to Sherman like a mockery of soldierly bond. It was all in hideous accord, the urban inferno and moral dismantlement of his army. (Doctorow, 2005:182)

Even the most disciplined veterans who have followed him hundreds of miles become "demons laughing at the sight of entire families standing stunned in the street while their houses burned" (182). In face of such disaster, Sherman murmurs to his adjutant Colonel Teack, "Christ, what are we doing in this war but consuming ourselves."(184) Teack feels embarrassed for the general as the latter debases the war, which is just and great in the mind of Union soldiers, to an act of self-consuming. Like Clark, Sherman also feels the "strange currents and self-expression" of army that cannot be represented by paper documents. He does not interfere with anything he sees, "possibly understanding that, in this state of anarchy, challenges to his authority might arise"(182). These details on the road of the March reveal the true pictures of the war, especially its cruelties and anarchy, thus "defying the surety and conviction of Sherman's narrative account of his army's conduct" (Seymour & Barrett: 2009: 50).

The discrepancy between historical record and reality arises not only from the use of language. Even photography, the medium purported to restore the past in an entirely verisimilar way, turns out to be subjective and ideological. In an interview, Doctorow tells the host that the Civil War is to some extent the first modern war in human history. In this war, modern technologies such as advanced weapons and telegrams were widely used. Furthermore, large amounts of photographs are left to restore the bloody scenes of the war. When Confederate solider Will Kirkland dies miserably in the arms of his friend Arly Wilcox, the most touching scene of the novel appears:

> Sighing, Arly put his arm around. And the two of them sat that way in the quiet of

burned air under the blackened trees, neither the dead man or the living inclined to move. (Doctorow, 2005: 171)

At this time, a U.S. photographer named Josiah Culp appears with his black assistant Calvin, carrying their instrument in a mule-drawn wagon. Arly is asked not to move so that the photographer can take a picture of them. According to Culp, the dead man is the perfect image he has been looking for. He knows it when he sees it. Culp's words reveal the ideas on photography in the last half of the 19th century: meaning is there only for people to discover it. According to Miles Orvell, the most desired effect in the nineteenth-century photography is "typification", the presentation of a "general truth" (Orvell, 1989: 73). Orvell further states that "[w] hat one finds, in short, is that even while the image was presented as a 'document', the photographer was constructing a general representation, a simulacrum of the real thing.... Verisimilitude was the goal, verity was the claim" (95). Thus, making photographs is sacred work, the possible way to access truth, as Culp's assistant Calvin later remarks, "It is fixing time in its moments and making memory for the future...There is no higher calling than to make pictures that show you the true world" (Doctorow, 2005: 308). Being able to fix images spontaneously and in a duplicative way, the art of photography erases the trace of human operation in the process, and thus obscures its role of complicity in social discursive construction. The manipulative nature of photography is reflected as the photographer chooses what he/she wants to shoot, from what perspective, and what poses the objects should take. After the death of Culp, Arly replaces his position and takes a photo of his dead companion Will in the uniform of southern soldier, in the hope of showing it to Will's family and letting them be proud of the young man who has sacrificed himself for the nation. But the truth is that Will is a coward deserter, who never fights a battle for his southern homeland. He dies in an accident rather than in the battlefield. In this sense, photography becomes the vehicle of manipulating truth by the photographers. Thus, in *The March*, photography ends up to be the perfect trope to interrogate the objectivity of official historical discourse. As Seymour and Barrett point out, with the use of this medium, the Civil War initiated an era of vicarious experience: "public faith in the identity between photographs and events made it possible for historical knowledge to be determined by an expert class of practitioners driven by ideological, economic, or political interests". (58)

As a result, the coherence and unity, which emerge from "the represented historical world", are "attributable to the writer's power as teller of history" (Cooper,

1993: 112). Thus, in Doctorow's novels, it is "the process of historical reconstruction itself, rather than what is being represented, comes to the fore" (112). Now that history is subject to artificial construction and manipulation, it is not historians' privilege to write it. Therefore, Doctorow claims, "history as written by historians is clearly insufficient" and novelists can write even better histories. According to him, the historical figures in his novel, like General Sherman, General Grant and President Lincoln are more real than the ones represented by historians. Unlike historians who insist on the objectivity of their account, at least the novelists admit that their works are fictional. So in *The March*, Doctorow portrays not only historical figures but also fictional ones, in the hope of writing better histories. These figures commingle with each other, their voices dialoging or contradicting, creat the effect of heteroglossia[①].

3. 2. A history from the below

In an interview with Donna Seaman, Doctorow expresses his appreciation of Shakespeare and Tolstory's fiddling with history. He thinks that in the United States, people tend to be naïve about history: We think history is "Newton's perfect mechanical universe, out there predictably for everyone to see and set their watches by" (Seaman, 1994: 239). But in fact, it's "more like curved space, and infinitely compressible and expandable time. It's constant subatomic chaos." (239) Every day around the world, history is compiled and manipulated in a malign way to meet the demands of dictators, politicians, and other privileged social groups. Outrageously, Doctorow gives the example of Japanese government who rewrites historical textbooks to eliminate the facts of their invasion of China, especially of the numerous atrocities they have committed. He realizes that George Orwell has already spoken out the truth in *Nineteen Eighty-Four*: "History is a battlefield" where battles are constantly fought over by different powers "because the past controls the present"(239). People at the center of power structure can write their history while losers have no history. That's why "[there] are no failed revolutions, only lawless conspiracies". (Doctorow, 1983: 24)

In Doctorow's novel *Ragtime*, the partial perspective of WASP (White Anglo-

---

① Heteroglossia is terminology in Bahktin's works, which means the variety of language or the hybridity of discourses, which stands opposite to a monotonous voice of the standard or official language. In "Discourse in the Novel", he makes the point in a very explicit way, " A stylistic analysis of the novel cannot be productive outside a profound understanding of heteroglossia, an understanding of the dialogue of languages as it exists in a given era." Bakhtin, Mikhail. *The Dialogic Imagination*. Ed. Michael Holquist. Trans. Carl Emerson and Michael Holquist. Austin: University of Texas Press, 1981. p.417.

Saxon Protestant) family that dominates social discourse in the Progressive Era is taken at issue. In the eyes of the white middle class family, "There were no Negroes. There were no immigrants." (Doctorow, 1996: 3). But the following chapters tell the stories of the Jewish immigrants and the blacks from their respective viewpoints, contradicting the so-called facts from the WSPA perspective of mainstream society. The same strategy is also employed in *The March*. In this novel, one event is often recurrently narrated from different perspectives, which diverge from and contradict with each other, demonstrating the limitation of the unified and coherent writing of official history. For Doctorow, "It may have been impertinent for a Northerner to have written this book but I think of it as a national novel and I gave voice to everyone in the book, I had to give everyone their justice, whatever it was" (Yee, 2005: 75). Politicians, generals, officers and presidents who constitute the main voice of the war in historical textbooks become minor characters in Doctorow's narrative while marginal groups like the black slaves, prisoners, powerless women, and trash whites are put in prominent positions to speak out their stories. It is these people who have a firsthand experience of the destructive power and cruelties of the war. Their accounts of the war are always in sharp contrast to the perspective of the "top". Their voices, as Peter Stallybrass and Allon White state, impose a counter-view in the construction of social discourse about the past that inevitably influences the distribution of power at present.

3. 2. 1. The absurd world of common soldiers

Confederate soldiers Arly Wilcox and Will Kirkland are among the most important characters in the novel. Both of them come from the bottom of the southern society. With the ability to disguise their true identity and shift their way from one side to other "as the situation demands"(Doctorow, 2005: 63), they are able to view the war with a perspective different from others. As the book begins, the two are imprisoned in the opposite cells of a Confederate penitentiary, Arly for sleeping on a picket duty and Will for deserting. Due to a lack of hands in militia, they are forced to sign a paper of allegiance to defend the Confederate government in exchange for freedom. When the battle starts, Arly and Will find the scene too horrible to bear and out of instinct for survival, they put on the blue uniform of Union soldiers, deserting the South army. On their way of fleeing, they join in the victory party of the Union troopers in Milledgewille, pillaging, gobbling and having fun. Awaking in the morning, they find the army has gone at midnight and they are left alone. Back on the road, they are unfortunately caught by their own men, forced to claim allegiance to the Confederate government again and assigned the task to guard the northern prisoners. At this moment, Arly and Will are able to witness the inhuman treatment these prisoners have received: they are herded in the freezing rain, "wet, bedraggled, skeletal", and starved to death (65). Rescued by Sherman's army, Arly and Will, who have put on the blue uniform of the dead prisoners, join the Union soldiers again and enjoy their carnival after the army's occupation of Sanvannah. But when they are indulging themselves in the whorehouse, the army is gone. In order to catch up with the marching troops, Will goes out to get a horse. In the dispute with a black man for the horse, he is severely injured and later dies in the arms of Arly. Arly takes the place of Culp Jossiah, the photographer who accidentally died of heart attack. Disguised as a photographer who volunteers to take a picture of Sherman and his officers, he plots to assassinate Sherman, which he believes is God's plan. When the assassination fails, he is shot to death by the firing squad.

Arly and Will's experiences in the war suggest an absurd world "where life is haphazard and meaningless" (Cai, 2013: 102). Their identity as grassroots from the bottommost of white society determines that "who they were, where they were, was [now] a matter of total indifference to the universe" (Doctorow, 2005: 97). Unlike the generals and officers who find their cause just and noble, Arly and Will is pushed to the battlefield by the ambitions of politicians. Their only concern in this war is survival. As Arly tells Will, "if it is any good reason for war, it ain't to save Unions, it certainly ain't to free the niggers, it ain't to do anything but have you a woman of your own ..."(99) Compared with the young Will who still has some impractical illusion about war, Arly is the sophisticated one who penetrates the mystified veil of it. Commenting on Will's naïve view on war, he cries in a sarcastic way: "I am standing with this boy here who thinks an army at war is a reasonable thing." (64). Apparently, to Arly, the world has gone crazy and people live in an insane state because of the war. Arly's opinion is complemented in the episode of Columbia when civilians and injured soldiers are transferred to the college campus as the whole city is set on fire. Hearing the asylum residents locked in the dungeon roaming, screaming and moaning in the dungeon, the refugees on the campus can't help feeling that the world is out of control and all is "fire and madness and death"(191).

However, despite their agileness, Arly and Will inevitably lose their life in this crazy war. In the mind of General Sherman, soldiers like Arly and Will are merely "a weapon" and the death of them "a numerical disadvantage, an entry in the liability column"(395). He admits that it is the generalship that reduces the weight of death, diminishing his imagination of it. The March that has butchered hundreds of thousands of life seems to Sherman merely an event that invests every town, every river, and every road of south with meaning. Compared with city life, he prefers the life of the March "where nobody could tell him to do" and "no envy", "no praise [will] explode in your face" (121). To Sherman's general of right wing Kil Kilpatrick, the March gives him a chance to hoard wealth, which he has amassed a lot from looting. During the combats, he even indulges himself in the romance with a southern belle and her mother. When he finds a slave Jean-Pierre good at cooking, he declares his freedom but immediately inducts him into the army as his personal chef.

Different from these officers from the higher rank of military hierarchy, Arly and Will's struggle for life in the March tells the cruelties of war on the side of common soldiers. Thus their account diverges from and even contradicts Sherman's viewpoints in both the novel and his memoirs. As Cai Yuxia notes, their ironic and absurdist narrative, a divergence from the perspective of Sherman's and his juniors, composes an "antithesis" to "the rigid and authoritative narratives of the mythic March" (Cai, 2013: 101).

3. 2. 2. Women in search of independence

To southern women like Emily Thompson and Mattie Jameson, Sherman's march means a nightmarish experience, in which they lose everything, including their beloved, their property, and the southern culture that has nurtured them. Attached to the marching army for survival, they begin to get rid of their past role as daughter or wife or mother, grow tough and mature, and eventually grope for the meaning of freedom and independence in this life of movement.

Emily is the daughter of the distinguished Judge Thompson. Her brother, enlisted in the Confederate army, has been killed in a battle. During Sherman's occupation of Milledgeville, her father Judge Thompson is seriously ill and dies in the night when Colonel Wrede Sartorius's medical column settles down in their house. In the eyes of Emily, men are "jungle creatures" who make the war and "gallop off waving their swords and screaming about honor and freedom" while women have to pay for their combative instinct. The death of Judge Thompson leaves her "hollowed out" and she feels the war has "wipe[d] her past"(34). Horrified by the scene of fighting and killing around, Emily finds solace and warmth in Colonel Sartorius, the surgeon who treats her kindly and always appears with his "impeccable manner". She follows the division of Sartorius's surgery wagon and becomes a nurse in his field hospital. Attracted by Sartorius's gentility and medical skill to save life,

Emily develops a sentiment toward him and becomes his lover, melting herself into the unstable life of the marching with the Union soldiers.

One day when the army is parading into a city, Emily feels herself gazed by the southern women whom she used to be a part of. They look at her as if she were a whore. Emily begins to scrutinize her life and contemplate on the issue of identity. The experiences in field hospital make her realize that Sartorius is not a doctor of compassion as she imagines. In a surgery on a raped victim, Emily fails to detect any "recognizable emotion" from Sartorius, who obviously takes the victim only as a medical object, a surgical challenge. Emily hence concludes that Sartorius is not a doctor at all but "a magus bent on tampering with the created universe", the "embodiment of cold-blooded science" (Doctorow, 2005: 189-190). This understanding propels her to depart Sartorius and pursue a life of her own. Emily's story ends here, leaving a mystery, which is unveiled very later from Arly's perspective. Arly's narrative line reveals the whereabouts of Emily after her jilting of Sartorius: she does not return to the "women of her class, the same whom she had lived among all her life" but becomes the patron of the southern children orphaned in the war in an orphanage (213).

Compared with Emily, Mattie Jameson is a more docile and impassive female character. Before the war, she is the perfect wife and mother in Jameson plantation—"the angel in the house"[①]. Married to a husband who is twenty years older than her, Mattie tolerates John's bad temper, cruelty, and infidelity. As she secretly confesses, she always has to "give in, to revise her opinions, to gainsay her own judgments" in front of John's overbearing nature, just as she submits to her domineering sister before marriage (Doctorow, 2005: 107). So the compliant Mattie turns a blind eye when John Jameson has an affair with their salve Nancy who gives birth to an illegitimate child Pearl. She does not stop Jameson when he lashes at someone in the plantation or sells slaves, tearing families apart. Feeling humiliated by Pearl's existence, she just ignores her, never showing her any kindness. When the family leaves Fieldstone at the eve of its fall, she is relieved that her husband has no inclination to take Pearl with them. As Pearl comments in a conversation with Stephen Walsh: the wife ma'm is "[a] weak thing"; She just likes to "play her piano and let the world be" (285). After the death of John in a dispute with a Union

---

① "Angel in the house" is originally a narrative poem written in 1854 by Coventry Patmore to dedicate to his wife. The imagery is used to describe the ideal femininity of his wife, who devoted herself selflessly to her children and to her husband, a symbolization of ideal womanhood in Victorian England. But later the idea is criticized by feminists as the embodiment of patriarchal projections on the role of women.

soldier, the grief-stricken Mattie falls into a "blessed state of dreaminess"(192). Only with the help of Emily and Pearl does she survive and stay in Sartorius's medical group, in the hope of finding her two sons with the procession. Facing Pearl, Mattie recalls her maltreatment of her back in their house. Now she secretly confesses that she is far from the "good Christian woman" she always considers herself to be. She realizes that "this child of her husband's sin" has come to "announce such upheavals of fortune as only God in his vengeance could design"(112). Meanwhile, the bloody scene of Sartorius's field hospital arouses in her the maternal instinct to nurture. It seems that her personal affliction is made indistinguishable by the world at war. She awakes from her numb state and learns to make herself useful as instructed by Pearl, comforting patients, folding towels, and nursing the injured. As an exchange of Pearl's kindness, she teaches the girl to read and write, making up her negligence in the past.

Finally, Mattie grows strong enough to endure the loss of her elder son John Junior. When Pearl has smuggled her little son Jamie out of his imprisonment, Mattie is able to unite with her only family member alive. Although there are numerous obstacles waiting on their way back home, with a mother's determination, Mattie, like other grieving mothers of the south, will rebuild their homeland and revitalize their culture.

In a sense, Emily and Mattie represent the upper-middle class women deprived of anything that they can rely on by the war. Before the war, they play the traditional roles of daughter, wife or mother as required by the patriarchal society, submissive and fragile. They are the hostesses of a prominent family, with crowds of slaves doing the household chores for them. The lady in the eyes of the public, they subject themselves to the will of the father or husband in the family. Forced to the front of fire and blood by the war, they have to learn to grow strong and independent. To a large extent, it is the war that has changed the public view on gender, destabilized the traditional social order, and forged their new identity. In this catastrophe initiated by men, they have suffered but won something more precious.

3. 3. 3. The ex-slaves' struggle for freedom

As Doctorow points out, there is no absolute protagonist in the novel. If there is, it is the March itself, a monster that has uprooted the southern civilization entirely, making life a floating experience[①]. When the marching troops approach to Fieldstone, the freed blacks in Jameson Plantation, Jake Early and Jubal Samuel, watch an unprecedented view: At first, it is the change of color in the sky that is "gradually clarified as an upward-streaming brown cloud"; then "the brown cloud took on a reddish cast", moving across the sky to the south of them (Doctorow, 2005: 9). When the sound of cloud reaches them, it is nothing that they have ever heard before, "like thunder or lightning or howling wind, but something felt through their feet, a resonance, as if the earth was humming."(9) The poetic description of the marching, with its color and sound, foreshadows the impact the March brings to these people will be "unprecedented", "as if the world was turned upside down" (9).

Pearl, the illegitimate daughter of John Jameson and his slave Nancy Wilkins, is also among the liberated blacks. Like Mattie and Emily, Pearl suffers from the psychological chaos brought about by the various changes in her life. In fact, Pearl's identity crisis comes not only from the male-oriented society, but also from her skin color. Disguised as a drummer boy in Clark's column, she feels ill at ease for her pretension as a white. She tells Clarke, "Sompun wrong bein a white drum boy" (43). But when the freed black men Jacob Early and Jubal Samuels come to search for her, Pearl blames them for their ostracizing her earlier in Jameson plantation and decides to remain with Clarke's company. In response to Early's accusation of her betrayal of her own people, Pearl says, "I ain't no Jez'bel". After the death of Clark, Pear volunteers as a nurse in Sartorius's medical column. The war makes her grow capable and mature, with the help of Mattie Thompson. When her father John Jameson is sent to the hospital, mortally injured, Pearl proclaims her self-emancipation in front of his deathbed. "I wish you was to wake up," she tells him, "so I could tell you I am free" (113). She helps her stepmother reunite with her brother Jamie, giving them twenty dollars (half of her savings) to get back to their home at Fieldstone. Facing her half-brother Jamie who once treats her crudely, she says: "[n] othin you will do in your life will be enough to pay us back."(291)

Despite her growth, Pearl is constantly confused by her double consciousness as half black and half white. She feels that she cannot be identified with the whites although she learns to speak in their way. But back to the camp of the black refugees, she feels upset by being taken as a white woman by her own folks. The sense of alienation always haunts her. Even with Stephen Walsh, the Union officer she falls in

---

① In a conversation with Colonel Sartorius, Emily Thompson talks of the war in this way: "I've lost everything to this war. And I see steadfastness not in the rooted mansion of a city but in what has no roots, what is itinerant. A floating world." (Doctorow, 2005: 61)

love with, she worries that this love will disempower her and continue to exploitate the past, making her a slave as her mother to John Jameson. Pearl is caught between the enslaved past and the freed present, and her predicament is not an exception.

Wilma Jones and Coalhouse Walker are among the black bondsmen who are set free after the coming of Sherman's marching troops. Embracing their newly gained freedom, they join the march in the hope of living a new life. But the episode of Ebenezer Creek makes them realize that if relying on the whites, they can never be free. Chased by the Confederate army, the Union soldiers destroy the pontoon bridge after they have all crossed the river, leaving thousands of black refugees to the hands of revengeful masters and guerrillas. As the witness of this event, Wilma is stunned to watch her people "screaming, praying, importuning God" (70). In despair, some even plunge into the water and drown themselves. Some, according to the later account of the Secretary Stanton, are murdered by guerrillas. Luckily, Wilma is able to board on a raft and gets rescued by Coalhouse when the raft is sinking. To Sherman, what happens at Ebenezer Creek is "military necessity". But from the perspective of the blacks like Wilma, the incident symbolizes their abandonment by the white people who claim to come to their rescue and to bring light to them.

After the twists and turns on the road of the March, Wilma Jones and Coalhouse Walker finally arrive at Savannah. They begin to discuss their future after the enactment of Sherman's Field Order Number 15. They have to make a choice between making a living in the northern big cities as Wilma has fantasized or by the forty acres on a farm promised to each freedmen head of household. Arguing that "a man who owns his own land is a free man", Coalhouse eventually persuades Wilma, who acknowledges that their former enslavers derive their power from land ownership (127). She comes to agree with Coalhouse that in "staking a claim, you stake out your freedom" (128). Wilma and Coalhouse's last appearance in the novel shows them crossing paths one last time with a parade of marching troops. As the literate Wilma completes the land application, she asks Coalhouse how he wants his name to appear on the document. He answers "Coalhouse Walker, Sr.," and then declares "Just come along to the preacher, if you please, and I promise you before you know it there will be a Coalhouse Walker, Jr." (128). Since their son Coalhouse Walker Jr. in Doctorow's other novel *Ragtime* becomes the victim of racial discrimination in the 1910s, the narrator seems to indicate that the freedom Wilma and Coalhouse has pursued is far from being fulfilled as their descendent still lives in the shadow of racism.

In the official history on the Civil War, narrative focuses are often placed on the people whose decision-making influences historical process such as the President, government officials, the marshals, the generals, etc. The blacks, the women, common soldiers and other characters from the bottom of the society are considered to be the other, often ignored and silenced in the historical record. To remind his countrymen of this fact, Doctorow thus portrays an injured soldier Albion Simms in the novel. With a spike in his skull, Simms miraculously survives but forgets everything that happened in the past moment. His amnesia and final demise "deliver a dire warning against too much forgetfulness" in American history (Adkins, 2014: 767). The spike, which causes his memory loss and decline in health, becomes the metaphor of the mental spike embedded in the body of the nation, making it forgetful of its ideals of foundation—equality and liberty. In Doctorow's *The March*, the voices of the marginalized come to the fore and their multiple voices interpret the history of the March from different perspectives by which "[t]he stable, authoritative, the serious" official history is "loosened, mocked, subverted" (Parks, 1991: 56). Their perspectives thus make a history from the below, which dismantles the status quo constructed by the history from the above, reminding American people that some voices, including the blacks, the women, and other disempowered in the war should never be forgotten.

Chapter Four
The Dialogic Voice:
Transgression of Genres

1. "The Great Divide" and Postmodern Transgression

The categorization of culture into high and low, or the Great Divide as Andreas Huyssen called[①], has always been there in the western society but it only gained momentum with Mathew Arnold's publications in the last decades of 19th century. According to Arnold, only a small group of cultural elites have access to the "the best that has been thought and said in the world" (Arnold, 1954: 6), which is culture. The mass of mankind, satisfied with "inadequate ideas", "will never have any ardent zeal for seeing things as they (the elite class) are" (Arnold, 1960: 364-365). So by culture, Arnold actually means high/elite culture, in contrast to the state of anarchy represented by the working class, which to him, is "raw and half developed" and has to "be suppressed by the harmonious influences of culture"(Arnold, 1954: 165). Arnold's ideas on the hierarchy of culture influenced scholars of several generations in cross-Atlantic countries, including F. R. Leavis and T. S. Eliot, who generally assume that "culture has always been in minority keeping" and it is upon them "depend the implicit standards that order the finer living of an age" (Leavis and Thompson, 1977: 3). Arnold, Leavis, and Eliot—the believers of the Great Divide— commonly acquiesce that the minority (elite class) represents the center of cultural power, and they "set the standard of taste" as well (Leavis, 1978: 191). In contrast, the mass and their culture (popular/mass culture) are considered to be lack of value, intimidating to the authority of the high culture. In this sense, the Great Divide, as Huyssen points out, is established on the principle of exclusion, and "an anxiety of contamination by its other: an increasingly consuming and engulfing mass culture" (Huyssen, 1986: vi).

---

① American sociologist Andreas Huyssen uses the term "the Great Divide" to refer to "the kind of discourse that insists on the categorical distinction between high art and mass culture" (Huyssen, 1986: 23).

Although it is difficult to give a clear definition of popular/mass culture, Raymond Williams suggests that the reference to popular/mass culture usually indicates the following connotations: well liked by many and created to win the favor of the mass public; easier to be comprehended and always considered as "inferior kinds of work" compared to high culture (Williams, 1983: 237). Both Leavis and Eliot's works mention standards or tastes which project rules and boundaries deliberately set up by the cultural authority to maintain the social order based on the dichotomy of privilege and degeneration. For French sociologist Pierre Bourdieu, taste is a highly ideological concept and it always functions as a marker of class. So the categorization of culture into high/low is "predisposed, consciously and deliberately or not, to fulfill a social function of legitimating social differences" (Bourdieu, 1984: 5). But as Foucault indicates, the existence of boundary inherently generates the desire to transgress it. The divide between high art and popular culture is never that clear. The twentieth century witnessed the constant interrogation of and ferocious attack on the Great Divide, with the rapid development of popular culture or mass culture, represented by movies, advertisemerts, science fictions, pop music, etc. Faced with the entrenchment of popular culture, traditional critics bemoan the decline of the great tradition and the loss of authority for the elitist minority, who can no longer "command cultural deference" (Storey, 2009: 23). Especially when it comes to the 1960s, a sentiment arises which celebrates the revolt against canonization in the cultural field. Q. D. Leavis's opinion on this situation is representative and pertinent to be cited here:

> One danger which I have long foreseen from the spread of the democratic sentiment, is that of the traditions of literary taste, the canons of literature, being reversed with success by a popular vote. (Leavis, 1978: 190)

According to Q. D. Leavis, the masses of uneducated or semieducated used to be contented to acknowledge the supremacy of the classics of their race. But somehow of late she has perceived some signs, especially in America, of "a revolt of the mob against" literary masters. She thus feels anxious that the revolution against taste will "land us in irreparable chaos"(190). The movement in the 1960s, with its sentiment of experimenting with the revolt against the dead classics, becomes what we commonly understand as postmodernism today. Frederic Jameson argues that postmodernism was born out of "the shift from an oppositional to a hegemonic position of the classics of modernism..." (Jameson, 1988: 299) Andreas Huyssen, on the other hand, points out that postmodernism operates "in a field of tension between innovation and tradition, renewal and conservation, mass culture and high art, in which the second terms (tradition, conservation, high art) are no longer automatically privileged over the first" (Huyssen, 1986: 185). Anyway, in this movement called postmodernism, the Great Divide is interrogated, challenged and transgressed. The transgression of the boundary, as John Jervis claims, is "reflexive, questioning both its own role and that has defined its otherness" (Jervis, 1999: 4). As a result, what has been previously feared and excluded as the other is accentuated and appreciated. What has been peripheral now comes to the center in this movement. The popular culture, which used to be labeled as "escapism", "sheer entertainment", "relaxation" (Storey, 2009: 183), begins to be taken seriously into postmodern art. Among the postmodern transgressor, Andy Warhol is the key figure in theorizing pop art. He claims that what is commonly held as "real" art is defined simply by the taste of the ruling class of the period. This implies not only that "commercial art is just as good as 'real' art—its value simply being defined by other social groups, other patterns of expenditure" (183). So the transgression of the Great Divide literarily reflects one of the central concerns of postmodernism, that is, to question the validity of boundaries and restore the voices of the excluded social group.

The influence of popular culture on Doctorow's works is everywhere to be discerned. On many occasions, Doctorow talks of the role popular culture plays in our daily life as well as in literary creations. He thinks that with the penetration of mass media into individual life, the rhythms of our perceptions have changed; it is a fact a writer should not ignore when he creates. Having realized that reading novels especially difficult ones requires "an effort of the will" and that the public who have got used to the fast pace of commercials or films may find it intolerable to finish them, Doctorow puts accessibility as a priority of his writing. "I've always wanted my work to be accessible," he claims in an interview, "[l]iterature, after all, is for people, not some secret society."(Baker, 1999: 2) In another interview, he complements this opinion, "I want working-class people to read it, people who don't follow novels.... I want the reader to be as unaware of committing a cultural act as he is when he goes to the movies." (Gussow, 1999: 4) Now that popular culture has become an indispensable part of our daily life, Doctorow thinks that he can make his works more readable by blending popular elements into it.

In *Ragtime*, for instance, the power of popular culture is given full play by Doctorow: as three most important icons of industrial America at the beginning of 20th century, the images of ragtime music, cinema and newspaper penetrate the book and they are closely intertwined with the spirit of the time. It is a time when mass production of culture has become the trend and a consumerist society was taking shape. The popularization of films and music has changed people's perception of the world. The reachability of newspaper makes it a superb platform to convey information and to disseminate socio-political ideologies. More than that, Doctorow' narrative, influenced by the rhythm and style of these mass media, both appeal to readers for its entertaining effect and leave them space to contemplate on some serious questions.

But Doctorow's aesthetic transgression happens not only between literature and other artistic forms but also between classic genres and popular genres. In the field of literature, the 1960s marked a shift in the hierarchy of genres within it, so that in this era of changes "genres which were originally secondary paths, subsidiary variants, now come to the fore, whereas the canonical genres are pushed toward the rear" (Matejka and Pomorska, 1971: 85). Thomas G. Evans, in his commentary on E. L. Doctorow and John Steinbeck, made a list of comparison between the normative generic definition of the best sellers (popular novels) and serious modernist novels. He contends that compared with serious modernist novels, popular novels are often more conventional in style and form. They generally support received audience values and tend to be mimetic or didactic in representational form while the modernist novel "is generally written from a stance chiefly concerned with the self-expression of the artist or with the self-sufficiency of the aesthetic object"(Evans, 1987: 72). Most importantly, the best seller aims for maximum reader involvement while the modernist "typically employs a number of devices to distance the reader from characters and events"(72). Novelists like Doctorow and Steinbeck, concludes Evans, represent those who have tried to make their work bridge the gap between the two different realms. In fact, besides Evans, many other critics also have noticed Doctorow's crossing boundaries between serious novels and popular genres in his works. J. Bakker, for instance, using Wister's *The Virginian* as an object of comparison, argues that *Welcome* engages "the tendency of popular Westerns" without retreating from "difficult moral or social issues" (Williams, 1996: 70)

In his works, Doctorow adopts many materials that are considered to belong to the realm of popular literature, such as criminal novel, science fiction, Westerns, detective story, the so-called "secondary paths" or "subsidiary variants". He creates *Billy Bathgate*, a novel on gangster life, possibly out of inspiration from *Godfather*, a series of very influential gangster movies in the 1970s. *The Waterworks* and *City of God* are to some extent detective stories, each centering on a mysterious event to be solved through the investigation of its protagonists. *Big as life*, a work considered to be a total failure by Doctorow, takes the form of science fiction. In *Welcome to Hard Times*, Doctorow skillfully integrates into his novel Western genre, a unique genre in American culture. The Western as a genre includes numerous legends, stories, films, TV series on the "western expansionism" and "a manifest destiny west of the Mississippi River" (Pirnajmuddin & Keivan, 2014: 34), which together form a myth about American ideals—ragged individualism, self-sufficiency, and limitless opportunity. This frontier story, set in the Dakota Territory in the 1870s, includes a cast of characters readers would expect to encounter in a Western. Besides, other elements typical in Hollywood Western movies are employed: desolate town in the prairie, violent revenge, community in danger and heroism. By giving the readers a familiar or predictable set of characters and scene of the west, Doctorow, as James J. Donahue notes, is "conflating literature and kitsch by writing a serious work of American fiction, addressing serious problems of narrative and its relationship to myth, in the form of a western, popular genre" (Donahue, 2007: 46). But Doctorow's version of the frontier is different from that in the classic Westerns. Here, heroism is frustrated and human efforts to conquer the evil seem futile in front of the pervasive and mighty power of evil. More importantly, the west, a symbol of freedom and hope in classical Westerns, becomes an infertile wilderness impossible to be tamed by the reason and order of human society. In this sense, Doctorow's *Welcome* both integrates and subverts the Western genre, questioning and altering the frontier myth constructed by American popular culture.

In all, Doctorow's strategy in these novels, as Michael Wultz points out, is the "infusion of disreputable genres into the domain of respects of fiction", which suggests "a deliberate interrogation of the traditional distinction between high and low art..." (Wultz; 2003: 521). The use of popular culture contributes to the accessibility of Doctorow's works, making him a writer "greeted by both popular and critical acclaim" (Rogers, 1975: 134). His deliberate transgression of genre line calls into question the validity of literary authority, specifically the standards of literature, which reflects the anti-traditional spirit of 1960s. For Doctorow, the 1960s which has nurtured his rebellious spirit, represents a major cultural revolution on multiple fronts:

> It wasn't until the 1960s and the rise of civil rights and counter-cultural movements that Black Studies was created as a subject, as a discipline in universities. Before that it was as if in the United States there has been no black people or no contribution

of black people to the building of the United States. … To this day, there is no concerned or large effort to understand historically the tremendous contribution of the Chinese people to the developing of the United States. The role of women in our history has only recently begun to be defined… (Doctorow, 1988: 40)

The 1960s, as Doctorow characterizes it, was a period of great social upheaval, whereby various institutions were re-examined with a critical eye as to what was being ignored, what was being rejected and what had been effaced in the historical record. The writers from this period, as Bevilacqua has argued, increasingly "centered on the assimilation into mainstream literature of such 'ephemeral' genres as science fiction, the detective story, pornography and the western." (Bevilacqua, 1989: 78) The process of assimilation is in essence the continual dialogue between serious literature and the "disreputable genres"—the previous subject and its other in the Great Divide. To Doctorow, this dialogue is only part of the "conversation that goes on among works of art" (Doctorow, 2003: 5). In fact, as he notes, "the artists of every genre" have to respond "not only to life around them but to the work that has gone on before"(5). Artistic history is swarmed with this transgressive conversation among genres as composers may respond to poetry, painters to music and film writers to novels and so on. Specifically in the field of literature, every book, however original, replies to an earlier book. French sociologist and critic Julia Christiva terms this "relationality, interconnectedness and interdependence" among artistic objects "intertextuality"[1]. It is due to this transgressive vision that the rigid hierarchy in literary system is broken down and the border of literature is opened to embrace a world of change and diversity.

2. *Ragtime* and Popular Culture

When E. L. Doctorow was writing his fourth novel *Ragtime* in 1975, he may not have anticipated that it would turn out to be such a success. In the words of Kathy Piel's, large numbers of copies were sold and cash poured into the pockets of both the writer and publishers in the ragtime rhythm. As for popularity, it took the first place on the *Publishers Weekly* list for 15 weeks and stayed at the top of the *New York Time Book Review* for 13 weeks. The publishing house Random House and the author himself were to share millions of dollars' worth of benefits in less than a year, which was amazing for a serious book, as "it's really the first time so much money

---

[1]   Quoted from Graham Allen's *Intertextuality*. Published by Routledge in 2000.

has been connected with a book of such high quality" (Piel, 1998:405).

Nor had Doctorow imagined that the work would lead to so many controversies from academic circles. People who like it think highly of its "stylistic innovation" as well as its creative interpretation of American history. For example, Stanley Kauffmann appreciated *Ragtime* very much and called it "a unique and beautiful work of art about American destiny, built of fact and logical fantasy" (Kauffmann, 1975: 20). Yet, there were also different opinions, with a conservative belief that "any book worth so much money couldn't have much literary value" (Piel, 1998: 405). Because of its relatively simple plot and language, some reviews claimed that the book was "all surface", a charge that would haunt the book for the following years. In Frederick R. Karl's opinion, the work can not even be called a serious novel, as it was "like those musical comedy entertainments turned out by MGM and RKO in the 1930s", which "catered to all tastes" (Karl, 1983: 514). Harold Bloom took side with Karl, declaring that the work was overvalued and it was "far from being Doctorow's most eminent work" (Bloom, 2004: 7). It seems that all these negative comments reached the consensus that *Ragtime* was not thematically deep and serious enough to be called a good novel. The consensus reflects the commentator's prejudice against popular culture: if a piece of work appeals to large numbers of readers and wins widespread popularity, then it cannot be judged valuable according to the standard of serious literature.

In fact, what these reviews list as the sins of *Ragtime* turns out to be aesthetics Doctorow has been pursuing. As revealed earlier in his interview, Doctorow always wants to achieve in his fiction a relentless narrative, full of ongoing energy. *Ragtime* serves as an example of his artistic ideal: With short, darting sentences in long paragraphs, the narrative moves briskly in disconnected imageries, shifting in scenes and perspectives (Ostendorf, 582); the characters, deprived of psychological depth, seem flat and almost allegorical; the language—"mock pedantic historical" as Doctorow called it—is deceptively simple and objective, with occasional tinges of mockery. In a way, it is "irreverent and populist" which bridges over the distinctions between serious literature and pop culture. As Rogers acclaims, in *Ragtime* Doctorow has discovered "a form that is experimental and accomplished enough to appeal to critics who demand innovation and yet familiar enough to attract common readers". (Rodgers, 1975: 139)

Set in the first fifteen years of the twentieth century, specifically ranging from 1902 to the eve of WWI, *Ragtime* is often called a historical novel for its restoration of a specific era of American past. Due to its disruptive temporal structure, shifting perspective, large numbers of characters and random arrangement of events, it seems impossible to outline the story in a few words. Generally, *Ragtime* centers on three representative families—the WASP family, the Jewish family and the Black family, who embody the cultural diversity and social turmoil of the period. There are also historical figures like J. M. Morgan, Harry Houdini, Henry Ford, Emma Goldman, and Booker T. Washington. The historically real and the fictive are interwoven into a peculiar scene. They come across each other, interact with each other, and even deeply influence each other's life. Meanwhile, the private events of the three families are involved in the stirring public affairs at that time such as Peary's exploration of the North Pole, Freud's visit to America and the sensational socialist movements like the Lawrence and Paterson Strike. In this way, the fate of an individual has been closely knitted with the common destiny of the entire society.

Dubbed as the Progressive Era, the 1910s is also a time when America was initiated into the age of modernization, with the rise of mechanical reproduction on a large scale. Based on the principle of interchangeable parts, Henry Ford invented the assembly line, which enabled the workers to maintain in the same position to do repetitive work, so that the efficiency of industrial production was greatly promoted. The technological developments such as the popularization of phonographs, efficient printers, televisions and cinematic devices gave rise to the prosperity of popular culture represented by ragtime music, motion pictures, baseball, newspaper, magazines, and others.

As the title of the book indicates, the imagery of ragtime music permeates the whole book. In the first page, Doctorow has Scott Joplin to tell us, "Do not play this piece fast. It is never right to play Ragtime fast."[1] The major character Coalhouse Walker is a ragtime pianist. In his encounter with the white family, he performs Scott Joplin's famous pieces like "The Maple Leave". Ragtime, a musical genre that originated from black community and enjoyed its peak popularity between 1895 and 1918, becomes the epitome of the time and the key image to apprehend the narrative structure of this novel. Another major character—Tateh from the Jewish family— is closely related to the imagery of cinema. Drawing inspiration from the flipping movement of a serial of silhouettes, he develops the idea of motion picture and turns to a successful filmmaker in the end. The popularization of films reflects a time when people are eager to learn about themselves. As a tool of duplicating reality, films satisfy their need for self-knowledge. In the novel, we also find the ubiquitous

---

[1]   The epigram of E. L. Doctorow's *Ragtime, A Novel.*

presence of news reporting and press: the shooting of the famous architect Stanford White by Harry K. Thaw preoccupies the headline in the New York City papers; the presence of Thaw's wife Evelyn Nesbit as a testimony in his trial is widely covered by newspapers and Nesbit becomes a celebrity chased by press for her beauty and intimate relations with the rich; Coalhouse Walker's terrorist attacks are firstly reported by journalists and the negotiation between his gang and the municipal office is completed through the medium of newspaper; the arrested Emma Goldman makes a speech about her socialist belief which will have widespread influence because of media exposure. In a way, newspaper plays the important role of bridging the individual and the public, disseminating social ideologies and consolidating class stratification. To sum up, Doctorow has newspaper, ragtime music and cinema as the three most important icons to present the age of mechanical reproduction[①]. Compared with traditional artistic forms, these media are associated with mass production and characterized by various forms of duplications—a central motif in the novel. More importantly, they become a shaping influence on the narrative structure, language and style of the novel.

In many interviews, Doctorow has elaborated his point of view on the relationship between media culture and literature. He contends that the development of mass media especially the optical technology has changed our way of perception. The public, now accustomed to the fast pace, discontinuity and explosive information a media society has brought about, may find traditional realist novels, with its chronologic order, fastidious language and leisure style, boring and a trial for their patience. Therefore, writers, in order to make their works reach the common readers, should open themselves to the influences of these popular cultural forms. By incorporating the popular culture into his novel, Doctorow restores an episode of American history when the rise of mass media had profoundly revolutionized people's way of perception and even characterized the mode of representation. As Michael Wutz points out, in *Ragtime*, Doctorow locates his narrative as "a technological medium within an ecology of other contemporary media against which it, like ambitious fiction generally, has to define itself" (Wutz, 2003: 516). By melting the elements of the subsidiary artistic form—the popular culture, which is

---

① Critics including Berndt Ostendorf have underlined that the novel's three explicit examples of mechanical reproduction are the player piano, the Ford Model T, and the cinema. Allan Johnson extend the proposition further with the reminder that "the iconic nature of these inventions derives precisely from their role in the rise of mass culture at the turn of the twentieth century and their implication in the in the rise of a vast social machine of commerce and commodity" (Johnson, 2015: 90).

considered to be shallow, superficial and frivolous—into literary tradition, *Ragtime* links the serious literature with the popular culture, interrogates the boundaries between the high and the low, and revigorates the genre of fiction with bold experimentation.

2.1. The Ragtime Pattern

Originally a kind of music from black community, ragtime is written in "2/4 or 4/4 time with a predominant left-hand pattern of bass notes on strong beats (beats 1 and 3) and chords on weak beats (beat 2 and 4) accompanying a syncopated melody in the right hand"[①]. It obtains the name "rag" because the performer always has the right hand to play syncopated melodies in a "ragged" fashion. This music became extremely popular in the first twenty years of 20th century, even among the white community. In the 1920s, the popularity of ragtime declined, possibly with the rise of Jazz and other musical forms to replace its position. Just like Fitzgerald who intended to show the spirit of the 1920s and 30s with the image of Jazz music, Doctorow perhaps had the same ambition when he entitled his novel with the name of a musical form. Born into a family of music-lovers, Doctorow more than willingly admitted the influence of music on his writing:

> Some music is useful for me. I was quite taken by ragtime music at the time I was writing *Ragtime*. For *The Book of Daniel*, I was listening to a lot of 60s rock music and folk acoustic music which doesn't have linear way of advancing. You hear the same piece endlessly with slight modifications. It's sort of oriental. Philip Glass uses this kind of formal approach. The narrative in my novella does not advance directly but spirals around and around. It uses six or eight motifs and each time it comes around to a new motif it changes cycle. (Bevilacqua, 1990: 130)

As rock music describes the restlessness of the 1960s in *The Book of Daniel*, ragtime best represents the spirit of Progressive Era in *Ragtime*, a time that adheres to convention and order but simultaneously moves toward change. A superb metaphor, ragtime's combination of repetition on left hand and syncopation on the right fits the description of the time. At the beginning chapter of the novel, Doctorow depicts the American society at the turn of century in a panoramic way, appealing to nostalgia and sentiments of the readers of some seventy years later. Apparently, this narrative is unfolded from the perspective of the WASP family who has just moved into the house in New Rochelle, New York. This family is made

---

①   Quoted from Wikipedia. https://en.wikipedia.org/wiki/Ragtime.

up of Father, Mother, the Little Boy, Mother's Younger Brother and Grandfather. Father is an entrepreneur who makes a fortune "from the manufacture of flags and buntings and other accoutrements of patriotism, including fireworks" (Doctorow, 2006: 3). At this time in American history, "[patriotism] is a reliable sentiment" and there are great demands for flags and buntings, so Father's business goes well and expands. The white family are able to live a cozy life and indulge themselves in the fantasy of prosperity and progress. With a limited point of view, they believe that they are the center of the American society, and there are neither Negroes nor immigrants. Compared with the Jewish family and black family who suffer a lot and wish to change their fate, the New Rochelle family are the most conservative group politically. For them, reason and order are the key words and life is about maintaining the status quo.

Father, for example, is such a conventional figure who try to resist the power of change. Following the great explorer Pierre to the North Pole, he finds the journey on the icy land tedious and intolerable, and he has to write a journal to keep everything under control. Father has a firm belief in system. He considers journals a system as well, "the system of language and conceptualization" (63). When he returns from North Pole, he finds that everything in his family has turned different: his father-in-law becomes senile, his son has grown taller and lost some fat; and the servant is "no longer efficient or respectful" (92). Even his wife, who used to be gentle and docile, has something new in her. To his surprise, she takes charge of his business well and "she was in some way not as vigorously modest as she'd been" when in bed (93). On her bedside table there are feminist volumes like *The Ladies' Battle* and Emma Goldman's pamphlets. Immune to the widespread feminist and socialist movements sweeping the country, Father fails to shake off his prejudiced opinions on race and gender. The inability to change makes him unsympathetic to the sufferings around him, thus he is gradually alienated from the other members of the family. Like "an immigrant as in every moment of his life", the end of the novel shows that Father loses his life in a shipwreck in his journey for business negotiations, "arriving eternally on the shore of his Self"(269).

In contrast to Father's immobility is the change and transformation undergone by a majority of characters. Tateh, originally a Jewish immigrant from East Europe and a socialist, becomes a successful businessman due to his occasional invention of movie books. Disillusioned with the socialist ideas, he extricates himself from labor movements and ends up as a Baron Ashkenazy (he buys the title). In the end Tateh is able to regroup a new family with the Mother in white family. Mother's Younger

Brother, a member of the prosperous white family, falls in love with the sexy model Evelyn Nesbit. Under Nesbit's influence, he makes friends with well-known Emma Goldman and becomes a socialist-sympathizer. The unfulfilled love with Nesbit turns the young man into a frenzy inventor of new firecrackers and explosives, which paves the way for his future role as a radical militant. He finally dies in a battle in the resurrection of Mexica. The black man Coalhouse, at first appears in front of the white family as a civilized ragtime player. On his way to meet his lover Sarah, he encounters a gang of racists led by Willie Comklin, who tries to blackmail him and have vandalized his car. Coalhouse goes to the police for help but is rejected and humiliated. After the municipal authority ignores his demands for apology and for the restoration of his car, he resorts to violence to fight for his dignity and legal rights. And his deeds encourage numerous black campaigners for civil rights to trace his way. There are other minor characters whose fates have been under drastic changes. At the end of the story, the readers are informed that the anarchist Goldman who has influenced generations of people is exported and the popular sex goddess Evelyn Nesbit has lost "her looks and fallen into obscurity" (270).

Technically, the musical pattern of *Ragtime* has shaped the structure of the narrative. "I became more aware of the possibility of the musical analogy and the form of the book," Doctorow points out in an interview, "It is divided in four parts, as rag is. A title is something to use up as you write the book, to give it some sort of resonance." (Gussow, 1999: 6) The narrative of the novel, structured in four different parts, resembles the four beats of left hand in ragtime rhythm. Echoing the alternating pattern of strong beats and weak beats, some characters of the three representative families are given prominent position, while others are merely briefly delineated, just as the background and foreground in musical dimension[1]. The strong beats and the weak ones alternate, accompanied by syncopation in the right hand, to produce melodies that "hung in the air like flowers" (Doctorow, 2006: 132).

The beginning opens with a rush of stereotypical images drawn from the first decade of the twentieth century—public names, references, conventional values and assumptions. Together, they provide a background against which the first of the novel's three generic families appear. This upper-middle-class family of New Rochelle, representative of the majority of Americans at this time, lives in an illusion that "There were no Negroes. There were no immigrants." (3-4) The prosperity and

---

[1] Susan Brienza reminds us, "in temporal and aural dimensions it might be said that ragtime also depends on this relationship between background and foreground."(Brienza, 1981: 101) The focus on some characters or evens and underplay of others is the expression of this relationship.

stability viewed from their limited perspective have disguised the dark side of the society: immigrants (represented by the Jewish family including Tateh, Mateh and the "Little Girl") and blacks (represented by Coalhouse Walker, Sarah and their child) barely scratch a life through continuous toil and hardship; workers have to labor long hours to earn a few pennies, strikes are happening everywhere, and children are employed to work in the assembly line, with their hands mutilated or legs crushed. The second part opens with Father's return from his exploratory journey to find everything changed in the house. Mother has adopted a black child and took the child's mother Sarah as a maid. Sarah's repentant lover Walker comes to the white house regularly to woo the girl back. One day, Walker encounters a group of racist led by Willie Comklin, his car being vandalized. This event leads to Walker's violent revenge, at the cost of his life and Sarah's. At this time, Tateh has joined a strike and gets busted in the head. Totally disillusioned on his socialist belief, he takes on a journey for a new life and finally discovers that he can support himself by making books of moving picture. The third mainly depicts Walker's terrorist attacks in several districts of New York City and his occupation of Morgan's library with the help of his gang. In the negotiation between Walker and the municipal office, Father serves as the messenger. Mother's Younger Brother, in despair of the failed romance with Nesbit, joins Walker's gang to provide bombs and explosives. In general, this part witnesses Walker's tragic fight for dignity and the disintegration of the white family. The last short section functions as a conclusion associated with the theme of death: Walker walks to his ruin after his requirement of having his car restored is fulfilled; Father dies in a shipwreck; Mother's Younger Brother is killed in the Mexican Revolution. Mother remains with the black kid, and she regroups a happy family with Tateh who has assured the death of his wife. The novel moves to its close as the First World War approaches. In the ending paragraph, the narrator tells us that the era has come to the end, so does the popularity of the ragtime music: "And by that time the era of Ragtime had run out, with the heavy breath of the machine, as if history were no more than a tune on a player piano"(Doctorow, 2006: 270).

Some parts of the narrative such as the episodes of Coalhouse Walker are stressed like the strong beats. As the only one who gets a special name in the three archetypal families that the author has fictionalized (Neumeyer, 2004: 58), Peter F. Neumeyer contends that Coalhouse Walker is "perhaps the most memorable character" in the book. As "the unifying narrational threads", he connects the three originally independent families together and provides important clues to the random events (Ditsky, 1983: 179). Compared with the fragmented experiences of other characters, Walker's story, taking up a large part of second section and penetrating the third one, achieves relative coherency. It's till the concluding chapter that the readers are able to perceive his tragic death. Diverging from the perspective of the WASP family, the perspective of Walker restores the voice of the black community, how they are prejudiced against and trampled in a white-centered society, how they struggle to defend their identity and dignity and how they fail in the 1910s when the civil rights movement has not emerged.

Other characters, such as Emma Goldman, Evelyn Nesbit, Harry K. Thaw, Standard White, Freud and his disciple Jung, J. P. Morgan, Henry Ford, to name just a few, appear and reappear, but only with a small part dedicated to them. There are also characters such as the newspaper reporter and reformer Jacob Riis, the great explorer Admiral Peary and the famous writer Theodore Dreiser who just show once and then never turn up again in the following narrative. They are like the weak beats in the ragtime music. With these weak beats interspersed, the strong beats of the major characters are strengthened and the chords are made diverse, full of inflections.

Literarily, a rag means tiny bits, or fragments, and it is often associated with something discarded. The image of rag appears several times, each time with different connotations. In Jacob Riis's color maps of Manhattan's ethnic population, different bits of color represent different race, which constitutes a "crazy quilt of humanity" (Doctorow, 2006: 16). Thus, the rag image here expresses the diversity of ethnicity that characterizes modern America and suggests the racial problems this diversity may bring about. On another occasion, in contrast to the miserable condition of workers and child laborers, the rich in New York and Chicago often give poverty balls, and the guests "came dressed in rags and ate from tin plates and drank from chipped mugs"(34). Ironically, these extravagant balls are held for the sake of charity. The lashing words of the narrator depict a picture of great gap between the rich and the poor, exposing the inequality and injustice of a capitalist society in the 1910s. The central protagonist of the narrative—the Little Boy, is also associated with the rag motif. We are told that he cherishes and collects anything that is discarded, including his father's Arctic journal and his uncle's silhouettes of Evelyn Nesbit, which he has found in the garbage. This habit of discerning value from the bits discarded gives him access to truth not discovered by adults. As a result, he becomes the insightful narrator who gets clues from various family documents to restore the history of the ragged time.

In ragtime music, "the syncopated melodies in the right hand are set over a regular repeating bass in the left.... There are call-and-answer figures and repetition. ... A rag is made up of a sequence of three, four, or even five strains, one or more of which is repeated. These do not develop out of one another but are more or less independent" (Rodgers, 1975: 141). Doctorow's narrative, as it were, consists of numerous rags like the pattern of the ragtime's syncopation. The encyclopedic materials are organized in "a series of forty swiftly delivered, short chapters averaging less than ten pages each" (Harter & Thompson, 1990: 55). The scene and plot are volatile and constantly shift, denying the readers the comfort of reading continuous line of development. For example, in the first chapter, the famous case of the shooting of Stanford White is presented in this way.

> In New York City the papers were full of the shooting of the famous architect Stanford White by Harry K. Thaw, eccentric scion of a coke and railroad fortune. Harry K. Thaw was the husband of Evelyn Nesbit, the celebrated beauty who had once been Stanford White's mistress. The shooting took place in the roof garden of the Madison Square Garden on 26th Street, a spectacular block-long building of yellow brick and terra cotta that White himself had designed in the Sevillian style. It was the opening night of a revue entitled Mamzelle Champagne, and as the chorus sang and danced the eccentric scion wearing on this summer night a straw boater and heavy black coat pulled out a pistol and shot the famous architect three times in the head. On the roof. There were screams. Evelyn fainted. She had been a well-known artist's model at the age of fifteen. Her underclothes were white. Her husband habitually whipped her. She happened once to meet Emma Goldman, the revolutionary. Goldman lashed her with her tongue. Apparently there were Negroes. There were immigrants. And though the newspapers called the shooting the Crime of the Century, Goldman knew it was only 1906 and there were ninety-four years to go."(4-5)

In this passage especially in the last few sentences, the correlation of sentences in sequence is loose. The subject matter shifts from Evelyn's occupation as a model to the color of her underclothes, and then to her husband's abuse of her. The readers are required to apply imagination so as to make sense of the text. Ostensibly, the color of Evelyn's underclothes has nothing to do with Harry K. Thaw's abuse of her. But in the context of the whole novel, we are informed that Evelyn has had an affair with Stanford White when she works as his model at 15. Jealous of their previous intimate relationship, Thaw thus "habitually whipped her" and eventually shoots White to death. Thaw's treatment of Evelyn insinuates his abnormal sexual indictment, which will be proved by the narrator's account of him in the later part. It turns out that he is a sadist and psychic. Similarly, the fact that Goldman lashes Evelyn with words seems in no way related to whether there are Negroes or immigrants. But soon, the episode on Goldman will show that she is a socialist who most acutely realizes the miserable conditions of the marginalized groups such as the immigrants and the blacks. So it is from her point of view, we are told there are both Negroes and Immigrants. Like the strains in a rag, the narrative of *Ragtime* is constituted with ostensibly disconnected images and sentences like rags. They keep independent from each other but all together make up a unit.

2. 2. The Cinematic Language

Like many of his contemporary writers, Doctorow's attitude on cinema is paradoxical. On one hand, he expresses anxiety on the rise of this visual art, which may change the significance of traditional reading in our life. Films, according to Doctorow, can sometimes be "regressive, non-verbal, simplistic" (Friedl & Schulz, 1999: 125). Due to its omnipresent influence on contemporary culture, young people are encouraged to perceive visually, which leads to the rise of illiteracy around the world. But more often, he admits having learned from films how to write:

> We've learned that we don't have to explain things. We don't have to explain how our man can be in the bedroom one moment and walking in the street the next. How can he be twenty years old one moment and eighty years old a moment later. We've learned that if we just make the book happen, the reader can take care of himself... (McCaffery, 1999: 81)

For Doctorow, cinematic language is characterized by discontinuity and showing. This is what he can use in the act of writing. Among Doctorow's novels, *Ragtime* is claimed to be the most cinematic. Michael Shiels thinks that Doctorow's books including *Ragtime* can be easily translated into cinematic language because they are structured in the "episodic and often counter-chronological" manner and "film composition, at least in conventional terms, is also structurally governed by these principles" (Bach, 1988: 167). *Ragtime* is a novel about filmmaking and writing as well. Thematically, it describes the creation of a film, which is closely related to the contrapuntal ideas of duplication and transformation—a central motif of the novel. Technically, the novel adopts many strategies that are often used in filmmaking or film editing such as framing, different ways of shots especially close-ups, and montage to create the visual effect of discontinuity and shift.

2. 2. 1. An art of duplication and transformation

In the novel, the art of film is closely related to the contrapuntal ideas of duplication and transformation, revealed from Tateh's perspective. Comparing Doctorow's work with *Humboldt's Gift*, Barbara Estrin sees in both books "the idea of film as a duplicable event, a mass entertainment deflecting the anxiety of the machine age with its own technology" (Williams, 1996: 54). In the conversation with the white family, Tateh explains to Mother the cause of films' popularity over the country:

> People want to know what is happening to them. For a few pennies they sit and see their selves in movement, running, racing in motorcars, fighting and, forgive me, embracing each other. This is most important today, in this country, where everybody is so new. There is such need to understand. (Doctorow, 2006: 215)

From Tateh's point of view, people flood to theatre because they want to know what happens in the world and they see film as a way of duplicating reality. In *Ragtime*, the man crucially related to the phenomenon of duplication in the modern era is Henry Ford, who invents the assembly line, making it possible to "break down the work operations in the assembly of an automobile to their simplest steps, so that any fool could perform them" (78). Just as another character J. P. Morgan has pointed out, the principle of the assembly line is the "interchangeability of parts", which is the basis of all duplicative events. In America, the value of duplication is everywhere to be perceived. The Americans appropriate the European art and architecture in an almost vulgar wholesale way, with "stones, statuary, tapestries, carved and painted ceilings, marble fountains and marble stairs and balustrades" successively shipped across the Atlantic Ocean from Europe to America. It seems that Europe has been dismantled, and "a new aesthetic in European art and architecture" is born in America grounded on "the uncluttering of ancient lands" (16). The famous psychologist Freud finds America a vulgar copy of Europe. When visiting the country, he says to Ernest Jones, "America is a mistake, a gigantic mistake" (34). The key character of the novel—the Little Boy also realizes the power of duplication in his life. He often studies his image in the mirror, not out of vanity of a young man caring for his appearance but because "he discovered the mirror as a means of self-duplication", due to which the integrity of an individual is destroyed, and "he was no longer anything exact as a person" (98). The pattern of duplication and repetition is reflected not only in the material sense, but also in people's outlook on their life and the world. For Houdini, a distinguished escapist artist in history, life is equated to a series of repetitive experiences of escape. He turns down any changes and alienates himself in a closed still world far from the contact of reality. So after his mother's death (death is part of the process of life, a reality he could not escape from), he collapses and becomes obsessed with the transcendental existence like ghost and soul.

The Jewish Tateh is the one who connects the art of film with the processes of duplication and transformation. Initially an improvised artist of silhouette, Tateh's inspiration for making film comes from his occasional discovery of turning over the silhouettes pages. He makes a hundred and twenty silhouettes on his daughter's skating and bounds them together with a string. So when the Little Girl turns over the pages it is as if she is watching herself skating away and back, gliding figure eight, returning, pirouetting and making a lovely bow to her audience. Tateh's design reveals the technological principle of filmmaking: films are photographs (photographs are duplication of reality in pictorial form) in dynamic forms and they show the process of transformation. The imagery of transformation also abounds in *Ragtime*. The Little Boy seems to possess an extraordinary perception about the transformations around him. Chapter fifteen gives detailed descriptions of the boy's fascination with the stories from Ovid, stories of transformation, say, "Women turned into sunflowers, spiders, bats, birds; men turned into snakes, pigs, stones and even thin air." (97) These stories told by his grandfather "proposed to him that the forms of life were volatile" and that everything in the world can easily change into something else (97). The boy also finds "proof in his own experience of the instability of both things and people", the statues in the square, for example, look seemingly the same every day, but actually they "turned different colors or lost bits and pieces of themselves". So it is evident to him that "the world composed and recomposed itself constantly in an endless process of dissatisfaction" (99).

2. 2. 2. Cinematic techniques

Almost every film maintains a consciousness about the frame of the movie screen and the frame of the camera. The importance of framing lies in that it reveals the cameraman's selection of the scene and the angle. The frame of the movie image forms its border and contains the mise-en-scene[①]. Normally, there are wide-screen frame and smaller standard frame. A wide-screen frame is "especially suited to catching the open spaces" such as prairie in the Western or the vast stellar spaces of

---

① A mise-en-scene refers to the arrangement of scenery and properties to represent the place where a play or movie is enacted.

sci-fi films (Corrigan, 2010: 65). The smaller standard frame is, perhaps, "best suited to more personal interior dramas or genres like the melodrama"(65).

As a filmmaker, Tateh is acutely conscious of the acts of framing in daily life. In Tahteh's first encounter with the white family at a hotel in Atlanta city, the readers are informed that he "carried on a chain around his neck a rectangular glass framed in metal which he often held up to his face as if to compose for a mental photography what it was that had captured his attention" (Doctorow, 2006: 214). Later he reveals to the white family that "[h]e was in moving-picture business and the glass rectangle was a tool of the trade which he could not forbear using even when on vocation. (214) Like a real cameraman, Tateh tries to take in the scene into his mental screen: "He held his rectangular class aloft, framing Mother and Father, the two children, the waiter walking toward the table and, at the far end of the dining room, a pianist and a fiddler who played for the patrons on a small platform decorated with potted palms".

In the history of motion pictures, many movies, such as Jean Renoir's "Grand Illusion" (1937) and Alfred Hitchcock's "Rear Window", fill their mise-en-scene "with the internal frames of windows or doorways or stage sets to call attention to the importance of frames and point of view in the story"(Corrigan, 2010: 65). Psychologically, the use of frame draws the attention of the audiences to the subjective inner world of individuals. In Doctorow's narrative, the cinematic method of framing is employed when Mother looks out of window of the hotel:

> [She] stood looking at the sun as it rose above the sea. Gulls skimmed the breakers and strutted on the beach. The rising sun erased the shadows from the sand as if the particled earth itself shifted and flattened, and by the time she heard Father astir in the adjoining room the sky was beneficently blue and the beach was white and the first sea bathers had appeared down at the surf to test the water with their toes. (Doctorow, 2006: 208)

The scene is shot from Mother's point of view. It is a frame in motion. In this mise-en-scene, the focalization moves from the gulls to the rising sun, to Father's astir in the adjoining room, and again to the sky and beach in distance. It looks as if the camera closely identifies with the character, with its repeated transition from medium shot to long short to close shot and then to medium-long shot again.

To Doctorow, writing also includes the process of framing. In the first chapter, the narrator briefly recalls Theodore Dreiser's attempt to find the proper alignment: sitting in a wooden chair in the middle of his room, the writer turns the chair again and again to align it properly. Unlike Tateh who frames with his glass rectangular, the writer frames with his eyes. Eventually, Dreiser fails: "he made a complete circle and still could not find the proper alignment for the chair"(3). Essentially, Tateh and Dreiser's experiences overlap for they both try to find the right angle of framing, one for film, the other for writing. The difference of the two lies in that film uses visual language while literature uses verbal one. In this sense, the use of framing reveals the self-consciousness of the writing process.

Furthermore, Doctorow's depiction of a special scene or a character emulates the method of cinematic shots. A close-up is a special way of shooting, with the camera pulled very close to the object. It includes very little of any background, with its concentration on an object, or an extreme close-up, a fragment of an object, such as the freckles on a human face. According to Louis Giannetti, close-ups often "accord great significance and symbolic value to the objects they portray" (Giannetti, 2008: 11). In the novel, the portrayal of Pierpont Morgan's nose is similar to the technique of close-up in movie shooting.

Pierpont Morgan, the classic hero of the 20th century in the eyes of American people, is seen as the "Napoleon of Wall Street". Like "a monarch of the invisible, transnational kingdom of capital whose sovereignty was everywhere granted" (Doctorow, 2006: 115), he takes control of America and spreads his power over the globe. However, in Doctorow's description, this great man, as if from Greek mythology, is distorted in a comic and ironic way. In appearance, his nose is abnormally huge as the result of the colonization of "a chronic skin disease"(116). As he grows older and richer, the nose also expands, like "a strawberry of the award winning giant type grown by California's wizard of horticulture Luther Burank" (116). Every time he makes an acquisition or manipulates a bond issue or takes over an industry, "another bright red pericarp burst into boom", but Morgan does not seem to be troubled by this flaw. Instead, he feels rather complacent, taking it as the only evidence serving to remind him of his humanity. In his mind, "the disfigurement of his monstrous nose was the touch of God upon him, the assurance of mortality"(116). Here, the nose, like the birthmark of Hawthorne's heroine Georgiana in "The Birthmark", is endowed with symbolic meaning. Like its master, its magnitude symbolizes the immense power of capitalist oligarch popular in this time. Through the close-up shot of Morgan's nose, Doctorow ironically depicts the image of a ruthless industrialist, who thinks that he represents the universal order.

The most noticeable cinematic technique employed in *Ragtime* is montage, as has been commented on by many critics. Montage is a technique in film editing in which a series of short shots are edited into a sequence to condense space, time, and information①. Originally a terminology in architecture, it was introduced to the field of cinema primarily by Sergei Eisenstein, and early Soviet directors used it as a synonym for creative editing. Through the use of montage, seemingly disconnected images are linked together to produce certain effects, and audiences are encouraged to wield their imagination to apprehend the motives of the filmmaker's editing art. As shots in a sequence are cut and pasted to regroup a unit, filmmakers can manipulate time, space and point of view in a freer way. Broadly applied in literature, the use of montage always produces shifted perspectives, parallel narrative lines and flashbacks.

In the first part of *Ragtime*, many clues and events are juxtaposed together in a peculiar way: One sunny afternoon, Mother's Younger Brother was walking idly on a beach, with his mind full of Evelyn Nesbit. Across the town the escaped artist Houdini's car occasionally broke into the community where the family lived in New Rochelle, resulting in causing the meeting of Houdini and the white family. At this time of history, Winslow Homer "was doing his painting"(4). He painted the light that was still available along the Eastern Seaboard. In the roof garden of the Madison Square Gaerden on 26th street, Harry K. Thaw took out his gun and shot the architect Stanford White to death due to his jealousy of the latter's intimacy with his wife Evelyn Nesbit. Although the newspapers called the shooting the Crime of the Century, the famous anarchist Emma Goldman knew "it was only 1906 and there were nighty-four years to go" (5). Ostensibly, the abundant materials bonded together give a sense of disparity, but together they constitute a picture that defines the time: it is a time when the middle class Americans live in a sentimental coziness; upper class celebrities are involved in scandals of sex; socialist and feminist movements are on the rise and they would sweep the country in the next few years.

When Houdini was about to depart from the white family, the Little Boy followed him to the street and stood at front of the Pope-Toledo "gazing at the distorted macrocephalic image of himself in the shiny brass fitting of the headlight" (9). "Warn the Duke", the boy said to Houdini and then he ran away. At that time Houdini was unable to figure out the meaning of the boy. Then the narrative line moves to the encounter of Houdini with Ferdinand the Archduke of Austria in the European continent. Still, the boy's words remained a mystery but readers may have speculated something ominous from the given clue. It is at the end of the story when Houdini was hanging upward down in the sky that he realized the significance of

---

①   Quoted from Wiki.

this episode many years ago. The year was 1914, and the Archduke Franz Ferdinand was reported to have been assassinated. It is at this moment that an image composes itself in Houdini's mind. The image displays a small boy looking at himself in the shiny brass headlamp of an automobile, who asked him to warn the Duke. Normally, the little boy will in no case know the assassination in 1906. But as the ending turns out that he is the narrator of the book so Houdini's flashback suggests the authorial manipulation of the narrative time by the grow-up Little Boy.

2. 3. The Journalistic Style

In the 19th century, new advances in printing technology, including the development of steam-powered rotary presses, significantly boosted publishers' of productivity. Meanwhile the dramatic expansion of railroads facilitated the distribution of books and periodicals across the nation. In addition publishing trade associations and publications, periodical depots and newsboys all promoted the sale of reading materials. Stimulated by these forces and the development in education, America was becoming a nation of readers (Canada, 2011: 3). Statistics shows that by the middle of the 19th century, Americans could choose from some 3,000 papers and citizens could buy a daily from a newsboy with a few pennies. The reach of the press was tremendous, as "mass and specialty papers extended the influence of journalism to all classes and segments of the population" (33). It is in the later period of 19th century that the newspaper "began to take its modern shape as a vehicle for reporting timely information on politics, crime, business, sports, and human-interest subjects for a mass audience"(3).

In Doctorow's novels such as *The Waterworks* and *Homer and Langley*, newspaper serves as a kind of crucial media bridging the internal and external reality. In *The Waterworks*, the narrator McIlvaine works as an editor for a newspaper called *Telegram* in the 19th century. For him, the newspaper world represents the objective world of printing words, which provides order to resist the alienation of the world of other around him. The weird brothers Homer and Langley live through most parts of the twentieth century. They reject the invasion of modern technology such as telephone and television but keep the habit of hoarding newspapers. Langley's quixotic project is "the collection of the daily papers with the ultimate aim of creating one day's edition of a newspaper." (Doctorow, 2009: 57) He aspires "to fix American life finally in one edition, what he called Collyer's eternally current dateless newspaper, the only newspaper anyone would ever need" (57). For Langley, newspaper works as a system based on which he tries to figure out a universal formula to explain everything in the world.

In *Ragtime*, as the most accessible media form, newspaper exerts great influence on forging individuals' mind and public consciousness. We are told that in Mother's Younger Brother's room, a newspaper drawing of Evelyn in profile is pinned on a prominent position of the wall. According to the news reports, Evelyn has caused the death of one man and wrecked the life of another. A reclusive young man, Mother's Younger Brother romanticizes the journalistic version of Evelyn and fantasizes about their relationship. Thinking of the disasters Evelyn has brought to men became of her enchantment, he deduces that "there was nothing in life worth having, worth wanting, but the embrace of her thin arms" (Doctorow, 2006: 5).

The reach of newspaper to every household makes it a perfect platform to contribute to the rise of commercial culture. Newspaper that has frequented every household serves as a perfect platform for the rise of commercial culture. When the trial of Harry K. Thaw begins, Evelyn, rather than the murderer or victim of the case, becomes the subject of constant focus for reporters. An embodiment of sexual beauty, her image as photographed on the newspaper creates "the first sex goddess in American history"(71). With Evelyn's face on the front page, the edition is completely sold out. Business communities realize from this fact that "there was a process of magnification by which news events established certain individuals in the public consciousness as larger than life". They think that "[t]hese were the individuals who represented one desirable human characteristic to the exclusion of all others"(71). Drawing inspiration from sensational effect of Evelyn's appearance on newspaper, they learn to connect commodities with individuals like Evelyn to promote sales. To some extent, Evelyn "provided inspiration for the concept of the movie star system and the model for every sex goddess from Theda Bara to Marilyn Monroe"(71).

Another group of people inspired by this event are various trade union leaders, anarchists and socialists, who accurately prophesizes that "she would in the long run be a greater threat to the workingman's interests than mine owners or steel manufactures"(71). They perceive that Evelyn's image on newspaper can only worsen the condition of the working class. How can the masses permit themselves to be exploited by the few? In response to the question, Emma Goldman explains in this way: "By being persuaded to identify with them"(71). She tells Evelyn in a letter: "Carrying his newspaper with your picture the laborer goes home to his wife, an exhausted workhorse with the veins standing out in her legs, and he dreams not of justice but of being rich" (71). In this case, newspaper becomes the battlefield where socio-political ideologies circulate and dispute with each other.

The intersection between journalism and literature has begun in an earlier time since the two genres share much in common. In both realms, the writers seek to capture some aspects of reality and convey them to the audience through medium. As Mark Canada claims, for reporters, columnists, poets, novelists and dramatists, along with every writer who ever sought to fashion some aspects of reality into a story, the most important thing is "material"—they must first "discover facts or impressions that will serve as the substance for their journalism or literature" (Canada, 2011: 23). Besides, journalists learn from literature techniques of writing such as the narrative structure, figurative speech, style and so on. In fact, the American literature in the 18th and 19th centuries enjoys a galaxy of writer-journalists such as Benjamin Franklin, Philip Freneau, Edgar Allan Poe, to name just a few. In the 20th century, the list is even longer and we have such influential figures as Theodore Dreiser, Earnest Hemingway and Jack London. To these writers, their career as a journalist means a lot to their literary creation. Dreiser, for instance, obtains materials of writing from news story, and his masterpiece *An American Tragedy* has its prototype in a real event reported in newspaper. Benefiting from his experiences as a journalist, Hemingway develops a style of economy, which is called Iceberg Theory by critics. Compared with literature, journalistic writings are characterized by simplicity, brevity, precision and emotional detachment. In order to convey a large quantity of information in a short time, journalists have to cut out superfluous decorative words and complicated psychological descriptions in a news report. Doctorow's style in *Ragtime* is apparently under the influence of journalist writings. He narrates Freud's visit to America in a journalistic way:

> Freud arrived in New York on the Lloyd Liner George Washington. He was accompanied by his disciples Jung and Ferenczi, both some years his junior. They were met at the dock by two younger Freudians, Drs. Ernest Jones and A. A. Brill. The entire party dined at Hammerstein's Roof Garden. There were potted palms. A piano violin due played Liszt's Hungarian Rhapsody. Everyone talked around Freud, glancing at him continuously to gauge his mood. He ate cup custard. Brill and Jones undertook to play host for the visit.

The description looks like a news report we will find in a daily. The sentences are declarative, simple in diction and rhetoric. Short, darting sentences are set "in tension with relatively long and leisurely paragraphs; the swift stabs of attention in one direction and then another demand from the reader a constant readjustment of perception" (Dawson, 1983: 205). All events are narrated in a matter-of-fact way, without any emotional investment. In fact, throughout the book, there are no quotation marks, seemingly no dialogue. But on scrutinizing, readers will quickly become aware that there is dialogue, though "it is contained in longer paragraphs and thereby hidden, made less unique, more integrated typographically; but just for that reason, it can be more unexpected—even at times, explosive (as, for example, at the end of Chapter I)". (205)

On the other hand, journalist writing differs from literature for its claim on truth. For journalists in the past and at present, factual accuracy is often considered as the central principle in journalistic ethics. They put the pursuit of truth as first priority, and for them, truth "usually involves the reporting of facts—that is, incidents, numbers, and other 'information', which can be observed, documented, and verified" (Canada, 2011: 15). Therefore, newspapers sometimes explicitly refer to their roles as bearers of "facts" and indeed come to be regarded as accurate, reliable sources of factual reality. In literature, truth in the eyes of writers can be something more abstract than factual truth. In the Preface to *The House of the Seven Gables*, Hawthorne points out a writer could approach "the truth of the human heart" without maintaining "fidelity, not merely to the possible, but to the probable and ordinary course of man's experience".

Like his contemporary writers, Doctorow is especially concerned with the relationship of facts and fiction. In "False Documents", he makes a comparison of two kinds of texts, one—the Navy's announcement—from *The New York Times* and the other from Nabokov's *The Gift*. These two texts actually correspond to two different genres—journalism and literature, and they also represent the different ways the medium of language is conceived. For Doctorow, the Navy's announcement refers to a verifiable world (the power of regime) with its precise expression and clear purpose while Nabokov's description inheres "a world that cannot be easily corroborated or verified"(the power of freedom)(Doctorow, 1983: 17). He further points out, we live in a society that counts its achievements from the discovery of science and which runs on "empirical thinking and precise calculations"(17). In such a society, language is "conceived primarily as the means by which facts are communicated". However, the boundary between facts and fiction is not that clear. In *Ragtime*, Doctorow mimics the objective principle of journalistic writing by deliberately "showing facts" of the society:

Millions of men were out of work. Those fortunate enough to have jobs were dared to form unions. Courts enjoined them, police busted their heads, their leaders were jailed and new men took their jobs. A union was an affront to God.... In the coal fields a miner made a dollar sixty a day if he could dig three tons. He lived in the company's shacks and bought his food from the company stores. On the tobacco farms Negroes stripped tobacco leaves thirteen hours a day and earned six cents an hour, man, woman or child. (33-34)

This documentary-like account of facts reveals the miserable condition of workers and blacks in the capitalist society. But they are only facts composed by a writer. They claim no more truth than the plot of Freud and Jung's riding a boat through the tunnel of love, Morgan and Ford's secret meeting to discuss the issue of immorality (both of which are fabricated by Doctorow). For a writer, the "truth of human heart" is more important than the factual truth. Therefore, in *Lives of the Poets*, Doctorow has the future-writer Edgar invent a story of his father's death in a letter as he thinks his invention is truer than reality. To Doctorow, facts do not only come from the outside world, claimed only by journalists, scientists, police officers; they are also "composed" by novelists (Trenner, 1983: 75). By creating a fictive novel with the journalistic representation of facts, Doctorow questions the validity of the objective truth in the power of regime (in this case, journalist writing), and his narrative breaks down the traditional categorization of literature and journalism.

3. Western Genre in *Welcome to Hard Times*

Welcome to Hard Times is Doctorow's first novel which was published in 1960, an initial attempt of him to render his imagination into American frontier experiences. The story is set in a small town named Hard Times in the Dakota Territory around the 1870s. It is supposedly narrated by Blue, the de facto Mayor of the town, who writes down the history of the town's destruction, rebirth and final destruction in three ledgers.

Blue's narrative begins with the town's invasion by a Bad Man from Bodie. The Bad Man named Clay Tuner literally plunders, rapes, kills and sets fire in the town, so the residents have to pack and leave for other places. The only ones who stay are Blue, an Indian John Bear, Molly the bar girl who is seriously injured by the Bad Man, and the newly orphaned Jimmy Fee. All traumatized, Blue, Molly and Jimmy regroup a symbolic family of three, which does not function well due to Molly's hatred toward the past. With the expectation to build a new town, Blue persuades the passers-by, a Russian bar boss Zar and his prostitutes, a storeowner Isaac and a couple Sweden and his wife Helga to settle down in the town. Their hope of building a prosperous town is based on the rumor that a railroad will be constructed nearby by a mining company. The settlers fetch wood from the ruins of other ghost towns in the prairie and build hotels, storehouses, stables and dugouts. After the devastating winter, they are able to gain new hope, as lots of newcomers crowd into the town wishing to get a job from the gold mine.

However, the ostensible prosperity does not annihilate the potential crisis that looms over the town. As newcomers gather around, chaos and violence also multiply. Finally the news comes that there is no gold in the lodes and the company decides that they will withdraw from the mining hills and no railroads will be built. Exploded by the news, the town goes into anarchy, with crimes everywhere to be seen, which incurs the Bad Man again. In the dual with the Bad Man, Blue is mortally injured. Molly dies in her frenzy revenge, after fighting with the Bad Man, both killed by Jimmy, who turns to the new Bad Man. Before his blood blows out, Blue writes down what happens in the town, in the hope that someday people will have a chance to read it.

The background of the novel is typical of the Western: small town in the bleak prairie, freezing cold long winters, scorching and drought-stricken summers, wagon trails in the sand, "a straggling line of tents and false-front wooden shacks that sheltered, among other things, a carpenter shop, an Indian's cabin, a general store, and a combination saloon, gambling joint and brothel" (Lewis, 2000: 56). In such a scene, the characters are what readers would expect: a bar boss and his prostitutes, a shooter, an Indian, miners, and pioneers who come to the town for getting-to-rich opportunities. The thematic concerns that recur in the frontier myth abound in the novel. For instance, the town Hard Times is exposed to the threats from the external evil force. The protagonist Blue wishes that the establishment of a real human community would help resist such evil. Molly's line tells the story of violence and revenge, which are common notes in a Western. Jimmy's fall is remindful of the failed nurturing. Undoubtedly, Doctorow is under the influence of the Western film when he creates the novel, as he claims in an interview "I admit to learning a lot of things from films"(Lubarsky, 1999: 40).

In fact, Doctorow was born and grew up in New York. He has never been to the area west of Ohio. In an interview, he confesses that the inspiration of the novel comes from his job as a reader of script for a motion-picture film company. Suffering "one lousy western after another", it occurs to him that "I could lie about the West in a way more interesting than any of these people were lying." (Yardley,

1999: 11). After reviewing Walter Prescott Webb's *The Great Plains*, Doctorow is struck by the image that no trees are out there. He claims excitedly: "I could spin the whole book out of the one image"(11). Therefore, this one image evolves into the opening chapter of *Welcome to Hard Times*. However, despite his use of "the stark and elemental background of the frontier" (O'Neill, 1999: 55), Doctorow's narrative is not as conventional as the genre itself. The Hollywood hero complex is nowhere to be found here since Blue the protagonist is a cowardly middle-aged man soaked in record keeping. This novel diverging from those typical westerns with the common ending of a restored order in the community, evil prevails in Hard Times, violence recycles and hope is extinguished, so Doctorow's version of the frontier is both an integration and subversion of the Western. As S. E. B. says, he "puts aside the shop-worn sentiment and melodrama" of the usual Western genre, and subverts the framework for the "creation of a serous literature structure" (S. E. B., 2000: 55). Doctorow's intention with this novel, as he announces, is to "take a disreputable genre, cheap materials of a nonliterary kind and ... fuse them in some way that was valid" to interrogate the myth of the society (Baker, 1999: 2).

3. 1. Western genre and Hollywood culture

American west is often associated with the land of freedom and infinite hope, far from the contamination of civilization embodied by eastern cities. This geographical signifier has generated extraordinary psychological and cultural significance to this nation. Whenever the word frontier is mentioned, people will naturally connect it to the spirit of self-sufficiency, ragged individualism, and revitalization. In his famous work *The Frontier in American History*, Frederick Jackson Turner vividly describes the west as the "safety valve": When the pressures of metropolis such as overpopulation and labor exploitation culminate, the frontier can be a place for the city-escapees to relieve themselves and move on. Since the end of the 19th century, the west has become a symbol in American culture, a shaping influence on American national identity. President Theodore Roosevelt (1901–1909), for instance, celebrated the "strenuous life" of the West and identified it with his own struggles as a rancher on the frontier. Artistic creations around the West bloom, which form a unique genre in American culture—the Western. As John G. Cawelty notes, of all the major popular genres, the Western seems most likely to "express some sense of the uniqueness of the American experience and of the imagined exceptionalism of America" (Cawelty, 1999: 43). Not until the middle of the twentieth century, Western symbols had become quite common in American culture, almost ubiquitous in

American institutions and national psychology.

According to Calwelty, popular arts like the Western are based on understood "conventions": "Westerns must have a certain kind of setting, a particular cast of characters, and follow a limited number of lines of action" to make it a particular genre (31). Conversely, if a Western "does not take place in the West, near the frontier, at a point in history when social order and anarchy are in tension, and does not involve some form of pursuit", people will not consider it to be a Western (31). It is commonly acknowledged that the Western originates from James Fennimore Cooper's *Leatherstocking Tales*. In his pentalogy centering on a pioneer hero named Natty Bumppo, Cooper identified the basic character types and motifs for the genre. In particular, the Western has such images as the "isolated town or ranch or fort by the vast open grandeur of prairie or desert and connected to the rest of the civilized world by a railroad, a stagecoach or simply a trail" (24). Other Western conventions include the typical characterization such as a hero, townsfolk, sheriff, the Indian and a virtuous heroine. The dramatic tension of a Western often comes from the conflict between civilization and savagery, good and evil, law and anarchy, which unsurprisingly ends with the victory of the positive side in the dichotomies.

As is known, the 20th century witnessed a rapid development of mass media. In this epoch of media, entertainment films and television programs became the most influential forces in shaping images of the American West. In these visual narratives, "Hollywood has interpreted American West to itself"(O'Connor & Rollins, 2005: 1). Jim Kitses (the author of *Horizons West: The Western from John Ford to Clint Eastwood*) considers the Western and the Gangster films as Hollywood's greatest inventions. The American Film Institute's (AFI) List of the Top 100 American Movies of the 20th Century, compiled and released at the turn of the millennium, included nine Westerns while several others on the list were apparently "informed by and owe debts to the iconography and themes of Westerns". (Merlock, 2005: X). Just as Turner argued, "the West was such a central force in American life that Hollywood producers used it as a backdrop for a myriad of dramatic relationships and situations that were characteristic of the American experience and American values—and therefore, presumably, especially appealing to American audiences"(O'Connor & Rollins, 2005: 6).

The Hollywood Western culture is closely related to literature since a lot of movies are adapted from Western literary works, so they inevitably inherit the convention or the pattern of the genre. However, on the other hand, they are endowed with the features unique in film industry. As noted by Rey Merlock, the

Western films are actually the filmmaker's "rethinking, reimagining, and realigning the Western with contemporary issues of race, class, gender, and violence that will lead to newly refined, freshly insightful critical, cultural, and historical analysis" (Merlock, 2005: XI). Therefore, in different times, the core elements of the Western films may vary, and the films, like literature, often serve as a projection of the social ideologies of that time. Commenting on the relationship between the Western and socio-political issues, John H. Lenihan contends that "the study of a single genre is especially revealing of how a particular form is modified in accordance with the constantly changing concerns and attitudes of a society" (Lenihan, 1980: 4). By refiguring the issues of nature, gender, race in a historical past, Western films provide a distance for reconsidering the present. As a result, the Westerns of the 1950s reflected cold war concerns; the Westerns of the 1960s and the early 1970s displayed an increasing cynicism and violence that were generated by the national experiences of war, assassination, riot, and political scandals like Watergate.

Welcome, written in 1960, suggests that the Western film in the 1950s may have exerted the greatest influence on Doctorow's idea of the book. In fact, the setting, characterization and even central themes of the novel are typical representations in Western, particularly suggest the influence of Hollywood Western culture in the 1950s. The 1950s, dubbed as "The Silent Generation" by *Times*, witnessed the mass of the country would like to keep reticent on politics and other social issues. As McCarthyism caused widespread panic and fear, consensus took over national psychology and people were encouraged to behave according to social norms. The Hollywood Western films in this period generally mirror the spirit of the time, so does Doctorow in *Welcome*. But Doctorow's creation is far more than a direct translation of cinematic language into words. He focuses more on subversion and renewal than on emulation. His deconstruction of the Western myth not only revitalizes the outmoded genre, but also foreshadows the coming of 1960s, a time when revisionist view is cast to the past and traditional concepts on history are interrogated and subverted.

3. 2. Integration

Critics such as Winifred Farrant Bevilacque unexceptionally focus on Doctorow's subversion of the traditional conception of the West, but his integration of the Western elements is often ignored in critical vision. The twentieth-century Western, as Jane Tompkins points out, is typically set on a barren and hostile landscape, which emanates an "aura of death both parodied and insisted on in place names like Deadwood and Tombstone" (Tompkins, 1987: 359). Doctorow's little west town Hard Time is such a place, with its name suggesting the hardship and trial of the frontier life. Amazed by the image of treeless prairie depicted in Walter Prescott Webb's *The Great Plains*, Doctorow presents to the readers the classic Western scene of vastness and bleakness in the second paragraph of the opening chapter:

> This town was in the Dakota Territory, and on three sides—east, south, west—there is nothing but miles of flats. That's how we could see him coming. Most times the dust on the horizon moved east to west—wagon trains nicking the edge of the flats with their wheels and leaving a long dust turd lying on the rim of the earth. If a man rode toward us he made a fan in the air that got wider and wider. To the north were hills of rock ant that was where the lodes were which gave an excuse for the town, although not a good one. (Doctorow, 1960: 3-4)

Besides the infertile of the land, the ornery weather on the prairie poses a challenge to the settlers there. As described in the novel, in the winter, "a storm would blow up for a few days" and every snow brings "its chinook to devil the skin"; there are days of pure coldness that it is "like swallowing frost to take a breath"(90). In the summer, the sun is scorching, sand flies around, and drought plagues every corner of the earth. The hostile nature is only one aspect of the threats, as the settlers have to occasionally face the evil forces like the Bad Man: "If the drought don't get you and the blizzards don't get you, that's when some devil with liquor in his soul and a gun in his claw will ride you down and clean you out. "(29). In such a harsh environment, the only creature that seems to survive is buzzard. They come in processing, circling around and preying on dead bodies. On the prairie, towns appear and die undiscernibly, leaving behind thousands of ghost towns. As one government surveyor says in the novel, "Over this land a thousand times each year towns spring up", but then "[t]he claim pinches out, the grass dies, the well dries up, and everyone will ride off to from up again somewhere else for me to charter" (142).

It is against this background that Doctorow's story of a town named Hard Times is unveiled. The most recurring motifs and features of the Westerns such as gunfighters, Indians, selfless sheriff or a marshal, townspeople, bars and saloons can all be found in this story. As each of the Western film has a moral center, in the novel, Blue represents the center as the events are narrated and commented from his point of view. He is a not-so-typical hero who tries to make a home out of wilderness. In his conversation with Molly, Blue expresses his wish to make a home against isolation and the wilderness, and he admits that "it wasn't the site but the settling of it that mattered." (209) For him, hope lies in community, in the ascendancy of civilization. His spirit is in accordance with the Western heroes, who always try to make the frontier a better place to live in. Molly, the bar girl severely injured during Bad Man's rampage, is a common prostitute figure that appears in a Western. The regular residents of Hard Times also include Zar, the saloon boss and whoremaster of Russian origin, Sweden, a honest man nicknamed for his nationality, his mad wife Helga, Isaac Maple, the storeowner who comes west to seek his brother and the deaf-mute Indian John Bear. According to the Western formula, there should be a sheriff. In the novel, a dumb gunman Jenks plays this role but fails in his assignment. Different from the set of white-oriented characters in Western films, the townsfolk of Hard Times demonstrate diversity in their nationality. It's obvious that Doctorow's Hard Times is representative of the whole mankind instead of a nation.

Blue's narrative begins with the coming of a Bad Man from Bodie, who kills, rapes and destroys, burning the small town to the ground. His mysterious appearance, out of nowhere, disturbs the peace and order of the small town in the Dakota prairie. As a miner reveals, the Bad Man named Clay Turner often rides into towns and disappears after his rampaging. He seems to embody the external force of pure evil. Blue, in his narrative, shows that the Bad Men are not "ordinary scoundrels": "they came with the land and you could no more cope with them than you could with dust or hailstones."(7) At the end of the novel, when the new town Hard Times collapses into chaos, Turner appears again, and this time, he multiplies. In the fight with Turner, Blue finds out to his surprise that Turner is a man of flesh and blood. When he is finally killed, Blue's foster son Jimmy Fee replaces Turner as a new Bad Man. The episode of Bad Man suggests that violence is a keynote of the frontier life, and it assumes "something unprovoked, meaningless, and unjustifiable, which descends on the settlers without warning and can in no way be prepared for, avoided, or overcome". (Bevilacqua, 1989: 82)

The invasion of external evil force is a typical Hollywood Western formula. Influenced by films of the Britich Empire, American Westerns develop the basic narrative structure of a righteous hero defending the safety and interest of his community. Classic Westerns, represented by John Ford's Calvary Trilogy①, are mostly about "taming the land and containing or exterminating savage elements, either Indians or outlaws, who threaten the well-being of the settlers." (McDonough,

---

① John Ford (February 1, 1894–August 31, 1973) was an American film director. He is renowned both for Westerns such as Stagecoach (1939), The Searchers (1956),

2005: 101) The Western films in the 1950s, including Fred Zinnemann's *High Noon* (1952), Anthony Mann's *The Tin Star* (1957) and Edward Dmytryk's *Warlock* are unexceptionally "law-and-order films", with the central conflict of "[a] virtuous individual, meeting the threat to community even with the potential for death that it entails" (Costello, 2005: 179). In this sense, Hard Times resembles the towns like Hadleyville and Warlock in these films, all of which face threats from outside the community. In *High Noon*, Marshal Will Kane, ready to retire and leave Hadleyville with his newly married wife, receives the news that Frank Miller, a vicious ex-con just released from the prison, is arriving on the noon train. Since Miller is sent to the prison by Kane, it is highly possible that he may come to Hadleyville for revenge, thus causing harm to the residents here. In *The Tin Star*, the external threat comes from the former defender of the community—Morg Hickman. Disillusioned with law and justice, Hickman returns to an unknown town similar to Hadleyville as a bounty hunter, to the fear and disgust of the townspeople. Only the young sheriff Ben Owens admires Hickman for his knowledge on law and his ability to cope with emergent situations. Under the guidance of Hickman, Ben succeeds in confronting the lynch mob led by Bargardus, and finally the order of the town is restored. In *Warlock*, the town bearing the same name of the title is a mining community surrounded by the San Pueblo ranch. The citizens are threatened by the vicious illegalities of the San Pueblo rancher Abe McQuown and his gangs, who have terrorized five previous deputies, massacred Mexicans, and killed the barber cold-bloodedly.

By comparison, the plot of *Welcome* is mostly analogous to that of *Warlock*. The image of Bad Man seems to have derived from the gangsters who terrorize a large area. In *Welcome*, Bad Man is portrayed as a monster-like giant; His skin is "shot red under the stubble" and he has "the eyes of a crazy horse", along with "a blaze on one cheeck" (Doctorow, 1960: 18). He moves faster than a cat, and demonstrates surprising power in his fight with the townspeople. But as the Bad Man reveals no emotions or motive behind his destructive behaviors, he is a quite abstract being, a pure embodiment of evil. This makes him different from the images of gangsters or outlaws in the movies. Doctorow seems to create this man from the numerous bad men of the Hollywood Westerns and make him an avatar of various evils.

According to John E. O'Connor and Peter C. Rollins, American people in the 1950s still lingered in the fear of the Korean War that just ended. The national anxiety worsened due to the rise of McCarthyism and the military competition with the Soviet Union, with the potential threat of the Sputnik and assertion of missile gap. The big screen finds the best emotional outlets for such widespread fear and anxiety. On the other hand, the 1950s was an unheralded period labeled as "the Silent Generation". In the 1950s, young adults tended to focus on their private life and to eschew politics. They were unwilling to render their voice heard even faced with the large-scale prosecution from McCarthists because activism may endanger their life, so in the Westerns of the 1950s, despite the heroic individuals' effort to confront evil, their community always fails to support them. The imagination of single-handed heroes in these films shows the Americans' desire for a redeemer to save their community from shame and disorder. For instance, in *High Noon*, the protagonist Will Kane has to confront Miller and his gang alone, because everyone around him has abandoned him—the town, his wife and his friends. In *Tin Star*, the noble individuals are further alienated from the community as throughout the film the town elders try to force Hickman to leave and threaten to remove the sheriff Owens from office if he continues to associate with him.

In *Welcome*, the failure of public virtue is full reflected. The first time when the bad Man walks into the bar and rapes the Bar girl Florentine, other residents of the town just scatter in the street "waiting for something to happen"(5). Nobody dares to stand out to stop the evildoings of the Bad Man. When Fee, informed by his son that a man has got his girl Florentine, impetuously rushes into the bar, he is killed immediately. In front of such violence, "[n]obody went back into the salon, we were all reminded of business we had to do."(6) In order to secure his place from being ravaged, the saloon boss Avery forces another of his bar girl Molly to go into the saloon to please the Bad Man. Molly turns to Blue for help but Blue just gives her a knife, telling her to use it by herself. Realizing the cowardice of the man in the town, Molly describes them as cowards "marching brave behind a lady's skirt" (16). In a burst of despair, she cries: "Christ that Bad Man's the only man in town!"(16) When Bad Man catches Molly and takes her upstairs, all the townsfolk are scared and escape into the flats. It seems the only resident who feels indignant about the savagery of the Bad Man is Major Munn, the old veteran. But as he is aged, he can do nothing but to curse Bad Man and then falls off his horse. Ironically, he dies of a stroke and his body is exposed to the buzzards.

In the rebuilt new town, situation is much the same as that in the ruined one. The relationship of the residents in the town is based on transactions instead of real human bondage. Zar and Isaac Maple stay in the town only for the possibility to make money here. When their business grows big and they have amassed tremendous wealth thanks to the newcomers, they refuse to invest the money into the impoverished job-hunters according to Blue's suggestion. Zar, when hearing that Blue offers free water to the travellers, even gets irritated for he has already hired men to dig a well himself. So in the context of Doctorow's narrative, the community is selfish and indifferent to the suffering of others. The failure of the public's response to external threats in Hard Times finds thematic resonance in the Western films, both offering a critique of the American society in the 1950s. Attacking community panic and conformity, Doctorow's novel thus can be seen as an expression of dissatisfaction toward national milieu of consensus during the period of McCarthism.

3. 3. Subversion

> LONE RANGER: Tonto, from this day on I'm going to devote my life to establishing law and order, to make the West a decent place to live.
> TONTO: That good.
> — "Enter the Lone Ranger," TV genesis episode of 1949

3. 3. 1. Failed heroism

In this famous line from the protagonist-hero Lone Ranger, the basic pattern of Westerns can be detected: Heroism is particularly reflected as an individual's devotion to his community. Born at Detroit radio station WXYZ in 1933, the Lone Ranger became a great mythmaking cultural product in the 20th century. His trajectory "ascended out of radio, comics, pulp novels, advertising endorsements, licensed merchandise, and fan clubs into the sphere of serialized television and the B Western". (Lawrence, 2005: 82). As a heroic figure admired by generations of American adults and youths, the Lone Ranger embodies the ideal American hero. He appears whenever the community is in danger and leaves when the emergency is relieved. He dedicates himself to the community but keeps distance from it. The Lone Ranger becomes the prototype of numerous superheroes in later Hollywood films. The heroes in *High Noon*, *Tin Star* and *Warlock* all follow this pattern: they brave the evil forces single-handedly and succeed in restoring order and justice in their community despite the failure of the community to support them. However, in *Welcome*, the pattern of individual heroism is parodied as neither the protagonist nor other male characters are able to perform heroic deeds in front of evil forces.

A middle-aged man, Blue tells readers that he has great expectations in his younger days as he tar-paints his name on a rock by the Missouri Trailside. Blue's expectation, as he later reveals, is to build a home out of wilderness. But as time passes by, he finds that the expectations "[wear] away with the weather" like his name has from the rock (Doctorow, 1960: 7). The depiction of Blue as a homebuilder makes him a candidate for heroic deeds, but his debility and cowardice in the face of the villainy turn him to an anti-heroic figure. As Christopher D. Morris points out, Blue apparently acts as an agent of civilization and he is "ludicrously naïve, self-deluded, impotent in the face of evil" (Morris, 1991: vii). According to Arthur Jaupaj, he seems to "be more talented in convincing the random travelers and fortune seekers to settle down in his utopian town than in handling guns and protecting his townspeople or his heroine" (Jaupaj, 2008: 37). When the Bad Man rides into his town, bullying and killing, Blue would rather get drunk than hold up his gun. Faced with Molly's cries—"I beg you, Blue, please Blue, Blue Blue Blue" (Doctorow, 1960: 152) —He offers no help but just walks her to the saloon where the Bad Man stays, and then quickly escapes to the flats with everyone else.

Compared with the heroes in the Hollywood Westerns, Blue is "unable to respond according to the ethos of violent heroism" (Bevilacqua, 1989: 84). He lacks skills in handling guns and fighting. He has a predilection for record-keeping rather than shooting. Described by Molly as marching behind women's skirt, Blue is not the type of protagonist with manliness: he is a man of words instead of acts. In reference to the Colt 45[①], Blue expresses his dissent from the popular opinion that a gun can settle all disputes and conquer evil: "Colt gave every man a gun, but you have to squeeze the trigger for yourself." (Doctorow, 1960: 32) Unlike his counterpart in a Western such as Will Kane in *High Noon* who would like to confront the outlaws with violence, Blue believes that violence cannot prevent the bad men from coming. Instead, like the female heroines in Western films, he insists that "a safe, settled community" is the best way to "prevent the appearance of Bad Men". It is based on this tenet that Blue sets up a temporary family with Molly and Jimmy. He also helps the union of the miner Bert and the China girl in Zar's whorehouse despite the impediment of Zar. As he claims, "I wanted to nurture something like that (human bondage), keep it going" (128).

After the destruction of the former town, Blue shoulders the responsibility to take care of Molly and Jimmy. He makes them a dugout, heals Molly's wound and gets them fed in the freezing winter. In the dugout, Blue "felt like believing we were growing into a true family" and he interprets this as a good sign of a bright future. (89) He tells Molly, when the next time the Bad Man comes "we'll be too good for him"(151). But soon he realizes that the good sign is only his imagination since Molly collapses into "madness" for revenge and Jimmy into "corruption"—Jimmy

---

①   The name of a kind of gun popular at that time.

becomes an instrument of Molly to fulfill her revenge. Blue's sense of unending futility intensifies when Jimmy learns from Jenks his shooting skills, grows wilder each day and develops hatred toward his foster father Blue. The relationship among the three is not naturally bonded but established on improvisational relations, so its dysfunction and eventual failure is doomed.

In a classic Western film, the sheriff is often the one who brings law and order to the community. But *Welcome* parodies the tradition by its portrayal of a rash and despicable sherriff, like Blue, who is also unable to be a heroic figure. Before his appointment, Jenks is a roamer in the town. He would flirt with the bar girl in Zar's whorehouse without spending a penny on them. He would eat in Sweden's eatery tent for free. However, appointed by the government agent as the sheriff for his well-known marksmanship, Jenks fails to protect Hard Times from falling into chaos. There are more and more fights in the town and no prison is available for the convicts. When the Bad Man reappears, Jenks is seen driving a cart with two prostitutes Mae and Adah, intending to flee the town. Persuaded by Molly's provoking words, Jenks decides he should stay and confront the Bad Man: "He was trotting like a hero" (203). However, in the gunfight with the Bad Man, before he has the chance to take out his gun, Jenks "was hit twice, the first shot took him in the chest and spinned him around, the second surely broke his neck."(205) As a symbol of authority, stability and order, Jenks should have been able to protect the town from the bad men. However, because good does not always prevail on the frontier, and because he has no practical experience as a Sheriff, Jenks loses this gunfight with the Bad Man and dies in an unworthy way. (66)

3. 3. 2. Undomestic Heroine

In the Western myth, the female is often stereotyped as the "repository of civilization." (Williams, 1996: 70) According to Mathew J. Costello, one kind of the typical women image in a western film is "the civilizing woman who seeks to end violence and endorse the community" (Costello, 2005: 179). Will Kane's Quaker wife Amy (*High Noon*) Nona Mayfield (*The Tin Star*) and Jessie Marlow (*Warlock*) belong to this group of civilizing woman. These wives represent feminine virtue and the temptation of domesticity, which lures the heroes to give up violence and return to family. In *Welcome*, the role is reversed as Blue turns to the domestic pacifist and his symbolic wife Molly becomes the outrageous revenger.

As the heroine, Molly's subversiveness mostly lies in her strong will to exact revenge. An Irish immigrant from New York, Molly comes to West with great expectations as Blue does. But somehow she ends up as a prostitute in Avery's bar. Although named after *The Virginian*'s sweetheart she bears no resemblance whatsoever to the classic heroine of the TV series. (8) During the first coming of the Bad Man, Molly gets raped and is severely injured in the fire. Healed by the herb of the Indian John Bear, she miraculously survives the holocaust and hence takes the role of a wife in the transitory family with Blue. In front of Zar's prostitutes, Molly behaves like a pure domestic wife. She dresses herself in the white wedding gown obtained from Adah and always wears a cross on her neck "as if invoking the western Heroine's gospel of love and reconciliation" (Donahue, 2007: 86). The victimhood makes Molly assume the role of Christ, who suffers for the sake of others (Cai, 2013: 55). But as Blue discerns, "what had happened in Avery's saloon could never be undone" (Doctorow, 1960: 36). Molly cannot shake off the shadow of the past even though the old town is buried and a new one rebuilt: she has been wedded to the Bad Man by hatred.

Disappointed at Blue for his lack of masculinity, Molly treats him coldly and indulges in her own world of revenge. Despite Blue's effort to make them a family of three, Molly derides him with lashing words. Protesting against Blue's promotion of the town to attract more settlers, she even gives up her domestic duty to cook, do laundry and answer the door when visitors come. Different from Blue who fantasizes that a settled community will resist the Bad Man, Molly clearly knows that no matter how prosperous the town seems, it is never immune to destruction. She points out to Blue: " 'Oh, Mayor', she said, 'if this town stretched four ways as far as the eye could see, it would still be a wilderness!'"(171) She calls Blue a fool for harboring hope in the future of the town and claims that they can never be good for the Bad Man because there are hundreds or even thousands of Turner: "And they are going to get me— they're all coming after me"(151).

Even Molly's maternal sentiment is motivated by self-interest. When Jimmy catches a fever in a freezing winter, Molly takes care of him like a mother would do, tending him overnight. But she works on influencing Jimmy, teaching him the importance of violence and training him to be ready for the coming of the Bad Man. In order to plant hatred in Jimmy's heart, Molly seduces Blue to her bed and then cries to Jimmy for help, pretending that she nearly gets raped by Blue. Under her influence, Jimmy becomes a "saddle fool wandering around with his grudge"(78). He listens to everything she says as if it was gospel, "no matter what she spoke of or how many times she'd said it before, he would drink up her words like they were mother's milk"(153). In this way, Jimmy has digested all Molly's malice on life and completed his transformation from Fee's boy to the Bad Man. In the end, Molly dies together with the Bad Man, in her death dance of retribution. Both are shot by the horrified Jimmy who pulls the trigger as he has been taught by his foster mother Molly. With the persistent will to seek revenge, Molly fails in her role both as a wife and a mother. In this sense, instead of serving a civilizing function, Molly's existence has only produced perverse and debilitating consequences, accelerating the disintegration of the community.

3. 3. 3. Untamable wilderness

Doctorow's narrative not only subverts the typical characterization of the Western myth, but also diverges from the common expectation of the West as a place of infinite hope, where wilderness can be tamed with reason and law of human society. In the Western movies of the 1950s, law and order is the key thematic concern. The story often ends with the victory of the good man over the bad one. Temporarily interrupted by the external evil forces, the order of the town will finally be restored by the righteous hero, so the Hollywood pattern is "peace-chaos-peace". But in *Welcome*, Blue's three ledgers tell the historical cycle of the Hard Times in the sequence of "destruction-rebuilding-destruction", which indicates that there is no hope for mankind to build a civilization out of wilderness.

As a survivor of Bad Man's rage, Blue chooses to stay in the ruins of the old town although most residents have left. The reason for his choice, as he explains to Molly, is that he wishes to "make a home out of nothing"(150). In fact, Blue is quite optimistic about his expectations. When standing in front of the tomb of the dead, another resident Ezra Maple advises him to leave but he responds: "We got a cemetery. That's the beginning of a town anyway."(28). In a conversation with a miner, he speaks of the town and believes it will grow like a weed in the prairie. Holding this belief, Blue persuades Zar, Isaac Maple, Sweden and a few other comers into settling down to build a new town. They take wood from other ghost towns, construct houses and make business in the hope of attracting miners nearby. As James J. Donahue comments, Blue becomes "the town booster, a kind of Chamber of Commerce representative" (Donahue, 2007: 60). Despite Molly's intuition that the Bad Man will come to destroy the town again, Blue thinks that as long as "business is good and the life is working", they need do nothing for "a settled town drives away" them (Doctorow, 1960: 152).

But what Blue does not realize is that the town collapses due to internal moral corruption. As Hard Times prospers and more job-hunters swarm into the town, disputes and fights also proliferate like a plague. Molly grows mad with fear and anxiety. Nurtured by Molly with hatred, Jimmy becomes wild and mean, even toward Blue. Blue feels unending futility of the integration of the temporary family and the community as a whole, and he claims, "Everything was come to nothing"(197). When the Bad Man reappears at the end of the novel, he finally comes to realize that they can never be ready for the Bad Men because they are a natural part of the wilderness: they "take to this land, they don't need much to grow, just a few folks together will breed 'em, a little noise and they'll spring up out the empty shells."(162) Another lesson Blue learns from the reappearance of the Bad Man is that he never leaves; he just hides himself in some corner of the town and waits for the right time to spring up. So the second coming of the Bad Man, as Saltzman claims, is "less the cause than the confirmation of the disaster: he arrives on the scene of a town already collapsed." (Saltzman, 1983: 78). Although Clay Turner is killed, he will be replaced by other Bad Men and this circulation will never end. Fed by hatred and violence—the darkness of human nature, Jimmy turns to a new Bad Man from Bodie. An embodiment of the untamable wilderness, he will continue the sabotage on civilization as he rides away to other West towns. The ending of *Welcome* is quite pessimistic. Before his last blood blows out, Blue writes down the sentence: "And I have to allow, with great shame, I keep thinking someone will come by sometimes who will want to use the wood." It indicates that the story of another Hard Times will be unfolded but the struggle between civilization and wilderness will go on and on.

Written in 1960, *Welcome to Hard Times* integrates the elements of Hollywood Westerns in the 1950s by offering typical characterization, scenes and key motifs that recur in a film. By describing a callous community where sufferings of the others are ignored and human relationship is based on transactions, the novel initiates a critique of The Silent Generation of the 1950s. On the other hand, Doctorow subverts the Hollywood pattern by introducing an anti-hero Blue, an untypical heroine Molly, and a pessimistic note on the image of the West. Doctorow's subversion of classic Westerns foreshadows the coming of the anti-traditional 1960s, when the Western myths about heroism, gender and hope were scrutinized and recast.

Conclusion

In his essay "Cross the Border—Close the Gap", Leslie Fieldler boldly proclaims the coming of a new age after 1955—an age opened with the death throes of modernism and the birth pangs of post-modernism. Since the time of old novels has ended and the old tradition gone, Fiedler points out, it seems evident that "writers not blessed enough to be under thirty (or thirty-five, or whatever the critical age in these days) must be reborn" in order to stay relevant to the moment (Fiedler, 1999: 274). The new direction for literature revival after the exhaustion of its forms, according to Fiedler, is the creation of a "New Novel" of "comic sacrilege" in which the sacred are profaned, the irrelevant are juxtaposed, the borders are crossed, and the gap "between high culture and low, belles-lettres and pop art" are closed (289).

In any case, E. L. Doctorow can be safely categorized as a writer of the New Novels defined by Fieldler. He stays relevant to the moment by keeping "a spirit of transgression" in literary creation. In his essay collection *Reporting the Universe*, he admits that nothing he writes will turn out well unless during the course of writing he feels "the thrill of transgression" by breaking the rules or playing a forbidden game. The practice has taught him that in order to produce a piece of work of "beauty or truth", a writer should always sin against something—"propriety, custom, faith, privacy, tradition, political orthodoxy, historical fact, literary convention, or indeed, all the prevailing community standards", without "fearing his work as a possibly unforgivable transgression" (Doctorow, 2003: 37).

For Doctorow, the boundaries are never that fixed because "Nothing's ever clear cut; every idea contains its opposite, some contradiction." (Seaman, 1994: 294) He believes in the artificial nature of social hierarchies, which are made natural by social discourses that turn to myths. Transgression, the movement from the side of law to the lawless, contains the power of subversion to step over the social taboos and prohibitions, the contents of which Doctorow suspects. All manifestations of transgression are marked by their own singular historicity, as Doctorow claims, "The radical ideas of one generation make up the orthodoxy of subsequent generations" (McCaffery, 1999: 84). Therefore, for a writer, transgression is never a negative act;

instead, it represents the power to suspect the system, to break from the clichés and conventions, and to innovate with something new. In fact, his works effect the "comic sacrilege" by deliberately transgressing the borders drawn in almost all aspects of society, be it psychological, ethical, discursive, or aesthetic. Moving from the center to non-center, from the law to the lawless, from the mainstream to the marginal, Doctorow overthrows the western ontology always which focuses on the center and establishes a logic of the "And".

To some extent, Doctorow's protagonists are almost unexceptionally narrators who are concerned with the issue of representation. Like Doctorow himself, the protagonist-narrators always realize that to obtain a narrative voice of their own, they have to step over the prevailing ideologies of the society (the norm, the standard, the boundary) to reach other possibilities. In their journey of artistic pursuit, they always have to sin against something, as Doctorow claims, that can be social norms, political orthodoxies or literary conventions. There is always a law to tell what is right and wrong, what we ought to do and ought not to. We're supposed to stay in one side of the law and are prohibited to step beyond the line. However, for a writer, it is necessary to cross the line for he/she has to renew himself/herself in the realm of unfamiliarity. "We're supposed to be able to get into other skins," Doctorow says, "We're supposed to be able to render experiences not our own and warrant times and places we haven't seen." (Seaman, 1994: 239) So the differential relation between the self and the other becomes the primary issue a writer has to address.

In *The Waterworks* and *Billy Bathgate*, Billy and Joe learn to look at their identity in a transgressive way. Billy and Joe, the two potential artists, have to sin against the complacent self (ontology) to create a narrative of their own. Both from a humble background, they embark on a journey to find who they are and their life tracks are intertwined with wealth, crime, evil, love and death. In this process, Billy and Joe inevitably find out that their identity is fluid, constantly subjugated to the forces of change and renewal. The so-called subject is based not on a unitary and closed self, but on the self's continual approach to and exchange with the other. For them, the key point is to "get outside" of oneself, to "exceed my being and my world, crossing over the boundary ... by proxy the events of another, of multiple others" (Wolfreys, 2008: 5). With this understanding, Billy and Joe succeed in producing a narrative of heteroglossic voices, which also symbolizes the composition of their identity.

According to Julia Wolfreys, the act of transgression primarily requires the perception to view skeptically at the categorizations and boundaries that constitute mainstream knowledge and truth system. A transgressor is necessarily a social outcast who dares to shake off the shackle of taboos to reach the realm of the peripheral. Daniel, the protagonist of *The Book of Daniel*, is such a figure with "the perception of a criminal." Faced with his tragic family history, he learns to be a traitor (his parents are convicted as traitors) who takes the position of a social outsider so as not to be assimilated by the prevailing ideologies. With the skeptical perception of the traitor, Daniel is able to scrutinize social values and moral judgments concerned with the case of his parents in a subversive way. On the other hand, Daniel accords with Doctorow's definition of a subversive writer, who realizes the close connection between esthetics and ethics. Employing narrative as a weapon of subversion, he resists the imposition of norms, values and truth defined by the society on him by providing a different version on truth and justice of the Isaacson case. In *The Book of Daniel*, Doctorow essentially traces how ethical discourses are formed under the multiple forces of politics, culture and individuals. In *The Waterworks*, he further examines how society, as the guardian of morality, alienates and suppresses the forces that try to transgress its rules and ethical codes. To the narrator McIlvaine, a thorny issue he faces is the limit of representation in a realist world to account for Dr. Sartorius' life stories, which eludes our common understanding of evil. McIlvaine's narrative, full of ellipsis and self-contradictions, can be seen as the ethical fissure to break down the monolithic discourse of the society in which Dr. Sartorius's voice is silenced. In the case of Daniel and McIlvaine, narrative plays an essential role to "piece through the thick veil of myths down to the common moral condition that precedes all diversifying effects of the social administration of moral capacity" (Bauman, 1993:14).

To Doctorow, the western society is structured by hierarchical thoughts. The high/low dichotomy characterizes every detail of social life and divides social discourses into the high discourse and low discourse, depending on the status of the subject in the socio-economic power. The high/low division in social discourse actually reflects the political relation of center and non-center in the power network. On many occasions, Doctorow warns that the public should recognize the artificial nature of these hierarchies and liberate their mind from the established order. Religious scriptures and official history are two kinds of high discourses Doctorow especially concerns about. A commonality of religious scriptures and official history, according to Doctorow, is that they are sacred texts claimed by the only and absolute author. In other words, they insist on the absolute authority of meaning and on rejecting the voice of the other. Like other metanarratives such as statecrafts, laws, ethical code, etc., they confine meaning to its enclosed, silent existence and try to validate knowledge and truth system of mainstream society. These discourses, if not "examined and questioned and dealt with constantly", will "harden and become dangerous", to use the words of Doctorow.

In contrast to the monolithic religious classics like the Bible and Augustine's *The City of God* where only God's voice is audible, Doctorow's protagonist-narrator in *City of God, A Novel*—Everett creates a petty narrative around the city of New York where the writing subject constantly disappears. Strictly speaking, Doctorow's *City of God* cannot be called a novel for it is a pastiche of materials including detective stories, scientific theories, songs, film scripts, and journals. The centrifugal energy that sustains the narrative structure also reflects its subject matter: it is a time when God has lost his position as the absolute writer; in this time of incredulity toward absolute faith, center is removed and what is left is the fragmented text with multiple voices, each complementing, dialoguing with or contradicting the other. In *The March*, the anonymous narrator takes a revisionist stance to reconstruct the history of General Sherman's famous March along the southern states. His/her narrative, a heteroglossic one, is made up of fragmented stories told from the various perspectives of marginalized people in the March such as the southern homeless women, the black ex-slaves and the soldiers of the lowest rank. By creating a history seen from bellow, *The March* challenges the status of official history as the transparent agent of representation by bearing witness to a historical epoch with a multiplicity of voices.

As earlier as in his college days, Doctorow noticed the interconnection of all things, based on the influence of E. M. Forster's idea "Only Connect". The intuition of interconnection enabled him to overstep the boundary of literature and non-literature, high art and popular culture, belles-lettres and pop writings to infuse into serious literary creation the energy of "disreputable genres". His works, as many critics have noticed, bridge over different genres, as well as high art and popular culture, thus establishing a conversation inside and outside literary system. In *Ragtime*, for instance, the narrative structure is greatly influenced by elements of popular culture such as ragtime music, movie, and newspaper. In *Welcome to Hard Times*, Doctorow smartly integrates and subverts the Western genre, especially that represented by Hollywood films, thus challenging the frontier myth constructed by popular culture. Doctorow's esthetics, as Wutz summarizes, is that of "heterogeneous formal assemblage that includes outlawed literary (or nonliterary) elements trashed and refused by critical-literary establishment" (Wutz, 2003: 521). Doctorow's stance is that of an outsider and transgressor, which enables him to step down the enshrined elitist altar and merge his art with the popular, thus departing from literary convention and practice. Finally, with his experimentation, the genre of novel is renovated and enriched.

Generally, Doctorow's focus has never been esthetics alone. In fact, on many occasions he blatantly declares that "all novels are political" and all arts are political. As Giles Gunn speaks, "the problem of representation is not only aesthetic but also ethical, not only epistemological but also political" (Gunn, 1992: 4). Doctorow's novels, by addressing the issue of representation, actually address the problems of politics and culture. His top concern is that some discourses, issued from those in the center of power structure, may hegemonize our society and perpetuate the current order, thus infringing the interest of the marginalized group who cannot have their voices heard. These discourses always invoke the concept of center, and they represent ontological privileges in the social hierarchy. In various versions, they can be called logocentrism. The discursive hierarchy, in essence, is the social projection of the spatial relation of center and periphery, thus pointing to the metaphysical issue of the self and the other.

For Doctorow, narrative provides a way of knowing, a possibility to penetrate the myth and invert the discursive hierarchy. His narrators, like himself, are mostly transgressors, who are invested with a skeptical view to look beyond the social system. Grabbing a voice of their own, they are enabled to create the narrative of "the saying" to interrupt the discursive hierarchy established by the monolithic discourse of totality. The narrative of "the saying" is characterized by its multiplicity of voices and opening to the voices of the other. The transgressive energy of a writer, therefore, is always necessitated by his concern for the other. Broadly speaking, this other refers to the external existence outside oneself. Politically, it includes the entire disempowered social group such as the blacks, the women, and immigrants especially in some specific time of American history. At the level of language, the other signifies the discourses or cultures that are defined as "low" "dirty" "trash" "surface". Therefore, Doctorow's works, by casting a transgressive outlook on ontology, ethical codes, social discourse, and literary convention, actually share with postmodernists their ethical project—a critique of Western culture's exalted notions of itself and an embrace of the other.

Works Cited

Primary Sources

Doctorow, E. L. *Welcome to Hard Times*. New York: Fawcett Crest, 1960. New York: Vintage, 1971.

——. *Lives of the Poets: Six Stories and a Novella*. New York: Random House, 1984.

——. *World's Fair*. New York: Random House, 1985.

——. *Billy Bathgate*. New York: Harper, 1989.

——. *The Waterworks*. New York: Random House, 1994.

——. *Loon Lake*. New York: A Fawcett Crest Book, 1979.

——. *City of God*. New York: Random House, 2000.

——. *The March*. New York: Random House, 2005.

——. *Ragtime*. New York: Penguin Books, 2006a.

——. *The Book of Daniel*. New York: Penguin Books, 2006b.

——. *Homer and Langley*. New York: Random House, 2009.

——. *Andrew's Brain*. New York: Random House, 2014.

Other Works by Doctorow

Doctorow, E. L. "False Document." *E. L. Doctorow: Essays and Conversations*. Ed. Richard Trenner. Princeton: Ontario Review Press, 1983.

——. "The Passion of Our Calling". *New York Times Book Review* 25 (Aug. 1985a): 21-23.

——. "The Beliefs of Writers." *Michigan Quarterly Review* 24 (Fall, 1985b): 609-619.

——. "Ultimate Discourse." *Esquire*. 106: 41, 1986.

——. *Poets and Presidents*. New York: Random House, 1993a.

——. *Jack London, Hemingway, and the Constitution, Selected Essays, 1977-1992*. New York, Random House, 1993b.

——. *Reporting the Universe*. Cambridge, Mass. : Harvard University Press, 2003.

——. *Creationists*. New York: Random House, 2006c.

Secondary Sources

Althusser, Louis. *For Marx*. Trans. Ben Brewster. New York: Random House, 1969.

Amani, Omid & Zohreh Ramin, "E. L. Doctorow's *The Waterworks*: A Polyphonic Novel." *International Letters of Social and Humanistic Sciences* 38 (Aug., 2014): 64-69.

Anderson, Sherwood. *Winesburg, Ohio*. New York: Penguin Books, 1976.

Arnold, Matthew. *Culture and Anarchy*. London: Cambridge University Press, 1960.

——. *Poetry and Prose*. London: Rupert Hart Davis, 1954.

Augustine of Hippo. *The City of God*. Ed. Philip Schaff. Trans. Rev. Marcus Dods. New York: The Christian Literature Publishing Co., 1890.

B., S. E. "Novels of Old West." Rev. of *Welcome to Hard Times*. *Critical Essays on E. L. Doctorow*. Ed. Ben Siegel. New York: G. K. Hall & Co., 2000: 55.

Baba, Minako. "The Young Gangster as Mythic American Hero: E. L. Doctorow's Billy Bathgate." *Varieties of Ethnic Criticism* 18.2 (Summer, 1993): 33-46.

Bach, Gerhard. "Novel as History and Film as Fiction: New Perspectives on Doctorow's *Ragtime*." *A Democracy of Perception*. Eds. Friedle Herwig & Dieter Schulz. Essen: Die Blaue Eule, 1988. 163-175.

Barkhausen, Jochen. "Determining the True Color of the Chameleon: The Confusing Recovery of History in E. L. Doctorow's *Loon Lake*." *E. L. Doctorow: A Democracy of Perception*. Eds. Herwig Friedl & Dieter Schulz. Essen: Die Blaue Eule, 1988. 125-147.

Barthes, Roland. *Mythologies*. Trans. Annette Lavers. New York: The Noonday Press, 1991.

Baker, John F. "PW Interviews: E. L. Doctorow." *Conversations with E. L. Doctorow*. Ed. C. Morris. Jackson: UP of Mississippi, 1999: 1-3.

Bakhtin, Mikhail. *The Dialogic Imagination*. Ed. Michael Holquist. Trans. Carl Emerson and Michael Holquist. Austin: University of Texas Press, 1981.

——. *Toward a Philosophy of the Act*. Trans. Vadim Liapunov. Eds. Michael Holquist & Vadim Liapunov. Austin: University of Texas Press, 1993.

——. *Problems of Dostoevsky's Poetics*. Ed. and trans. Caryl Emerson. Minneapolis: University of Minnesota Press, 1984.

——. *Rabelais and His World*. Trans. Helene Iswolsky. Cambridge, Mass.: MIT Press Press, 1968.

——. *Speech Genres and Other Late Essays*. Trans. Vern W. McGee. Austin, TX: University of Texas Press, 1986

Bauman, Zygmunt, *Postmodern Ethics*. Oxford: Blackwell, 1993.

——. *Postmodernity and Its Discontents*. Cambridge: Polity Press, 1997.

Bawer, Bruce. "The Faith of E. L. Doctorow." *The Hudson Review* 53.3 (Autumn, 2000): 391-

402.

Bercovitch, Sacvan. *The Rites of Assent: Transformations in the Symbolic Construction of America*. New York: Routledge, 1993.

Bergström, Catharine Walker. *Intuition of an Infinite Obligation: Narrative Ethics and Postmodern Gnostics in the Fiction of E. L. Doctorow*. New York: Peter Lang, 2010.

Berryman, Charles. "'Ragtime' in Retrospect." *South Atlantic Quarterly* 81.1 (Winter, 1982): 30-42.

Bevilacqua, Winifred Farrant. "Narration and History in E. L. Doctorow's *Welcome to Hard Times*, *The Book of Daniel*, and *Ragtime*." *American Studies in Scandinavia* 22 (1990): 94-106.

——. "The Revision of the Western in E. L. Doctorow's *Welcome to Hard Times*". *American Literature* 61. 1 (Mar., 1989): 78-95.

——. "An Interview with E. L. Doctorow." *Conversations with E. L. Doctorow*. Ed. C. Morris. Jackson: UP of Mississippi, 1990: 129-143.

——. "*Loon Lake*: E. L. Doctorow's Pastoral Romance." *Critique: Studies in Contemporary Fiction* 53 (2011): 49-65.

Bloom, Harold. Introduction. *Bloom's Guide to E.L. Doctorow's Ragtime*. Ed. Harold Bloom. Philadelphia: Chelsea House, 2004.

——. Introduction. *E. L. Doctorow*. Philadelphia: Chelsea House, 2002.

Bourdieu, Pierre. *Distinction: A Social Critique of the Judgment of Taste*. Trans. Richard Nice. Cambridge, Mass.: Harvard UP, 1984.

Bowen, Deborah C. *Stories of the Middle Space: Reading the Ethics of Postmodern Realisms*. Montreal; Ithaca, NY: McGill-Queen's University Press, 2010.

Brienza, Susan. "Doctorow's *Ragtime*: Narrative as Sihouettes and Syncopation." *Dutch Quarterly Review of Anglo-American Letters* 2.3 (1981): 101.

Bronson, Daniel R. Rev. of *City of God*. *World Literature Today* 74.3 (Summer, 2000): 593-594.

Buckiet, Melvin. "Stations of the Cross." Rev of *City of God*. *The Nation* (Mar., 2000): 2.

Busby, Mark. "E. L. Doctorow, Ragtime and the Dialectics of Change." *Ball State University Forum* 16 (1980): 39-44.

Canada, Mark. *Literature and Journalism In Antebellum America*. New York: Palgrave Macmillan, 2011.

Cawelti, John G. *The Six-Gun Mystique Sequel*. Bowling Green, OH: Bowling Green State University Popular Press, 1999.

Chances, Ellen. "The Reds and *Ragtime*: The Soviet Reception of E. L. Doctorow." *E. L. Doctorow: Essays and Conversations*. Ed. Richard Trenner. Princeton: Ontario Review

Press, 1983.

Clayton, John. "Radical Jewish Humanism: The Vision of E. L. Doctorow". *E. L. Doctorow: Essays and Conversations*. Ed. Richard Trenner. Princeton: Ontario Review Press, 1983: 109-119.

Costello, Matthew J. "Rewriting High Noon: Transformations in American Popular Political Culture during the Cold War, 1952–1968." *Hollywood's West: The American Frontier in Film, Television, and History*. Eds. Peter C. Rollins & John E. O'Connor. Lexington: The UP of Kentucky, 2005: 161-175.

Cooper, Barbara. "The Artist as Historian in the Novels of E. L. Doctorow". *Emporia State Research Studies* 29. 2 (1980): 5-45.

Cooper, Stephen. "Cutting Both Ways: E. L. Doctorow's Critique of the Left." *South Atlantic Review* 58.2 (May, 1993): 111-115.

Corrigan, Timothy. *A Short Guide to Writing about Film* (Seventh Edition). New York: Longman, 2010.

Critchley, Simon. *The Ethics of Deconstruction: Derrida and Levinas*. Edinburgh: Edinburgh UP, 1999.

——. "The Other's Decision in Me (What are the Politics of Friendship?)." *Ethics, Politics, Subjectivity. Essays on Derrida, Levinas, and Contemporary French Thought*. London: Verso, 1999: 254-286.

Critchley, Simon & Robert Bernasconi. *The Cambridge Companion to Levinas*. Cambridge: Cambridge University Press, 2004.

Dawson, Anthony B. " 'Ragtime' and the Movies: The Aura of the Duplicable". Mosaic (Jan, 1983): 205-215.

Detweiler, Robert. "Carnival of Shame: Doctorow and the Rosenbergs." Religion and American Culture: A Journal of Interpretation 6.1 (Winter, 1996): 63-85.

Diemert, Brian. "*The Waterworks*: E. L. Doctorow's Gnostic Detective Story." *Texas Studies in Literature and Language* 45.4 (Winter, 2003): 352-374.

Ditsky, John. "The German Source of *Ragtime*: A Note." *E. L. Doctorow: Essays and Conversations*. Ed. Richard Trenner. Princeton: Ontario Review Press, 1983: 179-181.

Drabinski, John E. *Levinas and the Postcolonial : Race, Nation, Other*. Edinburgh : Edinburgh University Press, 2013.

Donahue, James J. "Rewriting the American Myth: Post 1960s American Historical Frontier Romance". Diss. University of Connecticut, 2007.

——. *Failed Frontiersmen: White Men and Myth in the Post-sixties American Historical Romance*. Charlottesville; London: U of Virginia Press, 2015.

Edelman, David Louis. "E. L. Doctorow's *The Waterworks*." *Baltimore Evening Sun* (June,

1994): 57.

Eichelberger, Julia. "Spiritual Regeneration in E. L. Doctorow's 'Heist' and *City of God."* *Studies in American Jewish Literature* 24 (2005): 82-94.

Elie, Paul. "Augustine It Ain't." Commonweal Foundation 127 .9 (2000): 22.

Emblidge, David. "Marching Backward into the Future: Progress as Illusion in Doctorow's Novels." *Southwest Review* (Autumn, 1977): 397-409.

Evans, Thomas G. "Impersonal Dilemmas: The Collision of Modernist and Popular Traditions in Two Political Novels, 'The Grapes of Wrath' and 'Ragtime'." *South Atlantic Review* 52.1 (Jan., 1987): 71-85.

Friedl, Herwig. "Power and Degradation: Patterns of Historical Process in the Novels of E. L. Doctorow." *E. L. Doctorow: A Democracy of Perception*. Eds. Friedle Herwig & Dieter Schulz. Essen: Verl. Die Blaue Eule, 1988: 19-44.

Friedl, Herwig & Dieter Schulz. "A Multiplicity of Witness: E. L. Doctorow at Heidelberg." *Conversations with E. L. Doctorow*. Ed. Christopher D. Morris. Jackson: UP of Mississippi, 1999: 112-128.

Fiedler, Leslie A. "Cross the Border—Close the Gap." *A New Fiedler Reader*. New York: Prometheus Books, 1999: 270-294.

Fielding, Helene & Gabrielle Hiltmann. *The Other: Feminist Reflections in Ethics*. New York: Palgrave Macmillan, 2007.

Foley, Barbara. "From *U. S. A.* to *Ragtime*: Notes on the Forms of Historical Consciousness in Modern Fiction." *E. L. Doctorow: Essays and Conversations*. Ed. Richard Trenner. Princeton: Ontario Review Press, 1983: 158-178.

Foucault, Michel. "A Preface to Transgression." *Language, Counter-Memory, Practice: Selected Essays and Interviews*. Ed. Donald F. Bouchard. Trans. Donald F. Bouchard & Sherry Simon. Oxford: Basil Blackwell, 1977: 29-51.

——. *Foucault Reader*. Ed. Paul Rainbow. 1st ed. New York: Pantheon Books, 1984.

——. *Foucault Live: Collected Interviews, 1961–1984*. Ed. Sylvere Lotringer. Trans. John Johnston. New York: Semiotext, 1996.

Fowler, Douglas. *Understanding E. L. Doctorow*. Columbia: University of South Carolina Press, 1992.

Gentry, Marshall Bruce. "Elusive Villainy: *The Waterworks* as Doctorow's Poesque Power." *South Atlantic Review* 67.1 (Winter: 2002): 63-90.

Giannetti, Louis. *Understanding Movies* (11th Edition). New York: Pearson, 2008.

Gibson, Andrew. *Postmodernity, Ethics and the Novel: From Leavis to Levinas*. London & NewYork: Routledge, 1999.

Gross, Davis S. "Tales of Obscene Power, Money and Culture, Modernism and History in the

Fiction of E. L. Doctorow." *E. L. Doctorow: Essays and Conversations*. Ed. Richard Trenner. Princeton: Ontario Review Press, 1983: 120-150.

——. "E. L. Doctorow". *Postmodern Fiction: A Biobibliographical Guide*. Ed. Larry McCaffery. New York: Greenwood Press, 1986: 339-342.

Gunn, Giles. *Thinking Across the American Grain: Ideology, Intellect and the New Pragmatism*. Chicago: U of Illinois P, 1992.

Gussow, Mel. "Novelist Syncopates History in *Ragtime*." *Conversations with E. L. Doctorow*. Ed. Christopher D. Morris. Jackson: UP of Mississippi, 1999: 4-6.

Hall, Stuart. "Modernity and Its Futures." *Modernity: An Introduction to Modern Societies*. Eds. Stuart Hall& David Held. Oxford: Blackwell Publishers, 1992.

Harpham, Geoffery Galt. "E. L. Doctorow and the Technology of Narrative." *PMLA* (Jan., 1985): 81-95.

Harter, Carol C., & James R. Thomason. *E. L. Doctorow*. Boston: Twayne Publishers, 1990.

Hales, Scott. "Marching Through Memory: Revising Memory in E. L. Doctorow's *The March*." *War, Literature & the Arts* 21 (2009): 146-161.

Henry, Mathew A. "Problemzatized Narrative: History as Fiction in E. L. Doctorow's *Billy Bathgate*." *Critique* 39.1 (Fall, 1997): 32-41.

Holquist, Michael. *Dialogism: Bakhtin and His World*. London & New York: Routledge, 2002.

Hutcheon, Linda. *A Poetics of Postmodernism: History, Theory, Fiction*. New York: Routledge, 1988.

Huyssen, Andreas. *After the Great Divide: Modernism, Mass Culture, Postmodernism*. Bloomington and Indianapolis: Indiana UP, 1986.

Iannone, Carol. "E. L. Doctorow's Jewish Radicalism." *Commentary* 81. 3 (Mar., 1986): 53-56.

Iran, I. R. & Shafiqeh Keivan. "'Demythologizing' Hollywood Western: E. L. Doctorow's *Welcome to Hard Times*." *Teaching American Literature: A Journal of Theory and Practice* (Fall/Winter, 2014): 33-45

Jameson, Fredric. *Postmodernism, or The Cultural Logic of Late Capitalism*. Durham: Duke University Press, 1991.

——. "The Politics of Theory: Ideological Positions in the Postmodernism Debate." *The Ideologies of Theory Essays* (Volume 2). London: Routledge, 1988.

——. "Postmodernism and Consumer Culture." *The Anti-Aesthetic: Essays on Postmodern Culture*. Ed. Hal Forster. New York: The New Press, 2002: 111-125.

Jaupaj, Arthur. "The Rise of the New Western in the 1960s: E. L. Doctorow's *Welcome to Hard Times*." *European Journal of American Studies* 3. 2 (2008): 28-43.

Jenks, Chris. *Transgression*. London: Routledge, 2003.

——. "General Introduction." *Transgression: Critical Concepts in Sociology*. Ed. Chris Jenks. London: Routledge, 2006.

Jervis, John. *Transgressing the Modern*. Oxford: Blackwell, 1999.

Johnson, Allan. "The Authentic and Artificial Histories of Mechanical Reproduction in E. L. Doctorow's *Ragtime*." *Orbis Litterarum* 70.2 (2015): 89-107.

Karl, Frederick. "More Mid-1970s: Doctorow, Sukenick, Theroux." *American Fictions, 1940– 1980* (Jan., 1983): 514-520.

Kelly, Adam A. "Society, Justice and the Other: E. L. Doctorow's *The Waterworks*." Phrasis 47.1 (2006): 49-61.

Kramer, Hilton, "Political Romance". *Commentary* (Oct., 1975): 79.

Kurth-Voigt, Lieselotte E.. "Kleistian Overtones in E. L. Doctorow's 'Ragtime'." Monatshefte 69.4 (Winter, 1977): 404-414.

Kwon, Jieun. "Redeeming the National Ideal: Revisiting E. L. Doctorow's *The Book of Daniel* and Its Political Implications." *Studies in the Novel* 46.1 (Spring, 2014): 83-99.

Lawrence, John Shelton. "The Lone Ranger: Adult Legacies of a Juvenile Western." *Hollywood's West: The American Frontier in Film, Television, and History*. Ed. Peter C. Rollins & John E. O'Connor. Lexington: The UP of Kentucky, 2005: 81-98.

Leavis, F. R. & Denys Thompson. *Culture and Environment*. Westport, Connecticut: Greenwood Press, 1977.

Leavis, Q. D. *Fiction and the Reading Public*. London: Chatto and Windus, 1978.

Lenihan, John H. *Showdown: Confronting Modern America in the Western Film*. Urbana: University of Illinois Press, 1980.

Levinas, *Emmanuel. Ethic and Infinity: Conversation with Philippe Nemo*. Trans. Richard A. Cohen. Pittsburgh: Duquesne UP, 1995.

——. *Existence and Existents*. Trans. Alphonso Lingis. The Hague: Martinus Nijhoff, 1978.

——.*Time and the Other*. Trans. Richard A. Cohen. Pittsburgh: Duquesne UP, 1995.

——. *Totality and Infinity: An Essay on Exteriority*. Trans. Alphonso Lingis. Pittsburgh: Duquesne UP, 1969.

——. *Difficult Freedom: Essays on Judaism*. Trans. Seán Hand. Baltimore: Johns Hopkins UP, 1997.

Levine, Paul. "The Writer as Independent Witness." *E. L. Doctorow: Essays and Conversations*. Ed. Richard Trenner. Princeton: Ontario Review Press, 1983.

——. "Politics and Imagination." *E. L. Doctorow*. Ed. Harold Bloom. Philadelphia: Chelsea House, 2002: 51-60.

Levy, Zeev. *From Spinoza to Lévinas: Hermeneutical, Ethical, and Political Issues in Modern and Contemporary Jewish Philosophy*. Ed. Yudit Kornberg Greenberg. New York: Peter Lang, 2009.

Lewis, Oscar. "A Realistic Western." Rev. of *Welcome to Hard Times. Critical Essays on E. L. Doctorow*. Ed. Ben Siegel. New York: G. K. Hall & Co., 2000: 56-57.

Lincoln, Abraham. *The Life and Writings of Abraham Lincoln*. Ed. Philip Van Doren Stern. New York: The Modern Library: 2000.

Lorsch, Susan E. "Doctorow's *The Book of Daniel* as Kunstlerroman: The Politics of Art." Papers on Language & Literature 18.4 (Sept., 1982): 384-399.

Lubarsky, Jared. "History and the Forms of Fiction: An Interview with E. L. Doctorow." *Conversations with E. L. Doctorow*. Ed. Christopher D. Morris. Jackson: UP of Mississippi, 1999: 35-40.

Ludwig, Kathryn. "Postsecularism and Literature: Prophetic and Apocalyptic Readings in Don Delillo, E. L. Doctorow and Toni Morrison". Diss. Purdue U, 2010.

Lyotard, Jean-François. *The Postmodern Condition: A Report on Knowledge* (Theory and History of Literature, Volume 10) 1st Edition. Minneapolis, MN: 1984.

Matejka, Ladislav & Krystyna Pomorsk. *Readings in Russian Poetics*. Cambridge: MIT Press, 1971.

Merlock, Ray. "Preface." *Hollywood's West: The American Frontier in Film, Television, and History*. Ed. Peter C. Rollins & John E. O'Connor. Lexington: The UP of Kentucky, 2005.

Marchand, Philip. "Where Angels Fear to Tread." Rev of *City of God*. The Toronto Star (Feb. 2000): 321-322.

Marranca, Richard. "Finding a Historical Line." *Conversations with E. L. Doctorow*. Ed. Christopher D. Morris. Jackson: UP of Mississippi, 1999. 207-214.

McCaffery, Larry. "A Spirit of Transgression." *Conversations with E. L. Doctorow*. Ed. Christopher D. Morris. Jackson: UP of Mississippi, 1999. 72-87.

McDonough, Kathleen A. "Wee Willie Winkie Goes West: The Influence of the British Empire Genre on Ford's Cavalry Trilogy." *Hollywood's West: The American Frontier in Film, Television, and History*. Ed. Peter C. Rollins & John E. O'Connor. Lexington: The UP of Kentucky, 2005: 99-114.

McGowan, John. "Ways of Worldmaking: Hannah Arendt and E. L. Doctorow's Response to Modernity." *College Literature* 38. 1(Winter, 2011): 150-175.

McGowan, Todd. "In This Way He Lost Everything: The Price of Satisfaction in E. L. Doctorow's *World's Fair*." Critique 42.2 (Winter, 2001): 233-240.

Morris, Christopher D. *Models of Misrepresentation: On the Fiction of E. L. Doctorow*. Jackson: University Press of Mississippi, 1991.

Mohanmad, Marandi Seyyed & Zohreh Ramin, "Failure to Construct a Meaningful Border for Democracy in E. L. Doctorow's *The Book of Daniel*." *Life Science Journal* 10.1(2013): 2943-2947.

Neumeyer, Peter F. "E. L. Doctorow, Kleist, and the Ascendancy of Things." *Bloom's Guide to E .L. Doctorow's Ragtime*. Ed. Harold Bloom. Philadephia: Shelsea House, 2004.

Oates, Joyce Carol. "Love and Squalor: E. L. Doctorow Reimagines the Collyer Brothers." *The New Yorker* 85.27 (Sep. 2009): 80.

——. "I'll Take Manhattan." Rev. of Doctorow's *City of God. The New York Review of Books* (March 9, 2000): 3.

Oberman, Warren, "Existentialism and Postmodernism: Toward a Postmodern Humanism". Diss. U of Wisconsin-Madison, 2001.

O'Connor, John E. & Peter C. Rollins. "Introduction." *Hollywood's West: The American Frontier in Film, Television, and History*. Ed. Peter C. Rollins & John E. O'Connor. Lexington: The UP of Kentucky, 2005.

O'Neil, Catherine. "The Music in Doctorow's Head." *Conversations with E. L. Doctorow*. Ed. Christopher D. Morris. Jackson: UP of Mississippi, 1999: 53-58.

Ostendorf, Berndt. "The Musical World of Doctorow's *Ragtime*." *American Quarterly* 43.4 (Dec., 1991): 579-601.

Orvell, Miles. *The Real Thing: Imitation and Authenticity in American Culture, 1880–1940*. Chapel Hill: The University of North Carolina Press, 1989.

Ramya. B. "Parody on Ulysses-Telemachus: Father-Son Conflict in E. L. Doctorow's *Loon Lake*: A Postmodern Perspective." *The Criterion: An International Journal in English* IV. V (Oct., 2013): 1-8.

Parks, John G. *E. L. Doctorow*. New York: A Frederick Ungar Book, 1991a.

——. "The Politics of Polyphony: The Fiction of E. L. Doctorow." *Twentieth Century Literature* 37. 4 (Winter, 1991b): 454-463.

Patterson, David. "Mikhail Bakhtin." *Critical Survey of Literary Theory*. Ed. Frank N. Magill. Pasadena: Salem Press, 1987:82-84.

Piel, Kathy. "E. L .Doctorow and Random House: The Ragtime Rhythm of Cash." *Journal of Popular Culture* (Spring, 1998): 404-411.

Pirnajmuddin, Hossein & Shafiqeh Keivan. " 'Demythologizing' Hollywood Western: E. L. Doctorow's *Welcome to Hard Times*." *Teaching American Literature: A Journal of Theory and Practice*. (Fall/Winter, 2014): 33-45.

Reed, T. V. "Genealogy/Narrative/Power: Questions of Postmodernity in Doctorow's *The Book of Daniel*." *American Literary History* (Summer, 1992): 288-304.

Roberts, Brian. "Blackface Minstrelsy and Jewish Identity: Fleshing Out Ragtime as the

Central Metaphor in E. L. Doctorow's *Ragtime.*" *Critique: Studies in Contemporary Fiction* 45.3 (Aug., 2010): 247-260.

Rodgers, Bernard F. "A Novelist's Revenge." *Chicago Review* 27 (Winter, 1975/1976): 138-144.

Rodriguez, F.C. "The Profane Becomes Sacred: Escaping Eclecticism in Doctorow's *City of God.*" *Atlantis* 24.2 (June, 2002): 59-70.

Girgus, Sam B. "A True Radical History: E. L. Doctorow." *E. L. Doctorow.* Ed. Harold Bloom. Philadelphia: Chelsea House Publishers, 2002: 7-26

Sanoff, Alvin P. "The Audacious Lure of Evil". *Conversations with E. L. Doctorow.* Ed. Christopher D. Morris. Jackson: UP of Mississippi. 1999.

Sante, Luc. "The Cabinet of Dr. Sartorius." Rev. of *The Waterworks. New York Times Book Review* 1.13 (Jun. 1994): 10-12.

Saunders, George. "The Bravery of Doctorow." *New York Times* 23 (Jul., 2015): A3.

Sartre, Jean-Paul. *Being and Nothingness: An Essay on Phenomenological Ontology.* Trans. Hazel E. Barnes. Beijing: China Social Sciences Publishing House, 1993.

Saltzman, Arthur. "The Stylistic Energy of E. L. Doctorow." *E. L. Doctorow: Essays and Conversations.* Ed. Richard Trenner. Princeton: Ontario Review Press, 1983: 73-108.

Seaman, Donna. "The *Booklist* Interview: E. L. Doctorow." *Booklist* 91.3 (Oct., 1994): 238-239.

Seymour, Ericl & Laura Barrett. "Reconstruction: Photography and History in E. L. Doctorow's *The March.*" *Literature & History* 18.2 (Autumn, 2009): 49-69.

Schaff, Philip. "Editor's Preface." *St. Augustine's City of God and Christian Doctrine.* New York: The Christian Literature Publishing Co., 1890.

Sherman, William Tecumseh. *Memoirs.* Ed. Michael Fellman. New York: Penguin Books, 2000.

Shiels, Michael. " 'Look! It's James Cagney': Strategies of Cinematic Fictionalization in Milos Forman's *Ragtime.*" *E. L. Doctorow: A Democracy of Perception.* Eds. Friedle Herwig and Dieter Schulz Essen: Verl. Die Blaue Eule, 1988: 149-162.

Simon, Scott. "Interview: Author E. L. Doctorow on Religious Fundamentalism". *Weekend Edition Saturday* 15 (Sept., 2001).

Smith, Ned. "From *Ragtime* to Riches." *American Way* (Jan., 1981): 80.

Solotaroff, Ted. "Of Melville, Poe and Doctorow." Rev. of *The Waterworks. Critical Essays on E. L. Doctorow.* Ed. Ben Siegel. New York: G. K. Hall & Co., 2000: 137-143.

Stade, George. "Types Defamiliarized." *The Nation* 27 (Sept., 1980): 285-286.

Stallybrass, Peter & Allon White. *The Politics and Poetics of Transgression.* New York: Cornell UP, 1986.

Stark, John. "Alienation and Analysis in Doctorow's *The Book of Daniel*". Studies in Contemporary Fiction 16.3 (1975): 101-110.

Stephens, John & Robyn McCallum. *Retelling Stories, Framing Culture: Traditional story and Metanarrative in Children's Literature*. London & New York: Routledge, 1998.

Storey, John. *Cultural Theory and Popular Culture* (5th Edition). London & New York: Routledge, 2009.

Robertson, Michael. "Cultural Hegemony Goes to the Fair: The Case of E. L. Doctorow's *World's Fair*". *American Studies* 33.1 (Spring, 1992): 31-44.

Rodgers, Bernard F. "A Novelist's Revenge." *Chicago Review* 27 (Winter, 1975/1976): 138-144.

Rose, Charlie. "A Discussion with Author E. L. Doctorow." *The Charlie Rose Show* (Jan., 2006).

Trachtenberg, Stanley. "God's Little Acre." Rev. of Doctorow's *City of God*. *The San Diego Union-Tribune* (Feb., 2000): 1.

Tokarczyk, Michelle M. "The City, the Waterworks, and Writing: An Interview with E. L. Doctorow." *The Kenyon Review* 17 (Winter, 1995): 32-37.

——. *E. L. Doctorow's Skeptical Commitment*. New York: Peter Lang, 2002.

Tompkins, Jane. "West of Everything." *South Atlantic Quarterly* 86 (1987): 359.

Tourino, Christina Marie. "Sex and Reproduction in Contemporary Ethnic Literature". Diss. Duke U, 2000.

Trenner, Richard. "Politics and the Mode of Fiction." *E. L. Doctorow: Essays and Conversations*. Ed. Richard Trenner. Princeton: Ontario Review Press, 1983.

Vieira, Nelson H. " 'Evil Be Thou My Good': Postmodern Heroics and Ethics in 'Billy Bathgate' and 'Bufo & Spallanzani'." *Comparative Literature Studies* 28.4 (1991): 356-378.

Von Drehle, David. "E. L. Doctorow Great American Novelist." *Time* 186.5 (Aug., 2015): 19.

Wilde, Lawrence. "The Search for Reconciliation in E. L. Doctorow's *City of God*." *Religion and the Arts* 10.3 (2006): 391-405.

Williams, John. *Fiction as False Document: The Reception of E.L. Doctorow in the Postmodern Age*. Columbia: Camden House, 1996.

Williams, Raymond. *Keywords*. London: Fontana, 1983.

Williams, Bernard. *Ethics and the Limits of Philosophy*. Cambridge, MA: Harvard University Press, 1985.

Wolfreys, Julian. *Transgression: Identity, Space, Time*. New York: Palgrave Macmillan, 2008.

Woodward, Kathryn. *Identity and Difference*. London: Sage, 1997.

Wutz, Michael. "Literary Narrative and Information Culture: Garbage, Waste, and Residue in the Work of E. L. Doctorow." *Contemporary Literature* (Autumn, 2003): 501-535.

Yardley, Jonathan. "Mr. Ragtime." *Conversations with E. L. Doctorow*. Ed. Christopher D. Morris. Jackson: UP of Mississippi, 1999: 7-13.

Yee, Daniel. "Doctorow's Latest Novel Explores Burning of Atlanta During Civil War." *The Associated Press* (Oct., 2005): 75

陈世丹:《〈拉格泰姆时代〉:向历史意义的回归》,载《厦门大学学报(哲学社会科学版)》2003 年第 4 期,第 63-69 页。

蔡玉侠:《E. L. 多克托罗历史小说中的去神话改写》,上海外国语大学,2013 年。

胡选恩:《E. L. 多克托罗历史的后现代派艺术研究》,西安:陕西师范大学出版社,2012 年。

金万锋:《越界之旅——菲利普·罗斯后期小说研究》,北京:北京大学出版社,2015 年。

江宁康, 高巍:《清教思想与美国文学的经典传承——评 E.L. 多克托罗的小说〈上帝之城〉》,载《外国文学》2010 年第 6 期,第 72-77 页。

林莉, 杨仁敬:《美国历史的文学解读——评 E.L. 多克托罗的长篇小说〈进军〉》,载《当代外国文学》2007 年第 1 期,第 17-24 页。

李顺春:《论 E. L. 多克托罗小说中的 "大屠杀后意识"》,载《当代文坛》2013 年第 1 期,第 153-57 页。

李俊丽:《激进的犹太人文主义作家——E. L. 多克托罗》,载《西安文理学院学报》(社会科学版)2008 第 1 期,第 50-53 页。

——:《论 E. L. 多克托罗〈但以里书〉中的存在主义思想》,载《长春师范学院学报》2007 年第 7 期,第 112-114 页。

穆白:《一场被重塑的战争——多克托罗的〈大进军〉》,载《书城》2008 第 2 期,第 74-78 页。

王丽媛:《多克托罗小说犹太主题的发展轨迹研究》,上海外国语大学博士论文,2011 年。

王守仁, 童庆生:《回忆 理解 想像 知识——论美国后现代现实主义小说》,载《当代外国文学》2007 年第 1 期,第 48-59 页。

王玉括:《小人物与大历史——评 E.L. 多克托罗的新作〈霍默与兰利〉》,载《外国文学动态》2010 年第 1 期,第 27-29 页。

王维倩, 李顺春:《新现实主义视域下的宗教情怀——评 E. L. 多克托罗小说〈上帝之城〉》,载《外国文学研究》2013 年第 5 期,第 102-106 页。

鲜于静:《E.L. 多克托罗小说中的纽约城书写研究》,北京外国语大学博士论文,2015 年。

徐在中:《论 E. L. 多克托罗〈自来水厂〉和〈大进军〉中的美国科学伦理危机》,载《国外文学》2015 年第 2 期,第 135-160 页。

谢爽:《十年来国内多克托罗研究综述》,载《北方文学》(下半月)2010 年第 9 期,第 119-121 页。

杨仁敬:《关注历史和政治的美国后现代派作家 E.L. 多克托罗》,载《外国文学》2001 年第 5 期, 第 3-7 页。

——:《模糊的时空 无言的反讽——评多克托罗的〈皮男人〉和〈追求者〉》, 载《外国文学》2001 年第 5 期, 第 18-20 页。

虞建华:《美国犹太文学的"犹太性"及其代表价值》, 载《外国语》1990 年第 3 期, 第 21-25 页。

袁先来: 多克托罗《上帝之城》的反"神正论"叙事, 载《南开学报》(哲学社会科学版) 2014 第 3 期, 第 19-27 页。

袁源:《地方与感知的诗学: E. L. 多克托罗小说中纽约的"小小都市漫游者"研究》, 上海外国语大学, 2014 年。

张冲:《暴力、金钱与情感钝化的文学话语——读多克特罗的〈比利·巴思格特〉》, 载《国外文学》2002 年第 3 期, 第 113-116 页。

Acknowledgements

It is hard to be a scholar. It is even harder to be a mother and a scholar simultaneously. During the writing of this dissertation lasting for more than a year, I went through many difficulties and frustrations insofar as I once even thought about giving up. Luckily, I have great advisors, family members, and friends around me so that I can overstep these obstacles and finish My PH.D dissertation on time with their help and encouragement. The following are the people I would like to extend my sincere gratitude to.

Firstly, I want to thank my advisor Professor Guo Qiqing in Beijing Foreign Studies University. In the past four years, my advisor has given me selfless instructions and helpd in both my studies and my personal life. He teaches me that to be a scholar, I have to be open-minded to opinions of all sorts and never take an absolutist stance. Under his influence, I am always ready to accept new ideas, no matter how impossible they seem to be. An excellent researcher himself, Professor Guo also instructs me in how to abstract the main idea from numerous clues to write an academic essay. He would review my essay carefully and put forward pertinent suggestions, even though he was preoccupied with other business. Most importantly, Professor Guo shows me how to be a teacher with his charming personality. He is patient, warm and sincere. I have never seen a teacher with so deep concern for his students. I remember when I was struck by loneliness in the United States as a visiting student, he talked to me over phone, comforting me like a father would do. With his encouragement, I was able to write my proposal in America even when I became very sick due to my pregnancy. When I got back to China, Professor Guo helped me revise my proposal so that I can prepare the oral offense for the proposal in a short time. Returning to my hometown, whenever I felt anxious about the slow process of my dissertation, it is Guo who encourages me, asks me to ease, and to take care of my health and my baby at first. He is the example I want to become in the future when I start my career.

Then, I want to thank Professor Jin Li, Professor Chen Shidan, Professor Ma Hailiang and other professors who have offered precious suggestions to my dissertation. Professor Jin has given lectures to me for two semesters. I was deeply impressed by her style of lecturing and her life tenet as a strong and independent female. She was quite strict with her students and she pointed out many problems of my proposal. When writing my dissertation, I took in some of her opinions. Professor Chen is quite familiar with the writer I am doing a research on and he is a specialist in postmodernist studies. For this reason, he gave me much valuable advice for writing the dissertation especially on the choice of subtitles. In my oral defense for my proposal, Professor Ma also put forward many pertinent suggestions.

In addition, I'd like to give special thanks to my family, especially my mother-in-law and my husband. When I was pregnant, my mother-in-law took good care of me, making sure that I was healthy and carefree. When my daughter was born, she worked day and night to help me raise the baby and maintain the family. Without her effort, I would have never been able to finish my dissertation in several months. My husband also gave me unconditional support even though he could not be my side. When I was troubled by confusion and exhaustion, he was always there to warm me and comfort me with compassion.

Finally, my friends at BFSU also deserve my wholehearted thanks. When I was in Berkeley, I had Wang Dan who always discussed with me issues of my dissertation. Like an elder sister, she helped me a lot with my life. When it became inconvenient for me to walk around, she accompanied me to medical care, to attend conference, and to go shopping. When I was absent from campus, it is Feng Lei and Gao Ercong who always chatted with me over phone, providing useful information and guidance to me. Their friendship helped drive away the shadows of my heart when I felt that my life has hit the bottom. I'm really lucky to have them around all the time.